D0852688

The Great Hotel Robbery

BOOKS BY JOHN MINAHAN

A Sudden Silence

The Passing Strange

The Dream Collector

Jeremy

Sorcerer

Nine/Thirty/Fifty-five

Almost Summer

Nunzio

Complete American Graffiti

Eyewitness

The Great Hotel Robbery

TRANSLATION

The Fabulous Onassis

The Great Hotel Robbery

John Minahan

W·W·Norton & Company
New York · London

Published simultaneously in Canada by
George J. Mcleod Limited, Toronto.
Printed in the United States of America.
First Edition
The text of this book is composed in 11/13 Times Roman, with
display type set in Trump Bold.
Manufacturing by The Haddon Craftsmen, Inc.
Book design by Margaret M. Wagner.
Grateful acknowledgment is made to Ackee Music Inc. and Uncle
Doris Music Inc. for permission to quote lyrics from "Making a
Good Thing Better" by Peter Wingfield, copyright © 1976 by Island
Music Ltd. and Uncle Doris Music Ltd. DONT CRY FOR ME
ARGENTINA, music by Andrew Lloyd Webber, lyrics by Tim
Rice, © copyright 1976, 1977 by Evita Music Ltd., London, England.
Sole selling agent Leeds Music Corp. (MCA), New York, N.Y., for
entire western hemisphere. USED BY PERMISSION. ALL
RIGHTS RESERVED.

Library of Congress Cataloging in Publication Data

Minahan, John.
The great hotel robbery.

I. Title.
PS3563.I4616G7 1982 813'.54 82-8009

ISBN 0-393-01604-8

W.W. Norton & Company, Inc.
500 Fifth Avenue, New York, N. Y. 10110
W. W. Norton & Company Ltd.
37 Great Russell Street, London WC1B 3NU

1 2 3 4 5 6 7 8 9 0

Acknowledgments

I want to express my appreciation for the technical advice given to me by John Gaulrapp, Dan Forget, Happy Goday, Robert M. Cavallo, and the Police Department of the City of New York.

J.M.

For HAPPY GODAY,
who dreamed the dream
and made it come true.

If once a man indulges himself in murder, he comes to think little of robbing; and from robbing he comes next to drinking and sabbath-breaking, and from that to incivility and procrastination.

Thomas De Quincey
1785–1859

The Great Hotel Robbery

1

WHEN I SHOW UP, eight in the morning, May 29, there's a note on the squadroom door telling all detectives to report to the Hotel Champs-Elysées, Park and Eighty-fourth. We get up there, it's a real mob scene outside, squad cars all over, TV crews setting up, a rush-hour crowd behind the police lines. We go in the lobby and it's chaos. Emergency Service guys and uniformed officers are cutting handcuffs off hotel employees, suppliers, guests. Everybody's talking, shouting, women are crying, chief of detectives is there, all kinds of brass. By then, about twenty-five detectives are milling around, including Big John Daniels. Must be true that opposites attract, because you can't find two guys in the whole Nineteenth Precinct Detective Squad as different as us. I call him Big John because he's just that, six-foot-two, 205 pounds, a forty-nine-year-old Irishman who's been in the department since 1957, and he came up the hard way. He's been a detective sergeant since 1973, and when he chews you out, you stay chewed. Also, he's got this uncanny ability to sum up a person in one sentence and hit dead center. Like, he calls me "Quiet, smooth-talking Little

John with the steel-blue killer eyes." Not exactly the kind of epitaph you want chiseled into granite, but I can't really give him an argument. He's a pisser, Big John. We make a good team.

He's drinking coffee over near the front desk, wearing a light blue summer suit that looks like maybe a Pierre Cardin, but isn't, and the only way I can think of to describe his face that morning, he looks like Senator Daniel Patrick Moynihan contemplating the injustice of purgatory. He'd taken his wife to see *Sugar Babies* last night because she hadn't seen a show in years and she wanted to see Mickey Rooney and Ann Miller. It's one of the hottest musicals in town and they had to wait months to get halfway decent seats.

"So how was Mickey Rooney?" I ask.

"Funny little midget."

"Hilarious, huh?"

His eyelids go half-mast, he sips his coffee, thinks about it. "Funny little midget. Only fell asleep twice."

I glance around. "So what'd they get?"

"Don't know yet. Cleaned out the safe-deposit boxes."

One thing we all know, they came to the right place. The Champs-Elysées is forty-five stories of quiet money, one of the oldest and ritziest in the city, and 541 of its 826 units are now cooperative apartments of one-to-eight rooms. The large units sell for as much as $750,000. Remaining 285 units are rented to transient guests whose numbers include royalty, heads of state, multimillionaires, chief executives, movie stars, even politicians—on a slow night.

To keep undesirables out, the doors are locked from 1:30 A.M. to 6:30 A.M., but security guards are posted inside the Park Avenue and Eighty-fourth Street entrances to admit residents and guests.

Briefly, after interviewing everybody in sight, here's what we pieced together. Shortly after four in the morning, a black limousine rolls up to the side entrance. Two men get out, wearing tuxedos and carrying suitcases. Guard Thomas Gallagher is on duty. They tell him through the locked revolving door that they have reservations for a double room. Gallagher unlocks the door and the men enter the lobby. Now, in bright lighting, Gallagher sees that one of them is wearing a rubber nose, but it's too late, they both pull guns. A third man enters the lobby, also wearing a tuxedo and carrying a suitcase. Then the chauffeur comes in, and he's got two suitcases. According to Gallagher, all four of them wore disguises of some kind—wigs, mustaches, glasses.

Anyway, at that point, the men start rounding up employees, including four security guards, the assistant night manager, the room clerk, the bellboy, and the two elevator operators. All of them are taken into the red-carpeted executive offices, just off the main lobby, and forced to lie on the floor under a crystal chandelier. Next, they're handcuffed and three-inch-wide adhesive tape is stuck over their eyes and mouths.

While Rubber Nose keeps his gun on these people, his pals go to the cashier's office, down the hall and around the corner. They go into the adjoining vault area and find the night auditor, guy by the name of Adolph Reese, who's putting away some supplies. They don't have handcuffs or tape with them, so they tie his hands behind his back and tell him to sit on the floor.

Now, according to Reese, they go back to the cashier's office and find the list of people who have safe-deposit boxes. There are 215 boxes, so they use the list like a treasure map, select names with "M.D." or "Esq.," mostly co-op tenants, assuming these to be the most likely to contain cash and jewelry. A logical assumption. Then they start breaking into the boxes, using a crowbar, chisel, hammer, and metal punch.

Meanwhile, they're interrupted by all kinds of unexpected stuff. Like, the telephone at the front desk starts ringing. Rubber Nose grabs the room clerk, Albert Sale, removes his handcuffs and tape fast, hustles him to the desk, keeps a gun at his head as he answers the phone. A guy on the thirty-seventh floor says he's been waiting ten minutes for the elevator. Sale tells him it'll be right up. We learned later that it was a Brazilian banker who was staying there with his bride and mother-in-law after a honeymoon in Europe. The three of them had returned to the hotel shortly after three o'clock, gone to his mother-in-law's room on the thirty-seventh floor for a nightcap, and the man and his bride were trying to get back to their own room on the nineteenth floor.

To make a long story short, Rubber Nose ushers Sale back to the executive suite in handcuffs and tape, grabs a bellboy's jacket, removes his phony nose and takes the elevator up to the thirty-seventh floor, where he explains to the Brazilian couple that the regular elevator operator had a heart attack. Then he can't get the elevator to go down. Tries everything; can't get it to work. Now he escorts the couple back to mother-in-law's room, uses her telephone to call the desk. No answer, of course. Keeps trying. Finally, one of the gang answers, the chauffeur; Reese says he's a young guy with a fake mustache that makes him look like Hitler's kid. Rubber Nose explains the situation, asks him to take the other elevator up and get them. When Hitler's Kid arrives on thirty-seven, they both pull guns, go back, get mother-in-law, take the three of them down to the lobby, women dumping bricks all the way. Believe it. Bricks. Mother-in-law, she's swearing a blue streak in Portuguese; tough little lady. Into the executive suite, handcuff the three of them, tape their eyes and mouths. While Hitler's Kid is taping mother-in-law's eyes, she sinks her choppers into his fingers and won't let go. Hitler's Kid, he's yelling, slapping her with his free hand, punching, she's hanging on like a dog. Finally gets his fingers out. Now she's spitting on the floor like she tasted something rotten.

All through the two-and-a-half-hour robbery, all kinds of people are coming in, because the side door's still open. For example, one of the cooks arrives for work, then a kitchen helper, a magazine delivery man, a total of six cleaners from an outside firm. As each individual comes in and starts wandering around looking for other employees, one of the gang grabs him, takes him to the executive suite, handcuffs, and tapes him.

Now, except for the night auditor Reese, who's still on the floor of the vault, everybody's blindfolded, but they can all hear, and one of the things they told us afterward was that the robbers kept asking each other: "You get to the Princess's box yet?" Words to that effect. Okay, we ask the assistant night manager what princess they were talking about. No actual princess registered, but a lot of the employees called one of the cooperative tenants by that nickname. Her real name was Mrs. Nancy Kramer, apartment 3827, and she had two safe-deposit boxes, 118 and 119. More about her later.

According to Reese, the gang left the vault and the hotel shortly after six thirty. Reese was tied, not cuffed, and within a half hour he managed to free himself and call the police.

Of the 215 boxes, sixty-seven had been burglarized: thirty-seven cooperative tenants, nineteen transient guests, eleven employees. Naturally, we tried to interview each of the people who'd lost property, but twelve cooperative tenants were out of town at the time. Four were in Europe, two in the Caribbean, one in Mexico, and five were traveling in this country. So our initial estimate on stolen property was necessarily misleading. That first report, released to the press, estimated the cash loss at $289,651, including $155,000 in negotiable bonds, and the jewelry loss at $2,877,792. We knew the press would have a ball with those figures, incomplete as they were, because the rounded total of $3.2 million just happened to be a record of sorts, making this the biggest hotel robbery in American history. The previous high was an estimated $3 million in cash and jewels taken in the famous Hotel Pierre robbery of January 2, 1972.

The early afternoon editions of the *Post* and *Tonight* carried predictable front-page heads saying something like BIGGEST HOTEL HEIST EVER! Words to that effect. Later, when we finally reached all twelve cooperative tenants who'd been out of town, our "final" revised estimate put the cash loss at $397,891 and the jewelry loss at $3,011,563.

Of course, there's no question in my mind that the cash-loss figure was conservative. That's based on experience, combined with my observation of the reactions of various tenants when informed of the robbery. For example, a few prominent physicians and attorneys stated that their boxes had been completely empty, but they looked very, very upset. I can understand why. If somebody had, say, $50,000 or $100,000 in his box, in cash, and now it's gone (and there's very little hope of getting cash back), he'd have to declare it to IRS, then pay tax on something he hasn't got now. So, when you talk about a total figure of approximately $3.4 million, it has to be taken with a grain of salt. In my judgment, a more realistic figure would probably be $4 million. We'll never know.

Almost all the jewelry was insured, so that estimate was relatively accurate. The biggest single loss of jewelry was reported by none other than Mrs. Nancy Kramer, the "princess" they were talking about. Turns out the employees gave her that nickname because of her fabulous jewelry. Took two safe-deposit boxes to hold it all. Mrs. Kramer reported losses of $2,600 in cash and $800,000 in jewels.

Because of the various disguises worn by the robbers, trying to get even basic physical descriptions was difficult, to say the least. We have a total of twenty-three eyewitnesses trying to describe four men, and no two descriptions are alike. Which is par for the course. We can't even get a consensus opinion from the four intrepid security guards. Trained professionals. Big, beefy ex-cops in dark three-piece suits and squeaky cordovans. The head man, you would've loved this guy. Chief of security on the night shift, name of Leo Langdon. This is no shit, this guy looks exactly like James Cagney. Exactly. White hair and all. Looks like him, acts like him, walks like him, has all the gestures down. Resemblance ends when he opens his mouth. Ever hear a tape recorder played fast-forward? Guy sounds like a midget on amphetamines. Talks so fast he spits the words out, literally, I'm using my handkerchief listening to this guy. One long sentence without a comma and one digression piled on top of another until he forgets his own questions. If he ever knew. Talking with this clown is like trying to shovel smoke.

But when you've been in this racket as long as I have, you tend to listen to your instincts. I was intrigued by the M.O. of the robbery right from the start. Names and faces started coming to mind. Just three weeks before, the Hotel Waring had been hit, a much smaller joint up on Fifty-third near Madison, and we had a good line on that one. We knew who pulled it, we just couldn't prove it.

But to get back to the crime of the century, that afternoon at the Champs-Elysées, Chief of Detectives Walter Vadney calls his second press conference of the day, this time in one of the larger conference rooms. First one, he just gave out the facts and figures in order to make the early afternoon front pages. Now it's time for the feature event, because the TV boys and girls have deadlines for the six o'clock local news shows, and gentlemen like Dan Rather and John Chancellor and Frank Reynolds need time to decide if it goes network (which it did, on all three). So now we got a real grunt-and-sweat media event here with every major- and minor-league news team that can elbow into the room, plus New York's *paparazzi* crawling around with their Nikons and strobes, breaking wind, the usual. Chief Vadney shoves his way up to the lectern, checks his Omega Astronaut Moon Watch, clears his throat. He's in his element here. You have to know the chief, he's a John Wayne type guy. Shirtsleeves rolled up, tie pulled down, Smith & Wesson .38 Chief's Special holstered back on the right hip. Naturally, he's got the walkie-talkie in the black plastic case on his left hip. Man can fast draw with either hand, although modesty usually precludes demonstrations. His sky-blue eyes squint out at the battery of bright television lights, shoulder-mounted videotape cameras, hundreds of glistening zoom lenses that focus on his tanned, rawboned, weatherbeaten features. He leans toward the tangle of microphones taped before him.

"Ladies and gentlemen," he says.

Strobes flash like disco beats, shutters click, motor-drives whine.

"Down in front!" twenty guys yell.

"Ladies and gentlemen," the chief says. "If you'll just hold it down so we can get—"

"Down in front!" fifty guys yell.

Big John and me are leaning against the rear wall, smoking our cigars, enjoying the show. Chief won't allow us to be photographed because we're detectives. Crooks might see us. I glance over to my left. Through the hanging smoke I can see James Cagney leaning against the wall too, flanked by his three crack security guards, all of them playing pocket-pool, looking worried.

Then it happens. Now, don't get me wrong, this kind of thing doesn't happen to me all that often. Maybe once or twice a month for the past year or so, average, depending on the circumstances. I don't want to magnify this out of proportion. But what actually happens, it's like a kind of very brief hallucination. Makes me feel slightly dizzy and sick to my stomach for just a few seconds. I don't know this for a fact, but I think it's triggered by certain images. In this case, by Leo Langdon, who looks like Cagney. Question is, does he really resemble Cagney, or is it primarily in my imagination? Wouldn't bring this up if it wasn't important, so bear with me. Doesn't end with Cagney. But looking at this guy through the smoke in that room, hearing the chief's voice as he finally starts his spiel, I get the dizzy sensation, then I see like very quick flashes of scenes from when I was a kid, almost like very quick cuts in a movie, subliminal cuts like Rod Steiger experienced in *The Pawnbroker.* Remember that? That's as close as I can come to describing it. Plus the sick feeling.

I've never seen a doctor about this; to be honest, I just don't think it's that important. Still, it makes me wonder. Last July

30, I turned forty-seven. Been in the department twenty-six years now. Could've retired after twenty, but I wouldn't even consider it. Love my work, always have. Frustrations and all, they come with the territory. Think of myself as a relatively young man. That's the truth. Absolutely, positively, nothing wrong with me, thank God, except this one thing that happens every so often.

Cagney? James Cagney? Tell me about him. He's like an old friend, he's part of my growing up. This might sound strange, depending on how old you are, but we didn't even have television back then, back in my neighborhood, East Twenty-fourth Street. That didn't come until the early 1950s when I was in high school; most families just couldn't afford it. So we grew up on movies (called them movies, not films), a steady diet of them. Two bits got you into the usual double feature, serials in-between. Wasn't all that long ago either.

Maybe it's a cliché to say this today, but the fact is, we were much less sophisticated than most kids are today. I don't care what you say, I believe that. In the movies back then, we were exposed to a different world, a whole generation of us, for better or worse. We sat in darkened theaters for untold hundreds of hours and saw right and wrong all fairly clearly defined. In black and white, as it were. Okay, maybe too clearly defined, I'll give you that, no question. But we recognized the good guys from the bad guys without nine yards of psychological and socioeconomic qualifications. Needless to say, that exposure wasn't confined to the movies. Our whole value system was different. For better or worse.

Maybe that bothers me more than I think. In any event, Cagney triggers this hallucination, if that's the word, at the press conference, and that's not the end of them. Film at eleven.

Upshot of that press conference, Chief Vadney selects forty detectives to work full-time on the case, including Big John as supervisor and yours truly as one of the lackeys. Forty detectives sounds like a lot, I know, but there's an unusual amount of political pressure building up already and most of it can be traced to the media, who welcome a break from the doldrums of reporting all those boring murders and arsons and rapes every day in the city they love to hate. Now they got their fangs into a real cops-and-robbers caper in which the crooks are tuxedo-clad, limo-riding masterminds of disguise and intrigue who waltz into the famous Champs-Elysées and calmly pull off what's now gleefully dubbed "The Great Hotel Robbery," while New York's Finest are made out to be Keystone Kops commanded by Laurel and Hardy.

Big John and I work late that night, grab a cab over to Penn Station, agree to meet at the precinct noon tomorrow. Saturday work, what else is new? He lives in Garden City, I live in Bellmore, so we split to catch different trains. I'm in plenty of time for the 10:40, so I grab the late city editions of the *Post* and *Tonight,* plus an early morning "Extra" of the *News.* Front page of the *News* makes me smile. Big bold headline reads:

WHODUNIT?
COPS DON'T
HAVE CLUE!

Great Hotel Heist Nets $3.2M!

Directly below that, in a whacko departure for even the *News,* is a big cartoon of smiling Ed Koch, our mayor, riding a beat-to-shit camel in hot pursuit of a speeding Caddy limo and asking, "How'm I doin'?" He's followed on muleback by the chief in a ten-gallon hat, swinging a lasso with one hand, holding a telephone with the other, and hollering, "Hellooooo, Federal!"

When I'm settled down in the smoking car, I read the factual account of the robbery, which is reasonably accurate, but they've got a candid shot of the chief snapped at the precise second when he appears to be picking his nose. Next

I turn to the sports section. Yanks are in first place, Mets are last, strike is scheduled for June 12, but nobody really believes it'll happen. Too much at stake, we're talking about a national institution here, you kidding?

Train leaves on time, more or less, usual Friday night crowd. Despite the jokes, the Long Island Rail Road (yeah, still two words) isn't really as bad as it used to be, cars are modern, relatively clean, graffiti is scrubbed off the vinyl seats on a regular basis. Tonight happens to be an exception, seat directly in front of me has the carefully penned inscription, "I HATE GRAFFITI!" Below that, another clown has added, "I hate *all* Italian food!" Naturally, we're in off-peak hours now, so we make all the stops, but I'm used to it. We've lived various places in southern Nassau County most of our married life. Finally settled on Bellmore about two years ago, designed our own house, had it built, we expect to stay. Just twenty-four miles from midtown Manhattan, forty-seven minutes on the local, but it's like another planet. Nobody's ever accused me of being a snob, but I'll say this: Soon as you get past Kennedy Airport and out into Nassau County, you could be in almost any attractive suburban community in Connecticut or upstate New York. Relatively open spaces, lots of trees and grass, quite a few lakes and streams, modern supermarkets, shopping centers, malls, playgrounds, Little League ballparks, churches all over the place. Me, I wouldn't live in New York City. Any of the five boroughs. Much too dangerous. You could get killed in there.

We arrive 11:29 tonight, almost on time. Bellmore station is elevated, not steel girders, but modern reinforced concrete, clean and white, nice view up there. My house is within easy walking distance, about six minutes, so I rarely take the car to the station in warm weather. It's a pleasant walk, quiet, tree-lined, well-lighted streets, nice homes, lawns well kept. I don't know this for a fact, but I hear that quite a few cops live around the general area of Bellmore and the neighboring towns of Merrick, Wantagh, and Seaford, primarily detectives. None in our neighborhood, but I know two in Wantagh. We have our share of burglaries and robberies around here, but not many assaults or rapes, and only an occasional homicide. Maybe the underworld knows more than we think.

Our house is 117 Shore Drive. Although we're not on a shore of any kind, there's a small lake across the street within viewing distance. You'd like our place. Nothing fancy, strictly middle class, but nice. Exterior is natural cedar shingles, two stories, small white cement driveway, one-car garage with plenty of storage space. House is surrounded by shrubs and flowers, lawn is kept like a putting green, no exaggeration, I work hard on it. Four bedrooms, two baths, comfortably large living room, dining room off one side of the kitchen, family room off the other, with a fireplace that gets a lot of use in winter. Sliding glass door from the family room out to the backyard patio. Ready for this? We have a swimming pool. One of our few luxuries. Designed it ourselves, "free form," seventeen-by-thirty-six-feet, not exactly small, and the end by the diving board is nine feet deep. Had it built primarily with our son John in mind, he was five on December 14, our only child. He's not John Jr., he's John Christopher; I'm John Phillip. Pool is surrounded by a wide beige-colored dock material designed to stay cool in hot sunlight. Back of the house is bordered by shrubs and flowers, kitchen has a big bay window. Entire yard is attractively fenced in, we can't see our neighbors.

I come in quietly. John's been asleep for a long time, of course, and Catherine's sister Eileen, who's staying with us, usually turns in at a reasonable hour. I go back to the kitchen, look out the window. Pool's lighted, Catherine's sitting at the umbrellaed table by the deep end, reading a book in the bright blue glow from the water. She's poured a brandy nightcap for me. I slide the screen door softly, go out and join her. It's a pleasant ritual we have in warm weather when I work late. We usually sit there and talk quietly for a while and it helps us both unwind. In cold weather we sit in the family room, often in front of the fire.

You hear a lot about the high divorce rate for cops and it's true. Constant shifts, crazy hours, nature of the work itself all combine to make it difficult to have a normal family life. Catherine and I consider ourselves very lucky. Next January 26 is our twenty-fifth wedding anniversary. Hope to go off on the honeymoon trip we never had. We've been lucky, but we've also worked very hard at it, and we went into it with our eyes wide open. Or at least as wide open as you can expect to have them in your early twenties. We met in high school. Went to different schools, I was a year ahead of her. Our first date, I took her to her junior class dance. That was 1952. Didn't get married till 1957. We weren't ready for it and I'm glad we waited.

From the time I joined the department in 1955, I told Catherine I had one ambition and one only: I wanted to be a detective. Not a detective sergeant, not a detective lieutenant, not chief, just a detective, but a real good one. And we worked at that, we really went after it. I started as a patrolman in the Bushwick section of Brooklyn, shield number 23200, lucked into the double ciphers; add up the numbers, you get a lucky seven. Three years and four citations later, got recommended for a plainclothes position. We were married by now and Catherine was working, we needed the income. Went to the Police Academy, finished first in my class, was allowed to skip the intermediate assignments of precinct and division duty, got promoted immediately to what we call a "bank team" investigating organized crime. Finally a detective. Gold shield number 281. Add up the numbers, you get a lucky eleven. Now, 23200 and 281, that adds up to seven-come-eleven, what can I tell you? Didn't choose the numbers on either shield, of course, had no choice in the matter. Those numbers just seem to follow me around. Some guys lead a charmed life. Bank team for two-and-a-half years, then transferred to Brooklyn South.

Spring of 1969, two police officers were murdered in the South Bronx by a terrorist organization. Chief Vadney hand-picked forty detectives from the five boroughs to work the case, including Big John and me. Autumn of 1971, working as a team, we collared two men who were ultimately responsible for identifying the killers and breaking the case. Both of us received citations from the chief, plus transfers to the Nineteenth Precinct, fashionable East Side, much nicer class of crooks. Rest is history.

But to get back to tonight, we're sitting there by the lighted pool, I'm sipping my brandy, smoking a cigar, we're talking about our favorite subject, our son. He's a good healthy kid and he's up to the usual mischief of a five-year-old. Today he and his friend Peter put a frog in the pool. Funniest thing they ever saw. Try to get him out, can't catch him. Frog goes in one of the filter drains. They go up on the deck, take the lid off the filter, there's Mr. Frog. Reach in to get him, flick, he's in the pool again. In they go after him. Now he pulls a repeat performance. In and out they go, screams, laughter, takes the better part of the afternoon to rescue him. Meantime, John goes sprawling on the deck, skins his knee, draws blood and just a few tears. Catherine to the rescue, hydrogen peroxide, then two Band-Aids. Two. Stopped the tears instantly. Proud as hell of the two bandages. Off they go like a shot to show the other kids.

Well, if you have kids, you know what I'm talking about, something new every day. Quite a satisfaction for both of us. We wanted kids from the beginning, couldn't seem to get the right chemistry together, even considered adoption. When you have to wait nearly twenty years for your first child, and you've just about given up on the idea, it's quite a thrill. Tell you what, it's changed our whole lives around. Catherine's always looked young for her age, but now she even acts a lot younger. Difficult to describe someone you love. Light brunette hair worn relatively short now, bright blue eyes behind her glasses, fair complexion, shorter than me, thank God, lean and wiry. These days she seems happier than I've ever seen her, a definite spring in her step, laughter in her voice.

She gazes at the pool now, reflection of the water moving on her face. "Mat Murphy called about an hour ago. I didn't want to hit you with it right away. Good news and bad news."

"Let's have the good."

"The chief's authorized—Mat quoted him as authorizing 'virtually unlimited overtime, within reason.' "

I laugh softly, shake my head.

Catherine laughs too. "Now the bad. Every detective assigned to the case is expected to work seven days a week, no exceptions."

I smile, blow smoke toward the pool, think about it. "Christ, we'll be rich. Might not find the guys for years."

"Try and sleep late tomorrow anyway. You look tired."

"I am."

"Did you have any—?"

"Not today, no."

"You still don't think it's important enough to see a doctor?"

"No." I listen to the rattle of a train in the distance. Trees to the right of the house are black and heavy against the night sky.

"I know you don't want to talk about it."

"They're over in a matter of seconds, Cathy. I wouldn't even know what to tell a doctor."

"Tell him that you've had them on the average of twice a month for almost a year now. That you feel dizzy afterward. Isn't that right? Dizzy and slightly sick?"

"For a matter of seconds, yeah."

"You should really see a doctor."

I sip my brandy, look at the sky, remind myself that I never should've told her in the first place.

"I have the name of a neurologist," she says softly.

"A neurologist? Why not a psychiatrist?"

"Because I have a strong suspicion it's connected with the accident."

She's talking about an automobile accident I experienced on

the job in 1975. I was with three other detectives, we were in a high-speed chase situation in the South Bronx. Nothing as dramatic as *The French Connection,* mind you, but it was hairy. Our car was rolled three times. Nobody seriously injured, but we were all hospitalized for various cuts, bruises, and fractures. Two of us suffered mild concussions, including yours truly.

"I'd really like you to see him," she says. "Just once."

"Who's the neurologist?"

"Dr. David Cotton, one of the top men in his field. He's a neurologist at Mount Sinai, teaches in their medical school. He's got a private practice, with an office on Fifth Avenue."

I look at her. "Fifth Avenue?"

"Your insurance covers it, I checked."

"Okay, I'll think about it."

"Please do it, John."

"It'll have to be after this case."

"I know. I know that. Please do it for me."

I puff on the cigar. "All right, if it'll make you happy. But I think it's a waste of time, to be honest."

She takes a sip of my brandy. "You're a stubborn guy, you know that? Plug stubborn."

"Yeah, I know."

We go upstairs about midnight. Front bedroom to the left is John's, ours is directly opposite. Across the hall, Eileen has the rear bedroom, with the guest room opposite. I pause in John's doorway as Catherine turns on a lamp in our room. A soft rectangle of light throws my silhouette on his blue-and-red Spiderman curtains. His bed is in shadow to the right, but I can see he's pulled his matching Spiderman bedspread over him. He's sound asleep, breathing slowly, almost silently. Less than a year ago he had a Mickey Mouse spread and curtains and he confided to Catherine, "You know, Mom, I'm really too old for Mickey Mouse." He was right. So now it's Spiderman. Next year, the year after that? We don't know. We try very, very hard not to spoil him. But you know how it is. This afternoon, when he saw the chief in that TV news conference on the six o'clock news, he turns to Catherine and asks, "Is that Daddy's boss?" She tells him yes. After a few minutes, he turns to her again and says softly and honestly, "Daddy's boss talks like a nut."

Kid calls 'em like he sees 'em.

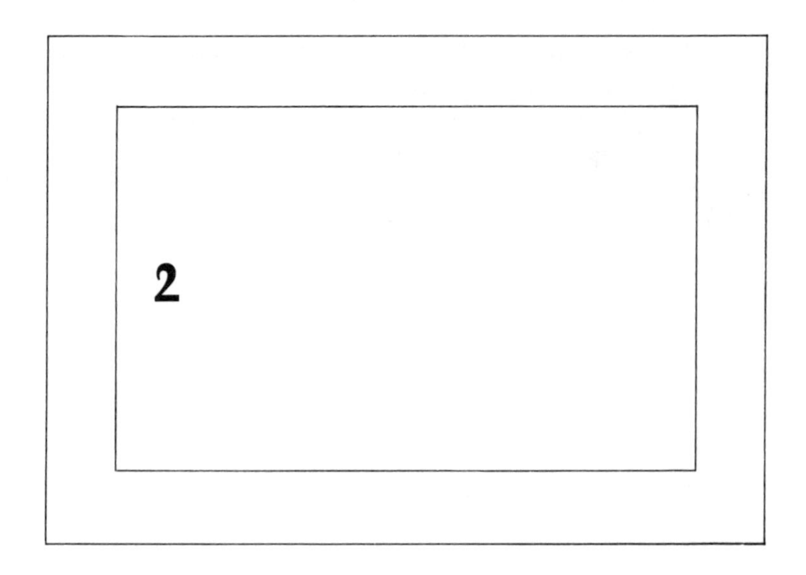

MONDAY MORNING, JUNE 1, chief sends Big John and me down to the FBI office at 26 Federal Plaza. We get down there and special agent Jim Maroney tells us they just got a tingle: Somebody's trying to fence a shitload of negotiable bonds to one of their long-time informants and he thinks they may be from the Champs-Elysées robbery. Now, the FBI doesn't have jurisdiction yet, they can't get into it officially, but they allow us to work with their informant, kid by the name of Bo Grasso.

Big John makes me contact man and a meeting is arranged that afternoon at a McDonald's restaurant, corner of Sixth Avenue and West Fourth Street. Grasso's described to me as: "White male Caucasian, twenty-nine years old, five-feet-eleven, 165 pounds, dark brown hair, dark brown eyes, wearing denim." Couldn't possibly miss him, right? Especially in a McDonald's in the Village. The FBI in peace and war. Sure glad they added the denim part.

I get there at the designated time, 3:30, and the downstairs part isn't crowded. Supposed to meet him upstairs. I'm wearing the appropriate undercover outfit, navy blue sweatshirt, faded Levi's, and Adidas. "Hill Street Blues." Haven't had lunch yet, so I buy a Big Mac, small fries, and coffee. Extra ketchup for the fries, please. Take my tray, go upstairs. Place is packed with children and mothers watching cartoons on the cassette-projector gismo hanging from the ceiling. Daffy Duck's on now. Also, there's a birthday party going full tilt in Ronald McDonald's area in back. Place is bedlam. Kids running around screaming, laughing, throwing food at each other. Daffy Duck's lisping up a storm. Noise level's almost unbelievable.

Grasso's not too hard to spot. The only twenty-nine-year-old, dark haired, dark eyed, white male Caucasian wearing denim in the room. He's sitting at a side table drinking a large Coke through a straw. You should see his eyes watching Daffy Duck. Hypnotized is the only word. The television generation incarnate. Kid could pass for a hitchhiker on a dead-end street.

"Grasso?"

He's startled. "Huh?"

"Bo Grasso?"

"Yeah, right, Bo Grasso."

"Name's Rawlings, John Rawlings."

He nods, frowns. "Yeah?"

"Jim Maroney sent me."

"Oh, yeah, right."

I sit down, uninvited, my back to the movie screen. He's still watching Daffy Duck. Mesmerized. I play it cool, open my Big Mac box, take the lid off the coffee, add cream and sugar, stir it. A ratty little boy runs past screaming, followed by a ratty little girl with her cheeks bulging. She catches him in the aisle and explodes a mouthful of chocolate milk in his hair. *Bon appétit.* I take a bite of the Big Mac, glance at Grasso's face. In the light from the movie screen, he looks like Karl Malden in *Streetcar.* Karl Malden with a fart caught in his brain.

"You got a tingle, right?"

He frowns. "Me? No, I just went. What kind of—"

"*Tingle.* Somebody called you—"

"Oh, yeah, right."

"Tell me about it."

He takes one last look at what Daffy Duck's up to, slurps the last drop of Coke through the straw, loudly. Now he glances around at the kids and mothers. "Guy named Nick calls me up, wants to unload some paper."

"Nick who?"

"Don't know. Calls me up last night, says he's a friend of Jerry G., so I know he's okay. Says he's looking to peddle some paper. Asks if I'm buying any paper these days. I says, 'Maybe.' He says, 'How much on the dollar?' I says, 'How much paper we talking here?' He says, 'A hundred and fifty grand.' I says, 'I'd have to sample.' He says, 'Forty cents on the dollar.' I says, 'Talk serious, friend.' He says, 'Look, this is very cold paper we're talking.' I says, 'Thirty-three, tops, but I got to sample.' He says, 'You interested in the whole hundred and a half?' I says, 'Maybe.' He says, 'I'd have to see the fifty.' I says, 'No problem.' He says, 'How big a sample?' I says, 'Fifteen hundred.' He says, 'Where and when?' "

I wait. "That's it?"

"Told him to call me tonight about seven."

"You got a bank?"

"Chase Manhattan, Broadway and Tenth."

"Checking, savings, what?"

He gives me this shit-eating grin. "Me, huh?"

"Don't play games with me, Grasso."

"A box, naturally."

"Be in the vault area tomorrow morning, eleven sharp. I'll have the fifty grand ready, serial numbers recorded. You count it in my presence, sign a voucher for it, place it in your box. When Nick calls tonight, tell him to meet you in front of the bank, noon tomorrow. Take him down, show him the money. Give him the five hundred, get the fifteen hundred sample. Tell him to call you in a couple of days."

One thing I'll say for the kid, he doesn't need a playback. Doesn't give me an argument, either. Nods, gets up, says, "See you," keeps his eyes on Daffy Duck until he passes the screen. I figure the FBI has its hooks into him pretty good. I go back to my Big Mac. Love junk food. Can't get enough of the shit. Wife hates it.

Bottom line, Grasso shows on time next morning, goes through the whole routine with me, then stands outside the bank at noon. He's never laid eyes on Nick, of course, but Nick says he'll be wearing a white turtleneck. Big John and me are in a car across the street from the bank's Broadway entrance. Our surveillance team at that point, all in radio contact, consists of another unmarked car one block north on Broadway, a pickup truck one block south on Broadway, and a van on the corner of East Tenth. Van has one-way windows, cameraman has a 200-millimeter lens focused on Grasso.

About five past noon, Big John points out this short, chunky clown standing in the alcove of a music store on our side of the street, about four doors north of us. He's wearing a Yankee baseball cap, sunglasses, a white turtleneck under a blue windbreaker, brown cords, and boots.

"Bingo," I say softly.

His name is Jimmy Ferragamo, a gentleman in his late forties with a rap sheet going back to 1954, primarily armed robbery. Dynamite character, know him well. Although it's been pointed out by a couple of comedians on the squad that Jimmy looks a little like me, the resemblance stops with his head. This sucker is completely bald. When he's not wearing one of his rugs, he's a mirror image of Telly Savalas. No exaggeration, ask anybody. Imagine Kojak turned crook, you got him made. Stick a lollipop in his mouth, forget it.

Remember I mentioned the Hotel Waring job? Little place on Fifty-third near Madison. We knew Ferragamo pulled that job, we got it on the grapevine. He used his buddy Wally Jones on that one, stickup man from Queens. Specialized in hotels. Some years back, I gave Wally a nickname, "Puddin' Head" Jones, after the one and only Puddin' Head Jones who played third base for the Phillies from 1947 to 1959, before he was traded to Cleveland and Cincinnati. Only resemblance between Wally and the real Puddin' Head, they both have a big mop of hair. Still, I liked the name, it seemed to fit.

Now, on the Hotel Waring, that was a beautiful job, that's when Puddin' Head used his wife. She cased the place for about a month, found out the night manager was a real swinger. Feeds the information to Ferragamo and her husband. They jump in, they find out the local gin-mill where the guy hangs out. They get friendly, they lend him money, they give him tips on the horses. When he's into them pretty solid for a good piece of change, they walk into the hotel one night, about two in the morning, and they got this gorgeous-looking hooker with them. They say, "Hey, we want to pull a gag on a friend, we want to take over the front desk for a while." They tell the guy, they say, "Why don't you take a break with our girlfriend here for a couple of hours?" The guy agrees, takes the girl up to a room. He comes down in a couple of hours, all the safe-deposit boxes are gone. I mean, they didn't just break them open, they hauled them all away. Loaded them in a vehicle and took off.

Okay, the night manager, he can't blow the whistle, right? So he tells us three black guys came in and stuck him up. Locked him in a room and took all the boxes away. We talk to a couple of hotel employees, they go, "No way!" This is how we got the story. They say, "No way, there was two white guys and one of them took over the desk." Well, the night manager, we can't tie him into it, he won't give us a thing. Naturally, he gets fired and all, but we come up empty. We have to get it on the grapevine that it was Ferragamo and Jones. As it turns out, they got peanuts on that job, about $15,000 in jewels, cash, and a few negotiable bonds. But, knowing these jokers, understanding their logic, if that's the right word, it occurred to me they might very possibly have pulled this one as a warm-up for the Champs-Elysées. To get back into harness again, so to speak, to get their nerve up. May sound a little weird to you, but that's the way characters like this operate. I also had a hunch that whoever pulled the Champs-Elysées probably had help from the inside. Too big and complicated to be completely researched from the outside.

But to get back to Ferragamo on Broadway that day, he stands there in the alcove of the music store, hands in his pockets, looking up and down both sides of the street. Traffic's heavy that time of day, sidewalks jammed. He checks his watch, melts into the crowd, walks north to the corner of East Eleventh, waits for the light to change. We lose sight of him for a few seconds as he crosses the street in the crowd. When we pick him up again, boom, he's walking slowly south on Broadway toward the bank. Big John's on the radio now, alerts the cameraman in the van, describes Ferragamo in detail. Cameraman picks him up in less than ten seconds, starts shooting. We can hear his motor-drive over the radio.

Grasso's leaning against the building, smoking, checking the bouncing tits, laid-back as you please. Now he spots Ferragamo, walks over and says something. Wish I could hear. Nick? Yeah. Bo? Yeah. How you doin'? Can't complain. What's happenin'? Nothin' I can't handle. They shake hands high-five. Young Karl Malden meets Kojak. Couple of clowns from the old neighborhood. Instant marriage. Usher each other to the revolving door. Ferragamo steps back, whips off his Yankee cap, bows, makes an elaborate sweep of his arm. Age before beauty. Don't mind if I do. What's shakin'? Nothin' but the bacon.

Exactly seventeen minutes later, Ferragamo comes out of the bank alone, spots a cab up the street, jogs over, jumps in. Cab shoots into the stream of traffic.

Now we have to move fast.

Tailing a taxi in midtown Manhattan during the lunch-hour gridlock is my second favorite occupation. Number one is hassling old ladies who refuse to use pooper-scoopers for their seeing-eye dogs. Fortunately, Ferragamo's cab snakes over to Sixth Avenue and stays on it all the way to Forty-seventh Street. Know the Diamond District? Forty-seventh between Fifth and Sixth. About 80 percent of the diamonds in America are bought and sold here, sometimes right on the street by these armies of bearded guys in black suits and yarmulkes, but mostly in little shops that have only one entrance. No back doors. Place is crawling with cops, of course, in and out of uniform. You can spot the plainclothes cops a block away because they look like Irish tourists in Tel Aviv. Safest street in the city for a pro like Ferragamo. What, me worry? Pickup truck closest to him on Sixth reports that he gets out of the cab and heads east on Forty-seventh. One of the detectives in the truck follows him on foot.

Big John and me are about six blocks behind the pickup truck. I'm driving. We get a radio message from headquarters to telephone Chief Vadney immediately. We expected that. I'd told Bo Grasso to call in the serial numbers of the bonds as soon as possible. Either they checked out or they didn't. I maneuver over to the right side of the road and we both start looking for a telephone booth. Big John spots one on the corner of Forty-second. I pull over and stop behind a double-parked truck. Big John gets out and makes the call.

When he comes back, his face is slightly flushed. Ever see Daniel Patrick Moynihan on TV when he's pissed off? Face just colors a little, that's all. That's all he'll give you. Can't quite control that. Still keeps the pixy expression in the eyes and the impish grin. That's John. Gets in the car, slams the door just a fraction harder than usual, stares straight ahead, pulls at his collar. He's had his usual inspiring conversation with the chief.

"Sheriff Loco," he says quietly.

"What'd he say?"

"Says, 'I want you and Rawlings on special assignment this afternoon.' I go, 'Special *assignment?*' He says, 'Yeah.' I says,

'Chief, we're right in the middle of a key *surveillance* operation here.' He says, 'I know that, Daniels, but this'll only take half an hour, tops.' He says, 'You remember Mrs. Kramer up to the hotel,' he says, 'the broad that lost all that jewelry?' I says, 'Yeah, I took her statement.' I says, 'Chief, what about *Grasso?* Did he *call?*' He says, 'Of *course* he called. We're checking out the serial numbers soon's Murphy gets back.' I says, 'Soon's Murphy gets *back?* Where in hell's Murphy?' He says, 'On his lunch break, back at one.' I says, 'Chief, we got eight detectives tailing Ferragamo, busting their nuts here, and Murphy's out to *lunch?*' He says, 'He left before Grasso called, what can I tell you?' He says, 'In the meantime, tell your men to stick to Ferragamo like stink on shit.' I says, 'Good analogy, chief, I'll tell them.' He says, 'Now, in the meantime, here's what I want.' He says, 'This Mrs. Kramer, she called, she's meeting with her insurance agent and her jeweler this afternoon, one o'clock sharp.' He says, 'She wants you there to verify the fact both her boxes were burgled.' I says, 'Chief, for Jesus Christ's sake, we're right in the middle of—' I says, 'Can't you send somebody else for crap like that?' He says, 'Daniels, she asked for you by *name,* what can I tell you?' He says, 'It'll take you half an hour, tops: Alistair Rodger Rare Jewels, Fifth and Seventy-first.' He says, 'Got it?' I says, 'Got it.' He says, 'Keep your men flat-out on Ferragamo and I want photographs of everybody he meets. Stink on shit now, Daniels, I mean it.' I says, 'Yes, sir, you got it. Stink on shit.' "

Embarrassing part is, chief has absolutely no sense of humor. Zero. You throw a line at him sometimes, just to break the tension, he looks at you. Gives you this quizzical look, like you dropped a fart in church. You feel like you're talking to an empty suit.

At any rate, after Big John coordinates the surveillance operation on the radio, we head up to Alistair Rodger's, one of the very oldest and most distinguished rare-jewel dealers in New York, complete with a uniformed guard outside. That whole routine. We identify ourselves and we're ushered directly to Mr. Rodger's private office on the second floor. He's actually Alistair Rodger Jr., son of the founder who's long-since croaked. Impeccably dressed and mannered chap in his late forties, ruddy complexion, happy eyes, receding hair, decidedly Scottish accent. Mrs. Kramer hasn't arrived yet, but he introduces us to her insurance agent from Lloyds of London, one Hamilton Harcourt, who has the unfortunate appearance and demeanor of a slim young lady in drag and a soft handshake that lingers just long enough to give you pause. We're just getting settled in small leather chairs around the glass-and-chrome coffee table when there's a knock at the door and Mrs. Nancy Kramer comes in.

First time you lay eyes on this broad, you know why the hotel employees call her "The Princess." Looks like one, dresses like one, even acts like one. Wears a dark gray, form-fitting thing that's got to be a Dior, Givenchy shoes to match, jewelry consisting of a diamond necklace, a slender gold bracelet, a tiny gold watch, a solitaire diamond ring, no wedding band. She waltzes in and, I swear to God, at first glance she reminds me of a young and thin Elizabeth Taylor. Lustrous dark hair, hazel eyes, flawless complexion, about thirty, thirty-two, and she's got a body to match the face.

We shake hands and sit down. I find it hard to keep my eyes off her. After Alistair Rodger lights her cigarette, she informs him very calmly that she wants her stolen jewelry to be duplicated as soon as possible.

For just a second, Hamilton Harcourt seems to have dumped his pants. Or panties, as the case may be. He recovers quickly, speaks in a crisp—if falsetto—British accent: "Don't you think it's just a bit early for that?"

"No, I don't," she says.

He clears his throat. "We normally wait a minimum of thirty days in such cases."

Mrs. Kramer looks directly at me. "Detective Rawlings, tell

me something up front. Do you honestly think I stand a prayer in hell of getting those jewels back?"

"It happens."

"Is that a fact?" she says coldly.

Big John to the rescue: "Depends on the circumstances."

"The circumstances?" She raises an eyebrow, turns to him. "The circumstances, Detective Daniels, would seem to indicate that this was an extremely sophisticated operation. Would you agree with that?"

"Yeah, I would."

She inhales deeply, blows smoke in his direction. "Would you also agree that, under the circumstances, you guys are expected to pacify victims with an attitude of guarded optimism, when in fact there's no basis for it?"

"Not necessarily, no."

"Detective Daniels," she says smiling. "Can you tell me the police recovery statistics for stolen property over the past few years?"

"Not off the top of my head, no."

"Detective Rawlings?"

"I'm afraid not."

"Maybe you're reading the wrong newspapers." She reaches in her black handbag with the white Courrèges label, takes out a clipping from a newspaper, hands it to me. "Would you be kind enough to read just the first few paragraphs aloud, so we all know what we're talking about?"

It's an article from *The New York Times,* Sunday, May 31, 1981, and the smaller clipping is from the front page. The headline reads:

BURGLARIES INCREASE, BUT ARRESTS FALL AS NEW YORK'S POLICE ATTEMPT TO COPE

I clear my throat and start to read aloud:

" 'Friday's record-breaking $3.2 million robbery at the

Hotel Champs-Elysées is perhaps the most spectacular example of an alarming trend in New York City that has been increasing over the past several years with apparently no plateau in sight.

" 'Burglary complaints in 1980, 70 percent of them from homeowners, apartment dwellers, and hotel guests, rose to 212,748, a record, according to police figures. During the same period, burglary arrests decreased by more than 1,000 to 19,320.

" 'A police spokesman said that last year the department closed only 6.7 percent of the burglary cases reported, in which residents lost an estimated $337.6 million in money and property.

" 'During the first two months of this year, burglary complaints were 12.1 percent higher than in the first two months of 1980. Arrest figures for that period are not available, a police spokesman said.' "

I take a quick glance at the rest of the article, a fairly long one, then hand it back to her.

"Six-point-seven percent of the cases are closed," she says. "I assume that means solved?"

"Correct," I say.

She nods. "It goes on to say that last year there was a burglary reported every three minutes in New York, that the police made one arrest for every eleven burglaries reported, and that less than one in eighteen of those arrested were actually convicted." She raises an eyebrow at me. "That sound accurate?"

"Sure, except it's misleading."

"In what way?"

"The truth is," Big John says, "the overwhelming majority of burglaries today aren't even investigated. Obviously, we don't have the manpower to to that. So we have to operate on the concept of what we call 'solvability.' Unless the burglary involves an institution—such as a school, bank, museum—or property worth five thousand dollars or more, we have to see fingerprints or clues that lead us to believe there's a chance of solving the case. In the absence of such clues, we won't even start an investigation. Unacceptable, I know, but we have no other realistic choice."

Mrs. Kramer puts the article back in her handbag. "I'm not trying to embarrass you men, I'm just trying to establish a few facts, okay? Detective Daniels, you took my statement at the hotel, correct?"

"That's right."

"Will you confirm to Mr. Harcourt that both my safe-deposit boxes were burgled?"

"They were both broken into, I can confirm that. I'm sure you can understand that I can't state they were 'burgled' in the sense that I know something was stolen, because I don't have positive knowledge of that. I know they were broken into and they're now empty."

She glances impatiently at the ceiling. "Fine. Mr. Harcourt, is that acceptable to you?"

"Certainly. The policy states specifically that the jewels in question must be kept in the safe-deposit boxes at all times. When not being worn."

"Fine," she says softly. "Now, the point I'm trying to establish is simple. My jewels have been stolen. Statistically, my chances of getting them back are negligible. It would be completely unrealistic to think otherwise." She smiles at Harcourt. "You agree with that?"

"From a practical standpoint, yes."

"Alistair," she says, "you see any problem in duplicating them?"

"Not really, Nancy. We have the individual specifications and photographs. I can't guarantee exact matching of the stones themselves, of course, but we can come very close."

"How long will it take?"

"I'd say four-to-five months, minimum."

"Mr. Harcourt," she says smiling. "Do you suppose Lloyds might honor my claim within that time frame?"

He returns her smile politely. "As I said, thirty days is considered adequate in most cases."

"Then let's do it, Alistair."

"I'll see to it personally."

"One more thing." She reaches into her handbag, takes out a black velvet ring box, tosses it across the table to Rodger. "How much do you estimate that's worth?"

He opens the box, inspects a solitaire diamond ring, stands up, goes to his desk. After switching on a small high-intensity lamp, he fits a loupe into his eye socket and studies the stone very carefully. "Difficult to say, Nancy."

"Approximately."

"I'd need an appraisal by the Gemological Institute, but I'd estimate about ten thousand dollars."

She stubs out her cigarette. "The cheap bastard. Sell it."

This gets a laugh out of Alistair Rodger, who obviously knows something we don't, so we join in half-heartedly. Meeting breaks up. Big John asks Rodger if we can use his telephone. It's about 1:15 now. He dials the chief's private number, then hands me the receiver fast. I take it, give him one of my steel-blue killer looks.

"Chief Vadney's office."

"Steve, John Rawlings, is he there?"

"He's on the line with the commissioner, John."

"Murphy in yet?"

"Hold on." Click.

I watch Rodger escort Harcourt and Mrs. Kramer to the door. Quite a package, Mrs. K. Big John's standing there staring holes in her Dior derrière.

Click. "Murphy."

"Mat, John Rawlings. Anything yet?"

"Hello, John, yeah. Looks like we struck out."

"Oh, shit."

"Not even close."

"Chief know?"

"Not yet. We pulled Ferragamo's B-number, pulled his rap sheet. Armed robbery going back to nineteen fifty-four, but nothing in this league. The guy's strictly a ground ball, John."

"Tell me about it."

"How many men you got on him?"

"Eight, counting us."

"Better pull them. We'll throw it back to Maroney."

"Check. Regards to the chief."

"Take care."

"Mat? Wait a minute. Wait a minute, do me a favor, huh? Remember the Hotel Waring job?"

"Three-four weeks ago, yeah. Small stuff."

"Some bonds reported, a few bonds, remember?"

He hesitates. "Yeah. I remember that."

"Do me a favor and just—"

"Hold on." Click.

Big John comes over frowning. "What's up?"

"We struck out."

"Knew it."

"I'm playing a hunch. Murphy's checking—"

"Knew it was too pat, knew it. Felt it."

"Murphy's checking the serial numbers of the bonds from the Hotel Waring."

"So? So what if they match?"

"So he hasn't got a hundred and fifty grand of those notes to follow through on, right?"

His green eyes dart to me. "Cold-paper sample."

"Minor-league hitter with major-league balls."

He grins, takes out a cigar, unwraps it slowly. "If you're right, I love it. Must say, it warms my heart. Little Jimmy Ferragamo finally makes the big time. After all those years in the bushes."

"Went to the best schools."

"Yeah, he did. Studied with all the heavy hitters."

Alistair Rodger closes the door quietly, rubs his hands as he walks over to us. His eyes look even happier than normal. I can understand why. Even in his league, you don't come up with an order for a cool $800,000 every day.

"Quite a lady," he says. "You gentlemen care to join me in a little pick-me-up?"

"No, thanks," we both say. Learned that from watching TV.

He opens a paneled cabinet, selects a cut-glass decanter and a glass that looks like a Waterford, pours himself a wee Scottish measure. No ice, if you please. "Yes, indeed, quite a lady, that Nancy Kramer, wouldn't you say so?"

Big John bites off the end of his cigar, drops it in the ashtray. "I'd say so."

Click. "John?"

"Yeah, Mat."

"Bingo. All of them."

I wink at Big John. "Okay, listen, Matthew. Tell the chief it's a cold-paper con up front. I think we got our man. When he gets back to Grasso, the deal is on. Con of a con of a con."

"Hi-yooo Silver!"

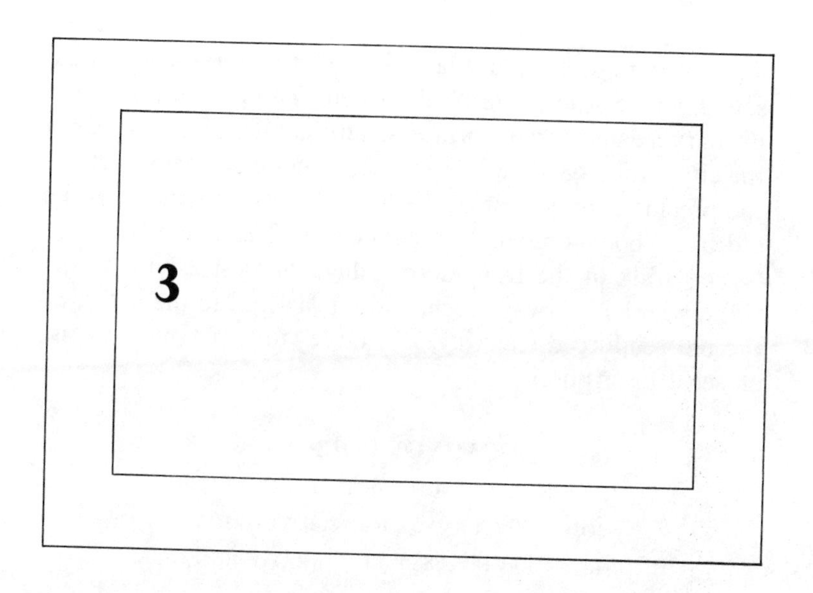

3

YOU'D LOVE THE NINETEENTH PRECINCT. That's our station, 153 East Sixty-seventh Street. Constructed in 1887 and it's still virtually unchanged after ninety-four years. Matter of fact, it's now a Designated New York City Landmark, which means the exterior can't be altered in any way without permission from the Landmarks Preservation Commission. Nice for history buffs, but not too thrilling for most of the cops who have to work here and find it unbelievably old fashioned, cramped, uncomfortable, cold in winter, sweltering in summer. Big John and I don't happen to agree with the majority opinion in this case. We like the joint. Has character and tradition. Gives you a sense of continuity and perspective. Go see it sometime and look around. Don't know what type of architecture it is, but it's got to be classic something-or-other. Five stories built with the kind of materials and craftsmanship you don't see nowadays. Main entrance is an enormous stone archway flanked by graceful lamps that hold bulbs now but were gaslights in 1887. Back then, the first electric lights, called "Brush arcs," were limited to Broadway from Fourteenth to

Twenty-sixth streets, and later in the area bordered by Nassau, Pearl, Spruce, and Wall streets. Horses were still the primary means of transportation; automobiles didn't appear in the city until 1898. Streets were mostly cobblestone or dirt. At the precinct, the lowest of the five stone steps still holds the old iron "boot-scrapers" on either side. Takes you back.

You walk in the front door today, the desk is still to the right, where it's always been, and on the wall to the left, near the old reinforced stairway, is a large stone plaque with the chiseled inscription:

COMRS OF POLICE

STEPHEN B. FRENCH. FITZ JOHN PORTER.

JOHN MC CLAVE. JOHN R. VOORHIS.

N.D. BUSH ARCHT 1887 J.H. BRADY BUILDER.

Wooden stairway creaks as you go up to the second floor. First door to your left is our squadroom. There's a glass window in the upper half of the door with a hand-painted sign that reads:

19th Detective Squad
DETECTIVE ON DUTY
Please turn knob and
walk in for assistance

Character? Tell me about it. Where else would you find a sign telling you to turn the knob of a door to get in? We take nothing for granted. If you could see some of the ying-yangs who walk in on us, you'd understand why. Squadroom itself is basically a large rectangular area, high ceiling with fluorescent lights, thick walls painted light blue, big windows with outside bars, light green linoleum floor, old-fashioned steam radiators. All the desks are little steel jobs, dark green with light green tops, if you please, but the filing cabinets are just about every color in the rainbow, some of them probably dating back to 1887, including the contents. Couple of years ago, we found a mustache cup in one of those suckers. No, that's true, ask anybody. Bulletin boards are jammed with the most recent "wanted" posters. Electric fans are all over the place. Off to the right, as you come in, is a little square cage that extends all the way up to the ceiling, called the "holding area," where the accused is kept out of mischief while we do the paperwork. There's no chair in the cage, no john, nothing. What if the accused has to relieve himself, you ask? He's told to hold it. Or sit on it, as the case may be. Regardless of what you read in the press, we don't pamper perpetrators. On the wall with the windows, directly below the clock, are nineteen small wooden plaques with the hand-painted names of every detective in the squad, arranged in the chain-of-command: Lieutenant on top, two sergeants below him, side-by-side, then sixteen detectives below that, separated into their various work shifts. Lastly, there are three private offices off the main room, the lieutenant's to the far right, the two sergeants' to the left.

Of the forty detectives selected by Chief Vadney to work full-time on the Champs-Elysées case, Big John and me are the only ones from our precinct. Which is a good thing, because the squad's so undermanned already it's ridiculous. Has been for years.

Now, the morning after our first day of surveillance on Ferragamo, we go down to headquarters first, pick up our copies of the best photographs, then drive up to the precinct to study them before our surveillance shift starts again at noon. Big John's a sergeant, so he's got one of the private offices. We go in there, we hang up our jackets, we turn on his fan first thing. It's only June 3, but the humidity's very high, feels like it might rain any minute. He boils water for instant coffee on his little one-burner range while I plaster two of his walls with photographs, all eight-by-ten-inch blowups, tons of them. Finally we light up cigars, sip coffee, walk around, and study each shot. Ferragamo jumps around a lot, but he only meets a few people we can actually photograph on the street. We can't identify any of them on the spot, so we're glad for the photos. First guy, call him Mr. X, Ferragamo meets him in the lobby of the new Grand Hyatt Hotel, Forty-second and Lexington. They take a cab down to Little Italy. We can't figure what they're doing, they jump around, they go to a total of seven restaurants down there in the space of three hours. We don't want to send anybody in to observe because it's too risky; it's the middle of the afternoon and the places are almost empty. So, that series of shots, we got them coming out of these restaurants along Sullivan, Minetta, Downing, and Thompson. Mr. X looks to be in his late twenties maybe, relatively tall, lean, athletic body poured into expensive sports clothes. We get some good closeups of this kid. Sensible haircut, honest eyes, square jaw. Little League coach from Tulsa. PTA all the way. In God we trust, all others pay cash. Hot damn, Vietnam.

Now they take a cab back to the Grand Hyatt. Mr. X goes in (we stick a tail on him); Ferragamo continues uptown to his only known residence, 236 West 106th Street. Comes out about 7:30, warm twilight, he's into his *bon vivant* role: White shirt, striped tie, dark blue blazer, light gray trousers, black Guccis—bright-eyed, devil-may-care, bald is beautiful. Next series of shots, he's coming out of Elaine's, no less, the celebrity haunt on Second Avenue up in Yorkville. The light's not too good now, but we're shooting with high-speed film, so we get a fairly decent shot of the guy with him as they hail a cab. Looking at the closeups, I have to laugh out loud. This kid is David Stockman. This kid is David Stockman City. Styled hair, high forehead, steel-framed glasses, baggy Brooks, club tie. Washington Whiz out of Congress out of Harvard Divinity out of Michigan State out of Fort Hood, Texas. Panache out of chutzpa. Strolling coolly out of the Oval Office after cutting the *cajónes* off some bleeding-heart Don Quixote. This kid doesn't wave for a cab, he snaps his fingers.

Next stop, Sirocco Supper Club, 29 East Twenty-ninth

Street. Now, anytime you're worried about the demise of the true international supersonic set, just take a gander at this spot. I've only been here once (in the bar, yet), but this place has a clientele of the United Nations Security Council. Actually, it's a Greek supper club and the décor is like an authentic replica of the dining room of a luxury cruise ship, complete with see-through portholes, the whole nine knots. Six-man Greek band, dance floor, and the entertainment includes an exotic young bellydancer who used to date Ferragamo. Maybe she still does.

In any event, when they go in the Sirocco, it's about 8:30. During the next half hour, Big John and me are replaced by a fresh surveillance team. Same with the detectives in the other vehicles. So now, in the morning, the next series of pictures are new to us, but they don't tell us much. Ferragamo and his David Stockman *Doppelgänger,* we'll call him Mr. Y, they come out late that night, they grab separate cabs, and both go home. Mr. Y goes into an apartment house at 201 East Thirty-seventh Street. Nice neighborhood. Fits the image. Night shift reports no movement of either man. Next shift takes over at 4:30 A.M. Status quo up to the present time, which is now about 9:45.

Big John and I can't identify Messrs. X or Y. Never saw them before. Now we call in the troops, Lieutenant Barnett, Sergeant Ferrante, and detectives Scanion, Roland, Fletcher, and Howard. Not by rank, but when they have a free minute. They come in, they study the faces. Nothing. Lieutenant Barnett recognizes Ferragamo, but that's about it. Never saw them before. Meantime, Big John gets a call from Sergeant Brideweiser of Midtown Precinct South. Thinks he recognizes Mr. X and he's running it through the computer. Thinks it might be Eddie Goliat, mob-connected kid from Detroit. Owns a couple of restaurants in Detroit. High-class fronts. Brideweiser will get back to us soon as possible.

Big John hangs up, tells me about it.

"He check the hotel?" I ask.

"Didn't say."

I grab the telephone book.

"You kidding?"

"Way too obvious, I know." I look up the Grand Hyatt. "How old's Sergeant Brideweiser?"

"Old enough to know better."

"I'm sure he's right. Big-time operator like Goliat? No way. 'Percy T. Goodfellow, Fairview Road, Ames, Iowa.' Cash in advance." I pick up the phone, dial the number, ask for the room clerk.

Big John's sitting back in his chair, blowing smoke toward the fan, enjoying this immensely.

Click. "Front desk."

"This is Detective Rawlings, Nineteenth Precinct. Who am I talking to, please?"

"Mr. Winslow."

"Mr. Winslow, I just have a couple of routine questions. You got a Mr. Goliat registered? G-o-l-i-a-t?"

"Just a minute." Clunk. Distant voices, bells pinging, a typewriter clicking. "Yes, sir, we do. Edward Goliat, Room eighteen forty-two. Would you like to be connected?"

"No, I wouldn't. Edward Goliat from Detroit?"

"Uh, yes, sir, that's correct."

"When did he check in?"

"In Monday, June first; out Wednesday, June third. Today."

Slowly, for Big John's benefit: "In Monday, June first; out Wednesday, June third. Many thanks, Mr. Winslow, appreciate your help."

Big John's got his head tilted back now, blowing smoke rings. Well, it goes without saying, Eddie Goliat becomes very low priority at this point. We don't pull his tail off, not until he leaves town, but my hunch is that he's not connected with the robbery. First, he's a mob guy and these days you find very few mob people getting into stunts as obvious as robbing banks or hotels; they don't need that kind of slapstick action anymore, they've outgrown it. Second, it's unlikely that Goliat was even in town on May 29. We don't know what the hell he was doing with Ferragamo in Little Italy, but life is full of little mysteries. We don't want to get sidetracked at this point.

Telephone rings at about 9:55. Big John answers. It's Lou Unright, one of the surveillance guys on Mr. Y. Big John tells him to wait a second until I can pick up on another phone. I go into the squadroom, grab a phone, punch the button.

"Okay, Lou."

"Okay, here's what's happening. First chance I've had to call. Nine twenty-five, subject comes out of his apartment, walks to the corner of Third, heads north on Third. I get out, follow him up Third. Marty follows us in the car, half-block distance. Subject is well dressed, gray suit, tie. Walks three, four blocks, goes into an office building. Six thirty-three Third Avenue. I follow him inside. It's about nine thirty-five, but the lobby's still pretty active. I get on the same elevator. Eight, ten people on it. He gets off on seven with a couple others. It's one of the floors occupied by National Airlines. I follow at a distance now. He goes down a corridor, passes through the public relations department, continues to a smaller area marked *Sunliner.* Okay, that's the name of their inflight magazine. He goes straight to a corner office, goes inside. I notice most of the other offices have little nameplates on the doors, but not his. Now I go up to one of the secretaries, tell her I'm trying to get a copy of the June issue of *Sunliner.* No problem, she goes off to a little storeroom, comes back, gives me the copy. I take the elevator down to the lobby, turn to the masthead page, look over the editorial staff. They got a staff of four, plus an art director who's at a different address. Also, advertising director, manager, all like that, also not in the same building. Editorial staff has two men and two women. One guy's the editor and publisher, the other's the senior editor. So, because of the corner office and all, and coming in late like that, I figure our man's got to be the editor and publisher. Name's William McCabe."

"Beautiful, Lou," Big John says.

"Terrific job, Lou," I add.

"Piece of cake. I'm in the lobby now."

"Okay, look," Big John says. "We'll run a make on William McCabe, see what we come up with. Marty parked outside?"

"Probably."

"Take a break, both of you. Call me in an hour."

As I'm dialing headquarters to request a computer check on McCabe, the other line rings, Big John picks up, and it's Chief Vadney. Now, the chief has been known to get antsy on the progress of certain cases, particularly when political pressure is being applied, but this time the boys and girls of the media are really starting to get on his tits, especially Vinnie Casandra of the *News.* Vinnie Casandra of the *News,* who happens to be managing editor of that ultra-conservative tabloid with the largest daily circulation in the city, the country, the world, and maybe the universe, depending on who you believe, got such a terrific public response from the initial cartoon of Mayor Koch and the chief that he decided to run a daily series of similar cartoons, under the title "How'm I Doin'?" This morning's cartoon, in typically understated fashion, finds our two heroes happily ensconsed in a hotel dining room, napkins tucked under their chins, holding menus labeled "Chauncey Lazy" and smiling moronically at a tuxedo-clad waiter who wears a false nose, a handlebar mustache, and says, "Excellent choice, gentlemen—turkey and crow."

Now, ordinarily, you couldn't accuse the chief of trying to maintain a low profile, publicity-wise, but we have it from reliable sources that he's so pissed at the cartoon series he actually calls Vinnie Casandra and asks him to turn down the heat for the good of the department. Casandra says, "No way." The chief drops the diplomacy and demands that the series be canceled immediately. Casandra asks him if he's ever read the First Amendment. The chief drops the demand and asks Casandra out to lunch. "You name the place," he says. Casandra says, "Okay, the Dimwit Cowboy, so you'll feel right at home." The chief calls Casandra a name. Casandra calls the chief a name. End of conversation. The series continues in earnest. The chief's going nuts now. Big John says he's been there for years.

But to get back to what I was saying, Big John's talking to the chief now, trying to calm him down. When he finally gets hung up on, he replaces the receiver slowly, puts his head down on the desk.

"What's the good word?" I ask.

He keeps his head down, closes his eyes. "I swear to God, this guy's blown his door. He says, 'Brief me, Daniels, and it better be good.' I says, 'We're making definite progress, chief, we got three men under separate surveillance now, around the clock, and we know each man's identity.' He says, 'That's not *good* enough, Daniels, I want *action* and I want it *today!*' I go, 'Today, chief?' He says, *'Today!'* I says, 'What kind of action we talking about, chief?' He says, 'I want *apprehensions!*' I says, 'Apprehensions? Chief, we got to wait till they do something.' He says, *'Do* something?' He says, 'James Ferragamo sold stolen bonds to our *informant!* You call that *nothing?*' I says, 'Chief, those bonds were stolen from a different hotel.' He says, 'John.' His voice goes low and shakes now, this is no shit, like he's going to cry or something. He says, 'John, you know what we're talking about here?' I don't know what to say now, I hate to hear a man cry, you know? So I say, 'I'm not sure I do, sir.' He says, 'I'll tell you what we're talking about here, John. We're talking about my job. We're talking about my career. They're after my badge, John.' "

"Oh, please. Not that routine."

"Close the door, will you?"

I close it, come back and sit down. "Who's *'they'?*"

Big John sits up now, braces his elbows on the desk, pretends like he's holding the phone. "I go, 'Who's *they,* chief?' He says, 'Who's *they,* huh? I'll tell you who's *they.*' He says, 'How long we known each other, John?' I says, 'We go back a long way, chief, you and me. Let's see, must be twenty-seven, twenty-eight years now, huh?' He says, 'That's why I'm telling you this, John, and this is for your ears only, understand?' I go, 'Sure, chief.' He says, 'Not your wife, not nobody.' I says, 'I got you, chief.' Now he whispers, 'I got the disease, John, and I think they know it.' I whisper, 'What disease is that, chief?' He whispers something real soft; I can't hear it. I go, I whisper, 'Come again, chief?' Now I can hear him cupping the phone with his hand, and he whispers: 'Herpes!' I let it sink in, then I whisper, 'Oh, boy.' He whispers, 'Herpes simplex, type two.' I go, I whisper, 'Type two, huh? What's that mean, chief?' He cups the phone real tight now, he whispers, 'Below the waist.' Okay, now I cup the phone myself, I whisper, 'Listen, chief, listen to me, I'm telling you this as an old friend, man-to-man.' I whisper, 'That's the most common VD in the entire world now. It's nothing. You got absolutely nothing to worry about.' He pauses, he whispers, 'Who told you that?' I whisper, 'Any doctor will tell you that. You been to see a doctor?' He whispers, 'You're damn tootin' I have. Outside the department, of course. Know what he told me? Told me the highest incidence of the disease is in *females!*' He's crying now, I swear to Christ, he's crying on the phone."

"Oh, no, come on."

"Swear to Christ. *'Me!'* he whispers. *'Me,* with a *female* disease!' I try to calm him down. 'Not only that,' he whispers, 'but there's no known *cure!*' Now he's sobbing, he's snuffing, I don't know what the hell to say. I go, I whisper, 'That's true, chief, but it can't kill you, it can't make you blind or nothing like that. It can be *controlled,* chief, everybody knows that.' He's still crying, he can hardly talk now. He whispers, 'I'm putting the ointment on every night, just like he said, but it itches like a son of a bitch, John. Itches like a son of a bitch. Can't help *scratching* all the time. It's embarrassing. Chief of detectives scratching his pecker in public.' Now he stops crying, he's quiet for a while. Maybe he's scratching, what do I know? Now he blows his nose, ka-*boom,* like right in my ear. Startles the crap out of me. Now, suddenly, he's back to his normal voice again. I'm sitting there, I can't believe this. He says, 'You got any idea when Ferragamo's meeting with Grasso again?' Just like that. Like I'm talking to two separate people. Stan Laurel to Duke Wayne. I go, 'Grasso told him a couple of days, chief. That was yesterday.' He says, 'Yeah, that's right.' He says, 'We can't make a move till the bulk of the bonds changes hands. Then we got something solid. In the meantime, we sit tight, Daniels, you got that?' I go, 'Got it.' He says, 'Around-the-clock surveillance. Patient, cautious, methodical police work, as usual, Daniels. Keep me up to speed on the big stuff.' He hangs up. Bang. No 'Goodbye,' no 'Take care now,' no 'Thanks, John, old friend of twenty-eight years, thanks for understanding.' Nothing. Squat. Bites my head off, cries on my shoulder, blows his nose in my ear, hangs up on me. I'm sitting here, I'm holding the phone, I'm asking myself how I ever got into this line of work."

"Never told you who 'they' are, huh?"

The elfin eyes of Pat Moynihan dart to me, then away, misted in mischief. Then the impish grin as he sits back, fingertips in the posture of prayer. "They? What 'they' might you be harboring in your brash little brain?"

"The 'they' who know he's—dare I say it? Uh, diseased?"

"Dis—? Bite your tongue, lad." He glances around to be sure we're alone. "Mustn't bandy that word about. Loose lips sink ships."

"Never mind. Think I know anyway."

"Well, I should hope so." He relights his cigar, which long-since went out, blows smoke thoughtfully toward the ceiling. "No. No, it's no good, I couldn't think of revealing such a—such an intimate confidence. Not to a blabbermouth like you, at any rate."

"Got to respect you for that." I relight my own cigar, look at him through the hanging smoke. "Not many guys left in the department who can keep secrets. Not like the old days. Three guesses?"

Checks his watch. "Against the clock. Loser buys lunch. Five seconds. Go."

"Commissioner and them."

"Nope."

"Mayor and them."

"Nope."

I hesitate. "Oh, God, no. Not—?"

"Time's up. You lose. Poor response time, very poor."

"Not—? Don't say it's Vinnie Casandra and them."

He leans back, puffs the cigar. "Afraid it's not that simple. He never told me who 'they' are. But then, I never said he did, did I? Not that I didn't try to find out. The truth is, he doesn't know who 'they' are. That's the murderous part. The mysterious 'they' who know his darkest secrets, and are out for his job, his career, his dignity, are the malicious goblins who haunt the nightmares of us all. Or most of us, at least."

"Yourself included?"

"No. Not any more."

"How'd you get them off your case?"

"Told them to take a hike. Came to the conclusion that my darkest secrets don't amount to a pile of shit in the barnyard of life. Truth is, I'm a delightful guy. Not to mention a fabulous detective." He stands up, checks his watch. "Let's go to work."

He's a pisser, Big John.

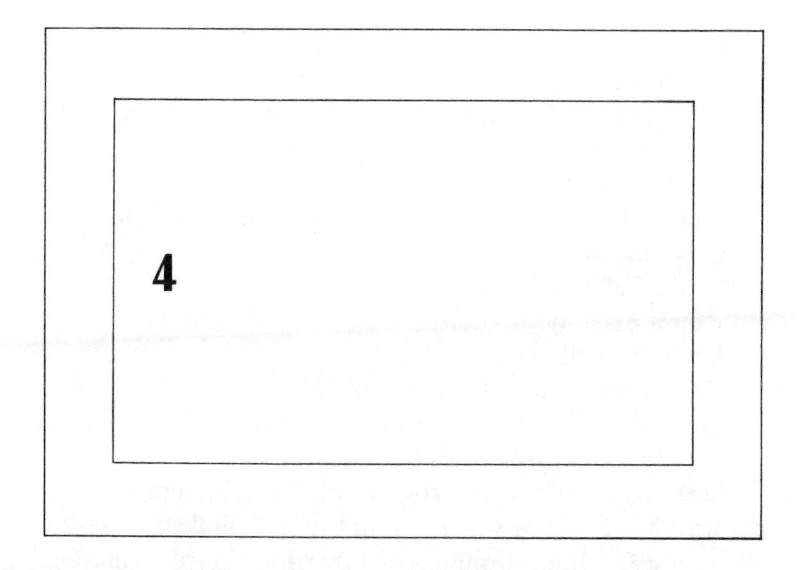

4

FERRAGAMO KNOWS ME FROM WAY BACK, so we have no choice today but to pick up the surveillance on McCabe or hang around the lobby of the Grand Hyatt waiting for Goliat to check out. We opt for McCabe, drive down to 633 Third. It's the Continental Can Building between Fortieth and Forty-first. We get there about 11:45. People are already leaving for lunch and some of them are carrying umbrellas. It's starting to get overcast and the air has that smell. Lou Unright's standing outside in front of the Chemical Bank that occupies the north side of the lobby. He's licking an ice cream cone. Good-looking kid in his late twenties, lightweight tan suit. His partner Marty Pederson is double-parked half a block south on the other side of Third. Big John's driving today, he lets me off in front of the Chemical Bank. Unright spots me, continues to lick his cone slowly, rhythmically, checking the passing tits.

"What're you licking, Louie?"

"Cooldown pussy."

"Sounds good."

He keeps licking and looking. "Variation on an old theme. Drop a scoop in the old cone, let it sink in, go to it, partner. Drives 'em wild. Try different flavors, never get bored. Better'n air conditioning."

"How about in winter?"

"Hot-fudge sundae time. You get a good-enough look at McCabe last night?"

"Yeah. Take off."

"Run a make on him?"

"Uh-huh. Nothing yet."

"Banker's-gray suit, three-piece."

"Go ahead. You got better things to do."

"Believe it. Regards to Big John."

He strolls to the corner, crosses with the light, jumps in the car with Marty. They shoot past in traffic. Couple of minutes later I see Big John turning the corner into Third again. He double parks in front of the Brew Burger, which has the south wing of the lobby. Just after twelve, the crowds start to pour out all three revolving doors. Within five or ten minutes, the sidewalk is jammed. Now, since McCabe didn't get to work until 9:35 or so, I'm guessing he might go out for lunch later than his staff, if he's any kind of real executive, so I'm prepared for a long wait. I'm wrong. About a quarter past, out he comes, David Stockman City, and he's got this healthy young blonde creature with him who has the potential to stop traffic at the Indy 500. Can't be any more than twenty-two, tastefully packaged, knows how to display the merchandise. Wears the same kind of glasses as Stockman/McCabe. Thin black steel frames. Identical. This kid's got to be his managing editor. Even has the walk.

McCabe ushers her directly to the curb. Couple of other guys are trying to flag cabs, so he strides south toward the traffic, one of those deals. Doesn't put his hand up for a cab, he sticks it out like a traffic cop. Stop! Look out, one swerves over and hits the brakes, screech. *What* other people waiting? Eagles soar, turkeys squat. As they say in China, it don't mean a ying if you ain't got the yang. Big John's ahead of the game, as usual, motor running as I walk toward him. Slam, squeal, they're off. Slam, squeal, we're off. Into that swift-flowing yellow river once again, midtown Manhattan in the lunch-hour gridlock two days running, déjà vu.

As it turns out, we get lucky again. Cab stays on Third all the way. Snakes around, but not too bad. Maneuvers over to the right up around Seventy-ninth, pulls over and stops on the southeast corner of Eighty-third. Little restaurant named Martell's. Been there for years. Big John slows to a crawl, waits for their door to open, stops maybe a hundred yards behind. I get out, he goes on to look for a space. They go inside. Nice looking place, has a little sidewalk café arrangement under a blue awning, tables enclosed by a low wrought-iron fence. Not many couples outside because it's getting darker now and the wind's starting to blow.

Inside, it's darker still, stereo playing softly.

"Table for one?" a girl's voice asks.

"Two, please."

"Fifteen- to twenty-minute wait."

"Okay, I'll be at the bar."

"Name?"

"Rawlings. Where's the men's room?"

"Straight back to the right."

I glance around as I walk. Candlelit tables, classy little joint. Can't spot McCabe and company. Go in the john, take a few squirts, come out, walk through the room behind the bar. They're sitting at a table near the fireplace. Romantic candle-light, faces glowing, specs gleaming. Waiter's just taken their drink order, removed one place setting, making it a table for three. I continue around into the bar area, take a stool, order a very dry Beefeater martini on the rocks, swivel around, look out the windows. It's starting to sprinkle now, but the few people at the outside tables stay put under the awning.

I'm enjoying the first few sips of the Beefeater when I see Big John walk up Eighty-third with his umbrella. He speaks to the girl at the door, looks around, folds up the umbrella as he walks toward me. I can tell by the way he walks that he has to take a wicked piss.

"Straight back to your right," I tell him.

He hands me the wet umbrella. "Order me a beer, huh?"

By the time he comes back, it's really raining. I feel cozy now, sitting there nice and dry, feeling the Beefeater go to work. Big John comes around from the front; he's passed through the room behind the bar. I was positive he'd do that. As he settles himself on the stool, I notice his face seems pale.

"You feel okay?" I ask.

"Not really." He starts to sip his beer, puts it down, waves to the bartender. "Give me a shot of Fleishmann's with this, huh?"

"What's wrong?" I ask.

"Didn't you see her?"

"See who?"

"At McCabe's table."

"No, they were alone."

"Jesus Christ. Like looking at a ghost."

"A ghost?"

He watches the bartender pour the shot, a good healthy one, picks it up quickly, tosses it down in one gulp. Makes a face, chases it with a swallow of beer.

I take a sip of Beefeater, get up, go around into the room behind the bar, head for the head. I look at McCabe's table. Now I understand. I can't believe what I'm seeing at this table. Sitting there between McCabe and the broad, face bright in candlelight, shadow flickering on the brick wall, is a woman who's got to be the identical twin sister of Joan Crawford. Identical! *Mean*-looking bitch. Dark hair yanked back, chalk-white face, arched eyebrows painted on, spider-leg lashes framing wide whacko eyes, lipstick-line circa 1945, teeth guaranteed to glow in the dark. Everybody's staring at her. Sends a quick little shiver from my neck to my asshole.

I get to the men's room, I lean on the sink, I look in the

mirror, it starts again. Second hallucination in a week and they usually occur only once or twice a month. Slightly dizzy, sick feeling. Then the very quick flashes, scenes from childhood mostly. Difficult to describe, but something like this: A nun walks slowly across the fenced-in playground of the Epiphany School on East Twenty-second Street. It's filled with children and she towers over them. She wears the old black uniform with the stiff white cowl and bib and a wide black belt with a heavy rosary hanging at her side and clicking. The bedroom I had as a boy in an apartment at 424 East Twenty-fourth Street. On the wall above the bed are large colored photographs cut from the magazine section of the Sunday *News:* Hank Greenberg, Bobby Feller, Red Ruffing, Charley Keller. A man I can't identify is washing a blackboard in a classroom at Cardinal Hayes High School in the Bronx. Whatever had been written on the blackboard has been erased first and the man is rubbing a wet sponge across the board in long, slow, horizontal strokes, changing the color from dull gray to glossy black.

It's over in seconds. The sick, dizzy sensation will last a little longer. I look in the mirror and shake my head slowly. It can't be the martini because it occurs without any physical common denominators except the images that seem to be triggers. In this case, Joan Crawford, of all people. As usual, I feel a little angry and frustrated. I also feel intrigued. What the hell is this shit all about?

I hear two men walk in, both laughing through their noses, then out loud when the door closes. I glance at them in the mirror, turn on the faucet, start to wash my hands. They go over to the urinals.

"Aw *right!*" the taller one says.

The other guy keeps giggling as he pisses. "Weird momma!"

"For a second, I thought it was Faye Dunaway!"

"She thinks she *is!*"

"See how she's lookin' at that *other* broad?"

"See those *choppers?*"

"Dracula Dearest!"

That breaks them up. Now they're shoving each other with their shoulders, saying, "*Duck,* man, she's *behind* you!" Shit like that. I dry my hands, straighten my tie, get out of there.

I take another long look at Joan Crawford as I pass through to the bar area. Even in candlelight, the hair and makeup and all is much too good to be the job of an amateur. Over the past couple of weeks there's been a lot of press-agent flack about the film version of *Mommie Dearest,* which is in production now, including pictures of Faye Dunaway who's been made up to resemble Crawford very closely, even to the shaved eyebrows. If this character at the table is an actress or model of some kind, or a comedian—which wouldn't surprise me—who's trying to cash in on all the hoopla, then it's a logical assumption that McCabe and company are also trying to cash in on the hoopla by doing a story on her for their magazine. Logical assumption. Still, one little thought flits across my mind that I decide to check out, just to satisfy my curiosity.

Big John's munching on peanuts, nursing his beer along.

"Mommie Dreadful," I tell him.

"The face that launched a thousand whips."

"What we have here is a serious identity crisis."

"Maybe she wants to be listed in *What's That?*"

I smile, sip the martini. "Maybe the old dear has more of a problem than we think. Know the Village Vamp down on Christopher?"

"Know *of* it, yeah."

"Transvestite joint. Nightly shows. Probably the best female impersonators in town."

He looks at me, shrugs. "Worth a shot."

I get up, walk to the back, find a pay phone, look up the number. It's about one o'clock, too early for a nightspot to answer, but I figure they might have an answering service for reservations. I'm right.

A young man's voice: "Village Vamp."

"Yeah, can you tell me the entertainers for tonight's shows?"

He speaks in a flat Bronx monotone: "Nine-thirty, 'Our Fine Fettered Friends,' featuring cuffs for toughs and gags for hags, choreography by Dizzi Pline, costumes by Hugh Mility, special effects by Pussy Tickle; ten o'clock, 'I'm Needing This Jock, I Ain't Got Enough Hangups Already,' featuring Muhammad Ali-Baba from Queens in the pink tutu with the robin's-egg blue stripes, and Reggi Jacksoff from Boredom in the watermelon-red jumpsuit with the fingerprint patterns; ten-thirty, 'Mommie Dearest, Spank Me in My Doctor Denton's with the Trap Door Open One More Time,' starring the tempestuous taskmaster Tanya Hide and the teen-queen wet-dream supreme Penny Tent; eleven o'clock, 'Tiptoe Through the Trollops,' featuring—"

"That's enough, thank you."

"So, you want a reservation?"

For just a second, I hesitate. "Yeah. Table for two at—say, ten-fifteen. Table in the back."

"Ten-fifteen, deuce in back. Name?"

"Williams, Tony Williams."

"That T-o-n-i?"

"T-o-n-*y*. Anthony."

"Okay, thank you, Mr. Williams."

No matter what you see on TV or read in books, most investigative work, police and private, is just plain boring as hell, and I mean that sincerely. The routine puts a lot of guys to sleep, particularly surveillance. Often lasts for weeks. Positively deadly. Come home after sitting in a car for eight hours or more, stinking of smoke and sweat and coffee and junk food. Glamorous occupation. Still, when you've been around long enough, the real uppers seem worth it somehow. At least for me. They don't come from getting a formal letter of commendation that goes in your file, or from reading your six-month evaluation report, they come at times you can't really anticipate. Like sitting in a little phone booth at the back of a crowded restaurant, looking out at couples in candlelight, smoke hanging in layers, rain beating on the tops of cars in heavy traffic, and getting this feeling deep in your gut that you've come up with something important.

Hard to explain exactly *why* I know it's important. All I can tell you, I just *feel* it. I'm the first to admit that the majority of so-called breaks in a case tend to appear accidential. In a sense, many of them are. But I also believe that you help to make your own breaks in this business. By that I mean you get to a point where you place a great deal of trust in your instincts rather than your intellect. It's like a kind of radar you develop when you hang around the street long enough. I trust that radar. I trust it because it's one of the things that's kept me alive.

Now I dial headquarters, ask for Mat Murphy, deputy chief, rather than the chief, because I know I can't possibly explain to Vadney what I'm doing. Transvestites, Duke Wayne doesn't want to know.

"Murphy."

"Mat, John Rawlings, how you doing?"

"Same old shit, John, what you got?"

"Anything on McCabe?"

"Yeah, hold on." I can see him holding the receiver with his neck, sorting through the mountains of papers that cover his desk every day. "Yeah, right, William McCabe. Nothing. Zero. Snow White."

"Thought so. Anything new on Ferragamo?"

"Last I heard, he hadn't left his apartment yet."

"How about Goliat?"

"Yeah, we got two calls on him. Wait a second. Eddie Goliat. Checked out of the Grand Hyatt eleven twenty-one, took a cab out to United Airlines, LaGuardia, arrived eleven fifty-six. First-class on the one-fifteen flight to Detroit."

"Okay, we're on McCabe now. Martell's restaurant, corner of Third and Eighty-third. Need a make. Almost positive this is a phony name, but run it through anyway, huh?"

"Go."

"Okay, now don't laugh, ready for this? White *male* Caucasian. Name, Tan-ya Hide."

"Oh, Jesus."

"Yeah, huh?"

"This on the level, John?"

"Afraid so. Tanya, think it's T-a-n-y-a. Hide, H-i-d-e. Could be H-*y*-d-e, but somehow I doubt it."

"Tanya Hide. One of *them* deals."

"How sweet it is!"

"You're a doll, John. They're gonna laugh me out of the office, you know that, don't you?"

"Comes with the territory, sugar."

"Have a nice lunch, tweetie."

When I go back and tell Big John, he's intrigued. Now we got some interesting possibilities going on here. First, if you've ever read an inflight magazine, you know there's no way in hell they'd touch a plastic fork to a story about a female impersonator. Folks out in Moral Majority City, who buy a shitload of airplane tickets every year, they don't want to know from a female impersonator, thank you very much. Ergo, McCabe and company are definitely not talking editorial here. Old friends meeting for a quiet lunch perhaps? Doubtful at best. Not with obvious straights like McCabe and company. So what's happening?

When we're finally offered a table, it's about 1:10 and it's at a front window where we can't see our subjects, so we decide to have sandwiches at the bar. We really don't have much of a choice at this point, because our subjects will undoubtedly finish long before us. Big John's not too delighted, since I'm buying, having lost our bet. We each go to the bathroom once more during lunch to check the progress.

Although I'd made those reservations at the Village Vamp for the surveillance team that's going to cover Tanya Hide that night, I ask Big John if he'd be at all interested in spending a half hour or so down there watching Tanya perform.

"What time's she go on?" he asks.

"*He* goes on at ten-thirty. Might be laughs."

"Yeah, what, an S-and-M routine?"

"Sounds like it, yeah. Might have some of his friends stop in, could be interesting."

He chews his tunafish-salad sandwich, thinks about it.

"What the hell," I say. "Some nice-looking broads down there, John. Might get lucky, y'know?"

He has to laugh through his nose to keep from spattering tuna all over the bar. Now he's wiping his mouth, giving me this look.

"Half an hour, come on. We'll sit at the bar, have a few, let the other team have the table. We need a break."

"Maybe. Depends what's on TV tonight."

"Already checked. 'Real People,' rerun; 'PM Magazine,' yuk; 'Charlie's Angels,' rerun; 'Merv Griffin'; 'Diff'rent Strokes,' rerun; 'Facts of Life,' rerun; 'Quincy,' rerun. You get the same shit at the Vamp, only live."

"I like Merv Griffin. Who's he got on?"

"Don't know. Catch his whole show, come down after. He's on eight-thirty to ten. All you got after that is a 'Quincy' rerun."

He agrees. After lunch, it's a yawn afternoon. We're outside in the car long before they leave Martell's, ready to split up if they do. Rain's developed into a steady spring drizzle, not so bad. About 1:35, out they come. McCabe flags a cab while they wait under the awning. All three get in. Up Third to Eighty-fourth, east to Second, south all the way to Forty-first (it's two-way because of the *Daily News* building's loading ramps), then back up to Third. McCabe and the broad jump out, head for their office; cab roars away with Tanya. We decide to stay with him. Up Forty-first to Lex, south down to Twenty-third, west to Seventh Avenue, then south down to Charles Street in the Village. Tanya gets out on the northwest corner, opens an umbrella, walks east on Charles. I'm out by now, using Big John's umbrella, walking on the opposite side of the street. Tanya goes into a high-rise apartment at 15

Charles. Nice red-brick building, clean white canopy. Uniformed doorman tips his cap smartly, opens the door, hi-ho. Doorman goes back to reading his paper. Looks like we got Tanya's address.

There's a little drugstore up ahead on the corner of Charles and Greenwich. I know we're probably going to be sitting in the car till our shift ends at eight, so I go in, buy a pack of Dutch Masters' panetellas. There's a phone booth in back. I'm 99 percent sure that Tanya Hide is a phony name, but I learned twenty years ago never to overlook the obvious, so I grab the book out of sheer habit and look up the name. Only seven listings for Hide in Manhattan. One of them reads: "Hide T 15 Charles."

The afternoon passes uneventfully. We're parked on the corner of Charles and Waverly with a good view of the apartment entrance. People come and go, speaking of Michelangelo. Rain stops about 3:45 and it's not so humid now. We have several cups of coffee. Big John starts walking back and forth between the car and the drugstore, making calls to headquarters mostly, checking on surveillance operations. We got a new team outside McCabe's building now; we don't believe the Indy-500 broad is worth tailing, so the guys have instructions to concentrate on McCabe when he leaves work. Ferragamo leaves his apartment about 4:15 to buy a newspaper, goes straight back again.

Around 4:30, I get a radio message to call Murphy. Surprise, they have a make on Tanya. Vital statistics: Hide, Thomas Nathan, aka. "Doctor J.," A.K.a. "Nauga," a.k.a. "Tanya." Last known address, 667 West 115th Street, Manhattan. White male Caucasian, twenty-eight years old, five-foot-seven, 134 pounds, brown hair, brown eyes, medium complexion. First (and only) arrest, Manhattan, 17th Precinct, March 7, 1976. Charge: "CPSP 165.50 1st." Translation: Possession of Stolen Property, first degree. Dismissed. Murphy says he figures the kid probably copped a dildo, got it stuck, then needed emergency corkscrew service.

Ever been to a transvestite bar? Can be very entertaining,

depending on the place. Village Vamp happens to be a class joint, as they go. Relatively selective about its clients. As the name may or may not imply to straights, it caters to males, although there's the predictable spillover. You come in here, you can't believe some of the stuff walking around. Some of them can easily pass for fashion models, actresses, receptionists, you name it. Easily. Wouldn't be at all surprised if some of them do. You look around, they're sitting at tables with their boyfriends, if that's what they are, they look like affluent young couples from maybe the upper East Side. And maybe some of them are, that's the catch. You can't really tell at a distance. Now you get up close, like at the bar, you look at their faces without seeming to stare, even then, most cases, you can't be absolutely certain. Obviously expensive hair styles that may or may not be wigs, extremely skillful makeup, not the slightest trace of a five-o'clock shadow, earrings and necklaces as subtle as their perfume. Average cleavage, some of it real, wide range of designer outfits, rarely flamboyant. Unmasculine arms, wrists, hands, manicured nails, tasteful bracelets and rings. Good female figures with the possible exception of the hips. Legs and ankles you got to see to believe, smooth as silk, shoes and handbags strictly *haute couture.*

First time you come in here, forget it. Maybe one or two exhibitionists on any given night, but they usually take the hints and leave. No matter what you hear or read or expect in your mind's eye, this place is guaranteed to give you second thoughts about shit like hormonal imbalance and chromosomal snafus. To put it another way, if these bimbos ain't girls, they sure as hell ain't boys.

Tonight, I arrive about 10:20 and the place is packed by now, ten o'clock floor show over, main events coming up. Tony Williams and Bob Curry, the relief team covering Tanya, are at their table in back and from the expressions on their faces I can see they're enjoying the assignment. Big John hasn't arrived yet. I go over to the bar, order a Beefeater martini, light up a cigar. Have to stand because all the stools have long-since been taken. Room has a little stage with a six-piece rock band. From there, a raised runway extends out maybe fifty feet into the audience, all at tables, something like at a beauty pageant, and ends in a circular area with a diameter of about ten feet, where the floor shows take place.

Air is heavy with the smell of pot and the rock band is just loud enough so I can't hear the conversations around me, which is fine. Big John shows about five minutes later. He's checking it all out as he ambles up to the bar. He's smiling. Never been here before, not used to such class. We exchange pleasantries, he orders a drink, lights a cigar, takes a good long look around. Pat Moynihan wanders onto a Fellini sound stage. I can tell he's just a bit uncomfortable. Although we're both dressed casually, the glances we're getting reveal that we've got to be: (a) vice squad; (b) narc squad; (c) convention delegates from Boise; (d) the ugliest bulldykes in the city. Me, I don't give a shit what they think. I'm having fun.

Almost exactly 10:30, houselights dim, band stops, crowd hushes, stereo system comes on with Bert Parks singing the "Miss America" theme. Yeah, Bert Parks. Now a bright circle spotlight follows the mistress of ceremonies from stage-center slowly out on the runway toward the performing circle. This mistress is a gorgeous dark-haired all-American kid in a dazzling sequined evening gown that sparkles like diamonds with every step. Ovation is tremendous. Walks regally into the circle and is handed a mike from below. Bert Parks fades. Mistress's voice is soft, sensuous:

"Ladies and gentlemen, once again, by overwhelming popular demand, Tanya Hide and Penny Tent in their lovely little sketch, 'Mommie Dearest, Spank Me in My Doctor Denton's with the Trap Door Open One More Time.' "

Loud applause as the spot dissolves, leaving the room in darkness. Now the stereo plays the soft overture to "The Girl from Ipanema." A pin-spot picks up the face of Penny Tent, center-stage, slowly widens to reveal the full figure. There's a sound from the crowd that can only be described as a simultaneous "*Ahhhhh!*" Penny starts his promenade along the runway. He's about seventeen, give or take a year, maybe five-foot-six, 115 soaking wet, classic features, very long dark hair. Wears a white string-bikini that accentuates a dark tan, a slim gold waist chain and a slim gold ankle bracelet. Has all the confident movements of a professional model as he walks, stops, turns side-to-side, then completely around, hair swirling, hands on hips. Even though it's a class joint, crowd noise is building to an edge of hysteria. All along the runway, hands reach out to touch and stroke the kid's ankles and legs. Every time the female vocalist on the recording reaches the line ". . . and when she passes, each one she passes goes 'Ahhh!'," this crowd explodes with "*Yeahhhhh!*"

Penny finally reaches the circle. Set up there is a little wooden hobbyhorse mounted on rockers. The kid mounts it, starts rocking slowly, luxuriously, knees in tight, eyes closed, sucking his thumb. I don't know if it's the pot or what, but people are starting to go bananas now. I take a quick look at the faces around the bar. These kids are sweating, saying stuff like, "*Pen*-nee, *Pen*-nee, do it, honey, *do* it!" Big John, he's standing there chewing on his cigar, he looks like he's going to bite through it any second. Me, I'm starting to get a rod on, I can't believe it.

Now the music segues into "The Best Is Yet to Come," with Tiny Tim tiptoeing vocal, yet. Instantly, a second pin-spot picks up the face of Tanya Hide, center-stage, and widens. Kid's unmistakably Joan Crawford, wild-eyed, wearing what may or may not be a replica of the famous black-lace negligee Crawford wore in her 1945 Oscar-winning performance in *Mildred Pierce.* In any case, he holds a gleaming gold Oscar high over his head with one hand. Other hand is behind his back. Mere sight of this guy brings the house down. Grand-slam home run, bottom of the ninth. Tanya doesn't even crack a grin, slinks down the runway, Oscar clutched to her bosom now, wide eyes staring fixedly at poor little Penny Tent who's obviously being a naughty kid. People along the runway are craning to see what Mommie's got behind his back.

We find out soon enough. Penny's rocking rhythm has picked up considerable speed now, like he's almost there. Suddenly, he realizes he's not alone. He opens his eyes wide, snaps the thumb out of his mouth. Mommie's standing over him. Tiny Tim's cut off in mid-sentence. Crowd goes almost silent. The dreaded confrontation. No mikes are used or needed.

"You little *bitch!*" Mommie shouts. "You're doing it *again!*"

Penny shakes his head, denying it, terrified.

"Don't you know that's a *mortal sin?!*"

Penny shakes his head, hair swirling.

"Don't you know you can be damned in *hell* for *eternity?!*"

Penny covers his face with his hands.

"All right, young lady. You haven't told the truth, so you must pay the consequences!"

Some spaced-out clown in the audience shouts: "Leave her alone, you rotten bitch!"

Fifty people go: "*Shhhhh!*" And you know they mean it.

"Pay the consequences!" Mommie commands.

Penny's off the horse in a flash, snaps to attention, head down, hair over his face.

Mommie removes the left hand from behind the back, tosses a small dark bundle at him. Penny catches it, unravels it, holds it up. Crowd goes, "Ohhh!" Words to that effect. It's a soft black leather version of Doctor Denton's pajamas, trap door, feet and all. Penny turns the pajamas upside down. Clink-clunk. Clink-clunk. Out fall two pairs of glistening nickel-plated handcuffs.

Mommie snaps his fingers, holds out the Oscar.

Penny takes it, places it carefully on the floor next to the handcuffs, then drops to his knees in front of Mommie. Silence. Now the stereo comes on, a faintly familiar, dreamlike overture—piano, electric guitars, bass, drums. For a few seconds, Mommie and Penny remain frozen in the spotlight, listening, waiting. At last we hear the lilting ultra-feminine voice of Oliva Newton-John in "Making a Good Thing Better":

Although I know our love is going strong,
Little surprises kinda help it along;
We mustn't let our lives become routine,
Don't do anything we don't mean.

Switch! Mommie sticks his right leg out submissively. Penny removes the slipper, fits the foot and legging on Mommie, pulls it up to the knee; black-lace negligee is no problem; Mommie lifts it shyly, just enough. Crowd's going wild now. Penny starts on Mommie's left leg.

There is no limit to love at all,
It can always get better, the deeper you fall;
I'm sure without that love we won't survive,
So COME on and SHOW it—let's keep it ALIVE!

Penny stands now, zips the front zipper up to Mommie's waist. Mommie removes the negligee over the head, flings it away with the right hand, covers his falsies with the other, utters an embarrassed little giggle. Much ado about nothing. Now he slides his arms in the sleeves. Out pop the little white hands. Penny zips it to the neck. Mommie's in!

And we'll be making a good thing better,
But with luck it's gonna last forever, you'll see;
Making a good thing better,
That's the way we're gonna stay together—you and me!

Everything goes smooth now as the orchestra picks up the cool, twanging, mellow theme. Mommie stands at attention, very slim in the tight black leather, hands behind her back, feet together. Penny slaps on the sparkling cuffs like a veteran cop. Mommie struggles, testing, tingling with excitement, realizing the awful humiliation to come. Now, slowly, Penny begins to unzip the big steel zipper on the trap door.

If we're to make each other satisfied,
Gotta keep on tryin', don't let it ride;
It all comes over in the morning kiss . . .

Trap door falls open, exposing Mommie's lily-white cheeks. Following the lyrics, Penny gives Mommie a soft slap first, then winds up and delivers a resounding WHACK:

. . . Don't DO it like THAT—do it like THIS!

Now the room's going totally nuts. Newton-John's belting out the theme, joined by her background vocals, but you can hardly hear them. Penny snaps his fingers, makes Mommie shuffle over to the hobbyhorse and stand by for action. You can see a pink blush on the right cheek of poor Mommie's ass. This kid doesn't fool around. Now he mounts the hobbyhorse, yanks Mommie down across his knees, begins rocking slowly, luxuriously, like before. He picks up the tempo fast when Newton-John comes back solo, begins spanking Mommie with both hands, giving it everything he's got, in rhythm with the cue word "better":

Make it so much better,
It's better, better,
Make it so much better,
Make it better, better, better,
Make it better, better, better,
Make it better, better, better,
Better, better!

Newton-John's back into the theme again as the spotlight dims very quickly, but you can hear Penny slapping away like a mad drummer. Now the spotlight goes out, leaving the room in complete darkness. A gradual hush. Newton-John and her background vocals are heard clearly, coming to the end of the song. *Click*—a very dim pin-spot needles down to pick up some kind of object on the floor. As the pin-spot gets a trifle brighter, you see it's the Oscar, but it seems to be standing on its head. Pin-spot widens slowly. Giggles, laughter, isolated voices: "What the hell *is* it?" Newton-John's voice starts to fade. Spot widens more. Some bitch hollers: "Harry, look, it's a big golden prick!"

But it's not a big golden prick. Directly below it, you can now see the dark outline of Mommie, flat on the floor on his stomach, with the Oscar stuck firmly in his asshole.

Typical Village Vamp *coup de grâce.* Stereo blasts out with "That's Entertainment," room goes berserk, high-pitched screams, whistles, cheers, sustained applause. "*Bravo! Encore!*" Opening-night audience at a smash Broadway musical. No curtain calls; Tanya, Penny, Oscar, and hobbyhorse have vanished in the dark.

When the houselights finally come up again and the rock band takes over, I glance at Big John. He's squinting through the hanging smoke, staring at the empty performing circle.

I wave my hand in front of his eyes. "Anybody home?"

"From here, four o'clock off the circle."

I look at the four o'clock position. At first I'm not sure. I jockey for a better view. No question. An attractive young thing is sitting alone at a ringside table for two, smoking, holding a glass of white wine. The kid wears a smart blue blazer, pale blue handkerchief in the breast pocket, white shirt, pale blue ascot. Has the subtle demeanor of a handful of others in the room, that of a slim, sophisticated young lady in conservative drag. We know this kid. This kid is Hamilton Harcourt, the insurance agent with Lloyds of London. Before we can get the attention of the bartender, pay our tab and leave, Harcourt's date arrives. Radiant, smiling, and with eyes only for Harcourt.

And her date is Penny Tent.

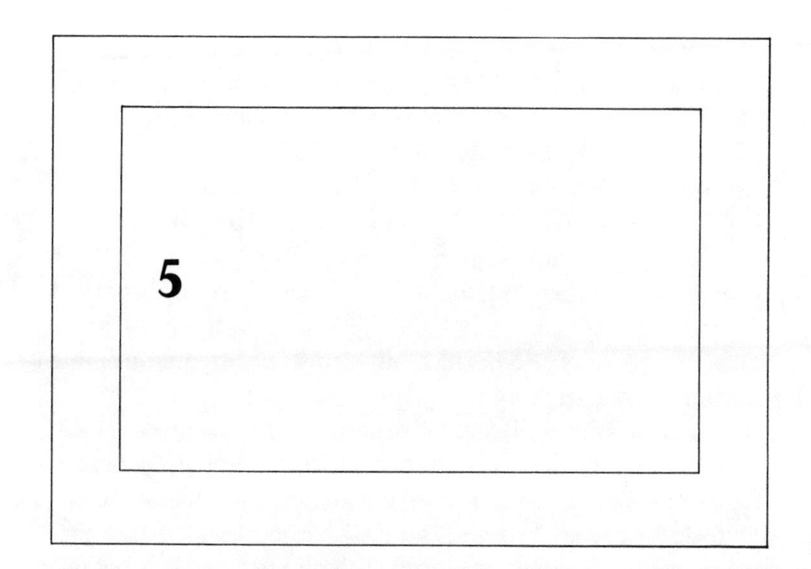

5

NEXT MORNING we get called to the chief's office down at headquarters. Compared to our precinct, the headquarters building at 1 Police Plaza is straight out of science fiction. It was opened in 1973 and it's undoubtedly one of the most modern police facilities in the world. From the street it doesn't look that imposing, fourteen floors of red brick, recessed windows. Kind of squats there in the plaza like a fortress. As you enter the enormous main lobby, off to the right there's an old wooden police wagon that had been horse drawn, vintage 1880, and it's the only touch of character in the whole place. Inside, it reminds me of a big modern hospital. Long, bright, antiseptic hallways, each floor color-coded, an atmosphere of efficient artificial cheer. Every police officer wears a plastic ID card clipped to shirt or lapel; every civilian employee wears a special ID card; every visitor wears a color-coded plastic pass, restricting admission to the floor of that color. Color-blind visitors are in deep trouble.

Chief's office is on the top floor, of course. Color-code red. Psychiatric ward. Big corner office. His assistant, Steve Adair, asks us to wait; chief's on the phone. We sit in the little reception area. I haven't read the paper yet, so I pick up this morning's *News,* turn to the "How'm I Doin'?" cartoon. I'm hooked on the series now. Today our heroes are in a white-tiled room with an elegant sign on the wall that reads "Le Can de Chauncey Lazy." They're sitting in adjoining stalls, doors shut, only their shoes and boots (with spurs) showing. Door to the left is marked "Hizhonor"; door to the right is marked "Hizhorror." Mayor's talk balloon says, "Anything?" Chief's talk balloon says, "No runs, no drips, no errors." Vinnie Casandra's been taking nasty pills.

Couple of minutes later, we're shown into the chief's office. Hizhorror's sitting in a high-backed leather chair behind a highly polished wooden desk that's innocent of clutter. "Cluttered desks cause cluttered minds," he once said. Appropriately, his desk is virtually empty. Telephone console is behind to his left. American flag is behind to his right. On the wall directly above his head is a framed photo of the commissioner, who's sitting in a high-backed leather chair with the American flag to his right; on the wall directly above his head is the bottom of a framed photo. Can't see who's in it, but I already know. It's a photo of the mayor, who's sitting in a high-backed leather chair with the American flag to his right; on the wall directly above his head is the bottom of a framed photo. Guess who's in that one? Right. The governor. By the time you get up to President Reagan, you expect to see maybe a portrait of George Washington, but you don't. Reagan's got a framed photo of his own personal hero up there, Ralph Bellamy, playing FDR in the film *Sunrise at Campobello.* That's a fact, you can check it out. High-backed leather chair, American flag, the whole routine. Guess it's all relative, right? Some guys set their sights higher than others.

But to get back to the chief, he waves us in, tells Steve to hold all calls except the mayor and the commissioner. Steve leaves, shuts the door. We sit down. Silence. Chief leans forward slowly, shirtsleeves rolled to the elbows, clasps his fingers together on the desk, studies them. Wrinkles his brows. Finally, the left eyebrow goes up and he's into the patented Duke Wayne down-home grin, left side of the mouth only, couple of molars gleaming.

"I got a—got a little problem," he says. "Been reading the surveillance reports this morning. Ferragamo and McCabe, all right. I can buy them, they're worth the manpower all the way. We're about to hit paydirt on Ferragamo, tell you about it later. These others—Jesus. I'm not second-guessing you, Daniels, you're supervising this thing, but I'm telling you I got problems with these others. Give me a quick rundown on these people, huh?"

Big John clears his throat. "Well, Thomas Hide, he's the guy met with McCabe, we ran a make on him, as you know. One arrest, possession of stolen property, dismissed. Now, my reasoning—"

"What's he do for a living, John?"

"A living?" Big John's face colors a little; he shifts his weight. "Thomas Hide's a professional actor, chief. As of last night, he's no longer a suspect anyway. I pulled Williams and Curry off him last night and put them on the two new suspects."

"Yeah, so I read. You were working overtime last night, the both of you?"

"Not officially, no."

"I see. But you were down to this Village Vamp club and you reassigned Williams and Curry on the spot, right?"

"That's—correct."

"Rawlings, let me ask you something. First off, let's call a spade a spade here. Let's back up a minute. This Thomas Hide you had Murphy run a make on. Wasn't the make under the name *Tanya* Hide?"

"Right. That's one of—"

"Yeah, an alias, I know, Rawlings. I know that. Now, is it true this guy's a transvestite *fag?*"

I hesitate. "Actually, he's—"

"A transvestite fag who actually goes around the streets in *drag?* Is that true?"

"Actually, he's a female impersonator, chief. As Big John said, he's a professional actor. He's made up to look like Joan Crawford for his act."

"Joan *Crawford?*"

"Yeah. See, there's a film coming out that—"

"Wait a minute, Rawlings. Just hold that thought a minute, let me get this straight in my mind. Now, when McCabe and his female companion finish having lunch with this—female impersonator fag, you guys somehow make the decision to tail the fag instead of sticking with McCabe who's a known associate of Ferragamo. Now, how in hell—what's that all about?"

"My decision," Big John says. "They were all in one cab. McCabe and the broad jump out at their office, Hide continues on. I decide it's more productive to follow him, try to get an address."

Chief nods, sits back, gives us a hint of the folksy grin. "Just between the three of us. Strictly off the record, okay? You guys have a couple of belts at lunch?"

"One beer," Big John snaps.

"Chief," I say softly. "We both had a strong gut feeling about Hide. As it turns out, the decision to go with him paid off. If we hadn't stayed with him, we wouldn't've established the link between Harcourt and Tent."

"Harcourt and Tent, yeah. I got *real* problems with *them.*"

"Harcourt's an insurance agent with Lloyds of London."

Chief knits his brows. "Nothing about that in the reports."

"Williams and Curry don't know it yet. We didn't have time to tell them last night."

"Okay, so what? What're you getting at?"

Big John sits forward now. "Harcourt's the agent who handled the insurance for Mrs. Nancy Kramer. Eight hundred thousand dollars. We met him up at Alistair Rodger Rare Jewels on Tuesday."

"*Harcourt?* You positive it's the same guy?"

"Positive," Big John says.

Chief frowns, opens the top drawer of his desk, rifles through some papers, pulls a couple out. "According to both Williams and Curry, they both describe Harcourt as—quote, 'possible female transvestite,' unquote."

"That's correct," I tell him.

"Oh, come *on,* Rawlings, for Christ's *sake!* An insurance agent from Lloyds of *London?* You telling me that a bone fide insurance agent from Lloyds of London is a *dyke* in *drag?*"

"More than possible," Big John says.

Chief's sky-blue eyes dart from Big John to me, then down to the reports again. "All right, let's put Harcourt aside for a minute. Now, Penny Tent. Both Williams and Curry describe this person as being a *male* transvestite. *That* correct?"

"Female impersonator," I tell him.

"Female impersonator, my *asshole!* What we're talking about here is *another* transvestite fag!"

I nod, shrug. "He's an actor. Does a sketch with Tanya Hide."

"Rawlings, look, do me a favor, huh? Let's drop all these fifty-cent cracker-barrel psychology words like 'female impersonator.' Let's call a spade a spade here. This person we're talking about here is an out-and-out *fag* in *drag!* That too gritty for you to say?"

"Fine with me, no problem. Fag in drag."

"Chief," Big John says. "We haven't seen those reports yet. Did they get addresses on those two?"

"Yeah. Apparently they—" He glances quickly at the window to his right, remains frozen in that posture for a few seconds, listening. A fly is buzzing around the pane. "Apparently they live together." He looks at the reports, runs his finger down one of them. "They got some kind of loft on—think it's Carmine Street. Yeah, here it is, Carmine. Twelve Carmine."

I take out my notebook, jot it down.

"One of the bells in the foyer is marked 'H. Harcourt.' Top

floor loft." Chief looks at the window again, listens. Now he pushes his big chair back, stands, strides to a nearby table that holds a stack of newspapers, grabs one, rolls it up tight, slaps it in his left palm as he walks to the window. Silence again. No sign of the fly. Chief looks around the pane carefully, begins to scratch his crotch with his left hand, almost unconsciously. When he speaks, his voice is extremely soft, just above a whisper, and with his back to us he appears to be talking to himself. "Commissioner Reilly, that suckass. 'I expect a verbal progress report on this case every morning, Vadney. Ten o'clock sharp every morning, is that understood?' Understood, suckass. So *you* can give *your* daily progress report to *Ed Koch.* So he'll think *you're* right on top of it." He stops talking abruptly, as if realizing we're there, glances at his watch.

Big John and I automatically glance at ours. Nine thirty-seven. This is no shit, it's embarrassing to be in this room now, we don't have a clue what this guy's going to say next.

He keeps his back to us, but makes a fair recovery: "So, like this morning, who's gotta tell Reilly all this weird shit that went down last night? *Me,* that's who. Not *you* guys. *Me.* Know what it's gonna make me look like?"

"Not true," Big John says. "Got nothing to do with you, chief. We're out there following leads like always. We don't know where they're going to take us anymore than you do."

Chief turns around slowly; a lock of hair is over his forehead. "Try explaining that to a suckass civilian like Reilly. Jesus Christ, I mean I got *forty* detectives on this case. *Forty* detectives, handpicked by me, best detectives in the city of New York. So what've we got so far? I'll tell you what we got. Right now, this minute, we got around-the-clock surveillance on four asshole subjects, three shifts a day. That's twenty-four men full-time right there alone. Tailing *what?* Tailing a ratass skinhead bush-league ground ball. Tailing an Ivy League intellectual editor of a halfass inflight magazine who gets his rocks off having lunch with a male transvestite faggot impersonator of Joan *Crawford.* Tailing a respectable insurance agent from Lloyds of London who's described by four of my best men as a *dyke* in *drag!* Tailing a Village Vamp bimbo actor who's actually a *fag* in drag! Real heavy hitters all the way, top-drawer shit, exactly the right combination to mastermind the biggest hotel robbery in American history."

"Chief, come *on,*" Big John says. "Now *you're* starting to talk like a civilian. You know that? That's exactly the kind of horseshit amateur psychology I'd expect to hear from some civilian or politician who got his police experience out of watching TV or reading whodunits. I'll listen to shit like that from a civilian, but not from you, Walt. You been around too long, you know too much. You came up the hard way, same as us. Don't talk that kind of nonsense, not to us."

Chief takes a swipe at his hair, looks at the rolled-up paper in his hand, examines it. "Maybe you're right, John."

"You know goddamn well I'm right."

Now the chief tosses the paper back on the table, goes over, sits on the edge of his desk, arms braced. "You guys understand that, I understand it. Try reporting to somebody who doesn't."

"Tell him the *truth,*" Big John says. "Tell him the truth as you *know* the truth only too fuckin' well. Those four whackos might not look to *him* like they're capable of pulling this off, but any cop who's worked the street as long as we have knows better. Talk about 'exactly the right combination'? What the fuck *is* the right combination? Look at this group we got here. Ferragamo's got all the experience you can ask for. Rap sheet going back to the mid-fifties. Plus he's a genuine loser, a lifetime loser who's probably dreamed all his life about pulling something this big, making up for it all in one swing, graduating to the big show. Getting the recognition he's always deserved. McCabe, this guy's so transparent, even Reilly could figure his angle. Bored intellectual who's wasting his life turning out a pissyass airline inflight magazine. Macho guy, ladies' man, out to impress, wants action, wants to hang out with crooks and cons and weirdos, loves the danger element. Needs a lot more money than the PR department of an airline can pay him. Expensive lifestyle. Harcourt? Now we're talking about the clown who probably had the original idea. He—or she—had to know Nancy Kramer had eight hundred thousand in jewels in those two safe-deposit boxes. Which would make it worthwhile for those two boxes alone. No guesswork involved; she *knew.* Now she needed help. She's living with Penny Tent who has all kinds of connections both AC and DC. Penny Tent, he's the only one we don't know much about yet, but we will."

"One thing's for certain," I add. "Both Harcourt and Tent are in *fact* masters of disguise. They have to be."

Chief nods, narrows his eyes, thinks about it. "That's true, they'd have to be. Can't argue with that. Interesting group, y'know? Got to admit we got an interesting group of people here. Maybe all this weird shit might hang together after all." He goes behind the desk now, sits down, opens the middle drawer again, takes out a yellow legal pad. First page is filled with his very large, bold handwriting, written with his thick felt-tipped pen. Many words are crossed out. He leans forward. Official police business: "Reason I called you two down this morning—"

"Okay if I smoke, chief?" Big John asks.

He gets a cold fisheye stare. "Daniels, do me a favor, huh? Don't carry this informality shit to an extreme. I'm cognizant we've known each other a long time, but you know as well as I do that I don't ordinarily permit smoking in this office. I'm no stuffed shirt, but I've *had* to lay down some rules around here to keep the animals in this building from turning my personal office into a fuckin' pigpen, which is what most of their offices look like." With that, he leans to his right, opens a bottom drawer, pulls out a large and spotless ashtray with a university insignia on the bottom and the legend "Duke Blue Devils," and places it on the end of his desk.

Big John, who I know is enjoying this to the hilt, mutters something like "Appreciate it, chief," bites off the end of his cigar, spits it in, plunk. I don't join him, not knowing the chief on such an informal basis, and not wanting to push my luck.

"Reason I called you two down this morning, we got a major break. Major break last night. Now, I'll explain it to you two exactly the way I plan to explain it to the commissioner at ten o'clock. Dealing with this guy, as you can well imagine, I've *had* to develop the habit of writing down exactly what I report to him every morning, literally word-for-word. Know why I'm forced to take that precaution? For the simple reason that, at this point in time, I'm convinced he tape records my reports. Unfortunate, but true. One time I actually saw his Sony telephone attachment still stuck on his receiver, with the little wire going down under the console to this Sony TCM-600 Cassette-Corder. I know what it is because I have one myself. Exact same thing. Unlike me, he forgot to remove it before I came in his office one day. I always make it a point to remove mine before anybody comes in here. As you may know, the attachment is perfectly legal, it's not a wiretap. At any rate, ever since the robbery, when he ordered me to give him a verbal progress report every morning, I've taken the precaution of, number one, writing it out, because I know he's recording it and I have no way of knowing who he plays it back for, of course. Ed Koch, no doubt. Number two, I also take the precaution of tape recording the conversation on *my* Sony TCM-600, primarily for the extemporaneous exchanges. Questions I'm sure he's written out in advance to see if he can catch me with my pants down. No way. Why do I say 'No way'? For the simple reason that I've already written down virtually every question he could ask on any given facet of the morning report and the progress of the case in general. And I've written my answers to those questions, of course. I realize all this might sound a little paranoid to you men."

"Not at all," Big John says. He's already lit his cigar by now and thick smoke is hanging. "Now I understand why you got to be chief and I wound up a sergeant."

Chief's left eyebrow goes up, then comes down when the left-sided grin goes up. "It's a necessity at this level, John.

Gotta cover your ass six ways from Sunday. At any rate, here's the report. Rawlings, I suggest you take notes."

"Will do."

He clears his throat, reads the first few lines to himself. "Commissioner insists I call him Bill, although I'd prefer not to, frankly. Anyway, here's the report: 'Hello, Bill, how you doing this morning? Good. Well, here's what's happening. Approximately eight forty-seven last night, I received a telephone call on my private line at home from Salaried Confidential Informant Six-dash-zero-eighty-two, who informed me that suspect James Ferragamo had telephoned him approximately fifteen minutes earlier. SCI was calling from a pay telephone, as instructed. SCI informed me at that time that suspect Ferragamo made inquiries pertaining to the so-called market value of the so-called paper sample that he, Ferragamo, had sold to SCI on Tuesday, June second. SCI informed suspect Ferragamo, as instructed, that the so-called market value was below his original expectations, but that he would be agreeable to purchase an additional quantity of the so-called paper, to wit: Seventy-five thousand at thirty cents on the dollar. That's twenty-two thousand five hundred dollars cash. SCI stated that suspect Ferragamo immediately balked at the suggested compromise offer, but made a counterproposal, to wit: One hundred thousand at thirty cents on the dollar. That's thirty thousand dollars cash. SCI rejected the counterproposal and made what he termed his final offer, as instructed, to wit: Eighty-five thousand at thirty cents on the dollar. That's twenty-five thousand five hundred dollars cash. Suspect Ferragamo, feigning reluctance, agreed to and accepted this offer. Now, as you know, Bill, SCI had my authorization to negotiate all the way up to forty-eight thousand five hundred cash, if, in his judgment, it was absolutely necessary, which is the amount remaining in his safe-deposit box in marked bills, but I cautioned him strongly against going that high, believing as I did that suspect Ferragamo, being a street-smart con, might smell something and split. As you know, we've got to play the game with these people, Bill, because they're paranoid as hell. In any event, suspect Ferragamo accepted the deal. SCI then suggested that they consummate the transaction the following day, today, June fourth, at two in the afternoon. The parties agreed to meet, as before, outside the main entrance of the Chase Manhattan Bank branch at Broadway and Tenth. They will then proceed to the vault room and make the exchange in one of the private booths. As soon as possible thereafter, SCI will telephone Deputy Chief Murphy giving the serial numbers of the negotiable bonds. If the serial numbers do in fact match the list of those bonds stolen from the Champs-Elysées, we'll apprehend suspect Ferragamo immediately. As usual, Bill, I'll keep you strictly up to speed.' "

"Excellent," Big John says. "What about the other—"

Chief keeps reading: " 'What about the other suspects?' That's the first question Reilly'll ask. I got it down as number one. Answer: 'I got a carefully planned, coordinated, and time-synchronized operation ready to go, Bill. Six-man teams for each suspect, search warrants signed and sealed, every legal technicality followed to the letter.' " He looks up. "That's *your* bag, Daniels."

"No problem. How you want it handled?"

"*I* don't know, I don't *give* a shit, that's *your* end of it." He continues reading: 'Give me a fast update on the others.' That's the second question he'll ask. For that one, I think I'll use your analysis, Daniels, if you don't mind. You know, when you said, 'Tell him the truth,' I liked that bit. I'll use that almost word for word."

Big John laughs softly. "Thought it was pretty good myself. Should've taped it, chief."

"I did."

"Did what?"

"Taped it."

Big John looks at him, glances around the almost-empty desk.

Chief grins. "Cold. Very cold."

Now Big John sits forward, bends, inclines his head to look around under the wide edge of the desk.

"Freezing cold," the chief says. "And you guys call yourselves detectives?"

I reach down, feel under the seat.

"Slightly warmer."

Big John reaches under his seat, feels with both hands.

"Hot."

"Chief, for Christ's sake." Big John gets up, face coloring, gets down on both knees, looks under the seat. Now he's on his hands and knees. Finally he reaches up, pulls out a slender tape recorder.

"Got a special holder and everything," the chief says.

Big John grunts as he stands up, brushes off his knees, hands the recorder to the chief. "So what else you get for Christmas? Pack-Man?"

Chief turns it off, presses the rewind button. "Sony TCM-600, latest model. Sony ninety-minute cassettes. Forty-five each side. High fidelity, auto-sensor, low-noise cassettes—'Captures the strength and delicacy of every sound,' as the label says."

"How long you been doing this?" Big John asks.

"Turned it on just before you came in."

"No. How long you been recording visitors?"

"I don't record everybody, Daniels. I'm selective about it. Picked up the idea in a management course I took about a year ago called 'Effective Retention of Verbal Communication.' FBI course, Murphy took it with me." Click. Rewind completed. "Teaches you to listen better. Most of us have relatively short attention spans. Teaches you to study the verbal techniques of others, learn from them. Each tape I record in here, I study it. Be surprised how much you can learn. Be surprised how many men rely on the four-letter word. Know why they do that?"

"They have shit vocabularies," I tell him.

"Exactly. Exactly right, Rawlings. They stopped building

their vocabularies back in grade school. Plus they're convinced it makes them sound tough."

"Unmitigated bullshit," Big John says.

Chief doesn't even grin. Presses the fast-forward button. "Think you started that shit about 'Tell him the truth' about ten minutes in." He checks the gauge, stops the fast-forward, plays it at normal speed. Out comes his own voice:

"—to keep the animals in his building from turning—"

Click. Too far forward. Rewind. Click. Forward. Chief's voice again:

"—explaining that to a suckass civilian like—"

Click. Too far back. Fast-forward. Click. Forward. Now Big John's voice comes out loud and clear:

"—might not look to *him* like they're capable of pulling this off, but any cop who's worked the street as long as we have knows better. Talk about 'exactly the right combination'? What the fuck *is* the right combination? Look at this group we got here. Ferragamo's got all—"

Click. "I'll transcribe it from about there, clean it up a little. That's it, men. Tell Steve to find you an empty office with a typewriter. I want a carefully planned, coordinated, and time-synchronized operation on my desk by eleven o'clock. That's your responsibility, Daniels. Six men on each hit team. Shotguns. Roof, front, back, alleys, hallway. Guy with the warrant goes in with shotgun and bulletproof vest. Rawlings, you type up the warrants. Get a copy of the robbery résumé, list all the property taken on each warrant, get the warrants down to the courthouse and signed by any judge you can grab. Let's go to work."

We get up fast, walk to the door.

"Daniels, one more thing."

"Yeah, chief."

"I'm the warrant-man on Ferragamo. He's mine."

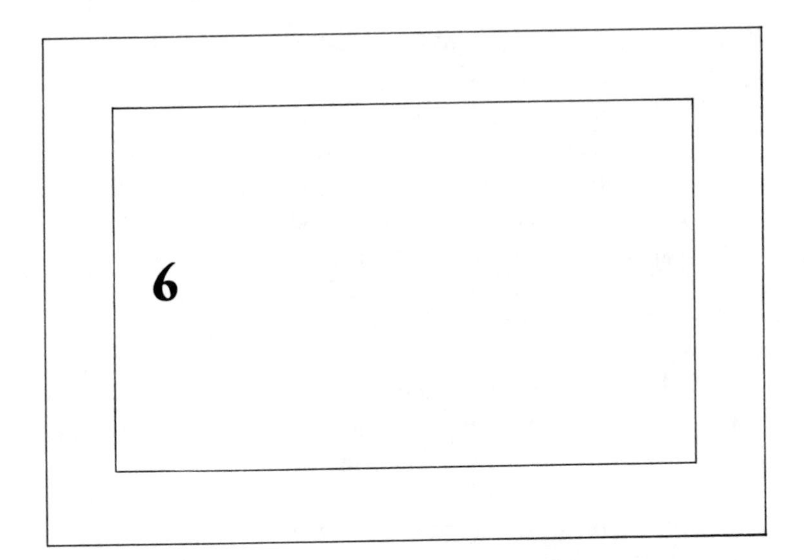

Now it starts to get hairy. At 11:35 that morning, the team covering William McCabe calls the chief to report that McCabe checked into Room 1154 at the Doral Inn, Lexington and Forty-ninth. Just one piece of luggage. What's he up to? Lunchtime shack? Lou Unright speaks to the assistant manager, manages to get into the nearest vacant room, 1157, keeps the door ajar; his partner Marty Pederson covers the lobby. At 11:56 McCabe has a visitor who Unright recognizes instantly, Jacob Benjamin, an old fence from the East Side, strictly diamonds. This is too good to be true, but it can also screw up our plans for Ferragamo and the others. Chief calls a quick meeting, Murphy, Big John, and me. Unright's holding on one of the chief's lines, Pederson's holding on another from a phone at the assistant manager's desk in the lobby. Obviously, we can't pass up the opportunity to hit on McCabe fast, but then we have to face the real possibility of blowing the rest of the operation. McCabe has the legal right to call an attorney, we know he'll demand to do it immediately, and it's odds-on he'll call Ferragamo.

We discuss it for about thirty seconds before the chief grabs the phone, punches one of the buttons. His tie's yanked down now and he's in his element, happy as a pig in shit.

"Unright? Vadney. I'm sending Pederson up. Don't play games with these assholes, I want weapons drawn. Knock, identify, gain entry, put the arm on these fuckers, see what they got. Arrest 'em, cuff 'em, read 'em their rights all legal. Now, listen, get this. When McCabe starts in about calling his attorney, tell him to stick it till he's booked. That's legal, that's Miranda. He gives you an argument, call me, I'll quote it to him: 'Accused must be fully informed of his rights and be permitted to contact counsel before *questioning.*' No questions till he's booked and I don't want these guys booked till at least two o'clock. It's just past twelve now. All right, Nineteenth Precinct has jurisdiction, you gotta get 'em up there, but you got unavoidable delays. First thing, your car already broke down, you gotta call the pool. We'll call first, tell 'em to put you on hold and forget about it. Now you call back, same shit. Now you call the Nineteenth Precinct, request transportation. We'll call first, tell 'em to give you a song and dance. By the time they get a car down to you, you've killed maybe the better part of an hour. Meantime, we call the desk sergeant up there, tell him to give you a stall on the book. They just had a bomb scare, the sergeant's got the diarrhea now, whatever. That should kill at least another half hour, now it's like one-thirty."

Mat Murphy's sitting there listening to this, he's drumming a pencil on the arm of his chair. Good man, Murphy, calm as they come. Strong resemblance to Johnny Carson, same facial expressions, same dry sense of humor. Only tip-off you get that he's nervous about something is the pencil bit. Taps it slowly, means some minor irritation with the chief. Medium speed, chief's getting himself into something moderately sticky. Full speed, like now, chief's up to his ass in alligators.

Click. Chief's on the other line now. "Pederson? Vadney. Just gave Unright the green light, he's waiting for you now. Get up there fast, he'll fill you in." Hangs up, turns to Murphy. "Who's on Ferragamo now?"

"Staucet and Lanifero. Last report, he hadn't left the apartment. Relief team at one-thirty, Arnsen and Jarvis. They go straight to Broadway and Tenth, wait for the pickup, stay with him while he goes to stash it. Probably his apartment. By then we should have verification of the numbers and you should be on your way."

Chief turns to Big John. "Your team set?"

"Ready to go. Harcourt left for work eight-fifteen, she's there, World Trade Center, Lloyds. We stay clear of the office, hit her later. That leaves Tent for the afternoon hit. Kazanski and Barnhart relieve at one-thirty, we join them at one forty-five—Telfian, Thalheimer, Rawlings, my car. We sit tight, wait for Code Green from Mat. I figure maybe two-fifteen, two-thirty, somewhere in there."

"Who's your shotgun?"

Big John jerks a thumb at me. "Kid here with the steel-blue killer eyes."

"Rawlings, do me a favor, huh? When you go down to the gun locker, tell the sergeant there we want twenty-guage Ithaca pump-actions."

I look at him. "Pump-actions?"

"Yeah, and five or six rounds of double-O buck each. Tell him it's my orders. He gives you any flack, tell him to call me."

"Will do, chief."

Just to fill you in a little, although it's standard New York City Police procedure for the warrant-man to go into a raid situation with a shotgun and bulletproof vest, we never use anything as exotic as twenty-gauge Ithaca pumps. That's strictly for the Emergency Service Division when they're going into something like a real bad hostage scene or up against a heavily armed mad-dog cop killer. Stuff like that. Normally, I'd use a twelve-gauge double-barrel break-action with twenty-six-inch barrel and modified choke, which is all the intimidation any rational human being needs. Now, the twenty-gauge Ithaca pumps (actually named Slide-Action) are something else again. Five-shell chambers, bottom ejection, full choke, raybar front sights, and twenty-inch carbine barrels that give them the classic "sawed-off" appearance. In police work, they're really intended for one purpose only: Blowing a man apart at close range. If you want to blow him all over the room, or the street, as the case may be, you use a high-base shell with double-O buckshot; each pellet measures .33 inches in diameter and there are nine pellets in a single shell, which means you're firing the equivalent of nine .33-caliber slugs simultaneously. Makes quite a bang.

Of course, I've been around too long to give the chief an argument about his choice of weapons. Although it might seem just a bit dramatic to use such heavy artillery on the likes of Jimmy Ferragamo, or even on mad-dog cop-killer types like Hamilton Harcourt and Penny Tent, the choice of weapons is only a small part of the psychological game going on here. If the chief has his way, this operation is going to be a class act all the way. With all his shortcomings, the chief understands the ground rules of the game he's playing. Those rules have been laid down not by police people but by politicians and media people who have already decided that the biggest hotel robbery in American history had to be conceived, planned, and executed by ingenious sophisticates of deception, disguise, and intrigue. Nothing less would do. Nothing less would satisfy political and mass-media needs. The NYC public out there in June 1981 is spit-up sick of third-class scumbag punks who spray-paint their names over the third-class scumbag-punk subway system and mug you and beat you and rape you and rob your apartment and get away with it because the police won't even investigate. The NYC public out there in June 1981 needs to pick up their *News* and switch on their TVs and see a touch of class for a change. Clean-cut class crooks. Tuxedos and limos and Gucci luggage. Multimillions in diamonds and sapphires and emeralds. Nobody hurt. Clean getaway. No clues. And then, before attention-spans lag—here comes the cavalry! Yeah, why not? That's what the Archie Bunker NYC public out there in June 1981 needs and wants to see. The crooks actually get caught. Those were the days, goils were goils and men were men, and the cavalry's led by J. Edgar Hoover.

That's the game, it's the only one in town right now, and the only serious question left is: Who plays Edgar Hoover? Smiling Ed Koch? Unlikely. Camels aren't noted for speed, even in an election year. Commissioner Reilly? Maybe, but he has to out-paranoid a man who analyzes the strength and delicacy of his visitors' farts. Most media men don't really *care* who leads the cavalry (Vinnie Casandra to the contrary notwithstanding), as long as it's somebody, anybody, who looks like he might have his shit together. Of course, from a media point of view, if this clown happened to be wearing a bulletproof vest and toting a classy-looking sawed-off shotgun as he collared the crooks—well, as they say in the trade, it couldn't hoit. Not necessarily a superstar, not a hero, not even an antihero, just some joker who gives the *appearance* that he's ready, willing, and able to do what the Archie Bunker NYC public out there in June 1981 has secretly dreamed of doing since the last time they were ripped off by some third-class scumbag punk: Blow the bastard apart at close range, blow him out of the room, out of the street, out of the subway, out of their lives. And if you don't think that's what they secretly dream of doing, you're definitely not a New Yorker.

Just some joker who gives the *appearance* that he's ready, willing, and able, that's all. The chief understands that. I understand it. I suppose that's why I seem to visualize a media mob scene in front of the old Nineteenth Precinct later this afternoon. What's happening? Someway, somehow, some canary in press relations leaked the rumor that three or four prime suspects in the Champs-Elysées robbery have just been apprehended in a clandestine guts-ball police operation. Maybe it's too late for the early evening front pages, but certainly in time for the six o'clock local TV news, and with plenty of time to spare for three- to five-minute edited segments on the seven o'clock network news shows. Look, up the street: A lone unmarked car with portable emergency lights flashing on the roof. Roars up Sixty-seventh, stops in front of the precinct, instantly surrounded. All four doors swing open, men jump out, videotape cameras roll, shutters stutter, motor-drives cry, everybody's shoving and shouting, you can hardly hear our correspondent on the scene: "Can't get close enough to see much, but that's Chief of Detectives Walter Vadney in the white bulletproof vest leading—from here the suspect appears to be bald, a short baldheaded man, his face is averted. As they go up the steps, you can see now, Chief Vadney appears to be holding a shotgun in his right hand." And away we go. Hizhorror becomes HizHoover in one swing of the shillelagh, the shot heard 'round the world. How quickly they forget. Vinnie Casandra, eat your heart out.

Back to the world of reality. Good news at 12:20, Unright calls to confirm the collar on McCabe and Benjamin. Real paydirt, the chief's showing molars we never knew were there. McCabe was fencing a shitload of diamonds, Unright estimates maybe a quarter-million dollars worth, all removed from their settings. Ordinarily, this makes common gems difficult to trace, but in this case almost all the jewels are heavily insured, so the precise specifications and flaws are recorded. As expected, McCabe's demanding to call his lawyer. He's allowed to speak to the chief, who listens politely, then recites the appropriate line from Miranda, assures him he can call as soon as he's booked. Unright tells the chief his car's got transmission problems and he's got to call the motor pool. Curtain comes down on Act I. Critics are all smiles.

Act II starts at 1:30 when the relief team of Arnsen and Jarvis go straight down to Broadway near Tenth and wait for Ferragamo to meet Grasso outside the bank at two. Soon as the transaction goes down, they'll stick to skinhead while Grasso phones the numbers to Murphy. Chief waits in the wings to move his team in for the collar.

Big John's team plays Act III and I finally get a shot at instant stardom. After signing out for my clean-white bulletproof vest, Ithaca Slide-Action Model 37 and five double-O shells, all of which I stash in the trunk of the car, we drive up Sixth Avenue to Carmine Street with detectives Telfian and Thalheimer in back. We arrive about 1:45, spot the car with Kazanski and Barnhart parked on the northwest corner of Carmine and Bleecker near a church, which seems appropriate for this assignment. As we pass, we see they're in postures of meditation, both munching apples. Twelve Carmine is about six houses west of Bleecker, south side of the street. We double park way down the block near Bedford. Big John grabs his walkie-talkie, calls Kazanski and Barnhart using the class-act code names added to the operations plan by the chief.

"Able One to Able Two. Acknowledge. Over."

Barnhart's voice: "Able Two here, over."

"Able Two, you in PSP on subject Red Apples? Over."

"Able One, uh, positively negative on PSP, over."

"Able Two, state source of negative SP, over."

Now Kazanski comes on with his excellent fag imitation: "Hi, able one, I'm able too. Actually, source of negative SP happens to be a darling little FV near your present location, over."

Everybody in our car's laughing now. Kazanski's known for pulling shit like this. Funniest part, this guy's like six-foot-three, maybe 195, one of the meanest-looking dudes in the division.

"Able Two," Big John says. "Request clarification on F as in Frank, V as in Victor, over."

"Uh, rodger-dodger, able one. Clarification as follows: F as in Fruit, V as in Vendor. Put 'em all together, they spell Mother, a word that means the world to me, over."

We're breaking up now, we're rolling up our windows. Big John can't respond to save his ass. He tries a couple of times, can't do it.

Kazanski comes back on: "Uh, able me to obviously unable you. Opinion here, silence indicates possible CGYT situation, is this positive, over?"

"Request clarification CGYT, over."

"Rodger-dodger, able one, it's right in the code book, dear boy. C as in Cat, G as in Got, Y as in Your, T as in—well, you know. Put 'em all together, they spell Kissy-Cat, a word that makes my pussy purr, over."

We're howling now, but that's it. Big John doesn't even try to respond, he's had it. Don't get me wrong, we don't goof around like this all that often, but most of the guys in the division today have a pretty good sense of humor, which is a healthy thing. Surgeons joke in the operating room, right? Keeps everybody loose, nothing wrong with it. In this situation, we got six detectives involved in a raid that's not exactly what you'd call dangerous, collaring a cuckoo like Penny Tent, what can I tell you? Maybe you think it's a little absurd to go in there with six men, but it's by the book. It's kept people alive in situations that looked like a piece of cake from the outside. Truth is, you never know what any clown might do with his back to the wall, particularly the weirdos. I keep remembering what a semipro baseball manager told me one time, black guy named Art Mitchell who played in the old Negro National League all his professional career. He said: "Never underestimate the hitter, no matter who it is. Anybody standing up there at the plate with a bat in his hands should be considered dangerous." He was so right. God, was he ever right, but I had to learn it the hard way. Good old Mitch, I can see him now. Used to yell at us from the dugout: "Keep your head up in there!" Learned a lot from that old guy. Don't think I ever thanked him for it, not really. I was a cocky little squirt, thought I knew it all. Too soon old, too late smart. Story of my life.

As it happens, we have a couple of former semipro ballplayers in the car today, and not by accident. Both a lot younger than Big John and me, not by accident either. We worked with Telfian and Thalheimer on special assignments before, they're always our first choices when they're available. Rick Telfian, tough little Armenian, around thirty-five, works out, stays in pretty good shape. Doesn't smoke, doesn't even drink that much, got a nice family, three boys. This kid's no angel, never has been, which is fine with us. Always had a gambling problem, almost compulsive when he was younger, he'd lay you odds on anything that moved. Gene Thalheimer looks a lot like Gene Kelly in his prime, bright kid, understand he writes plays in his spare time, dramas, I think. Both went to Cardinal Hayes High School; not in the same class, Gene was a year ahead. Played on the same varsity baseball team, keystone kids one year, Ricky at short, Gene at second. The one year they played together, Ricky makes all-city shortstop. Next year he switches to third base because nobody's ever made all-city at two different positions, and he does it, he pulls it off. Followed him in the papers, good power for a kid his size. Thalheimer didn't get that much press, but he was also starting quarterback on the football squad. Tough, scrappy type kid. Both went on to play semipro baseball for a few years there, worked at odd jobs before joining the department. Without going into the whole nine yards about these guys, the point I'm trying to make, we know them, we know where their heads are, where they're coming from. We trust them. Same with Kazanski and Barnhart. Although we don't know them as well, we know them by reputation. You can depend on these guys in a tight situation.

We got at least a half hour to kill, so we take turns keeping an eye on the front door of the apartment, which we can see pretty good from where we are. Normally, when we're going to hit an apartment where there's been no previous surveillance, we get a detective to go up there the day before we hit. He goes up to the street, looks around, checks the ethnic makeup of the neighborhood, then goes right in the building. He's looking for a relative, whatever. Checks the layout of the floor we'll be on, whether we'll have adequate room for cover if the guy's a nut case and decides to fire through the door, shit like that. It happens. Depending on the circumstances, the detective often gives us a diagram to study. Then, after we have the building staked out—front and rear exits, roof, alleys, fire escapes, whatever the case may be—we get a uniform squad car, park it out front where the guy can see it. Sometimes two cars. More often than not, we already got the guy's telephone number. Now we're all set, we call him up. If we need a Spanish-speaking cop, whatever, we get one. We call him up, we identify ourselves, we say, "Hey, Mario, look out the window." He looks out, he sees the squad car or cars, the uniformed officers out front. We say, "There's cops on the roof, there's cops out back, around in the alleys, there's cops in front of your door in the hall with shotguns and bulletproof vests. You can't get out. Why don't you come out nice and easy? We don't want to blow you out of there. We'll gas you, then we'll kill you if we have to. Make it easy on yourself, we don't care, it's your choice." The psychological effect alone is usually enough.

Unfortunately, in this case we don't have that kind of psychological advantage. First, we don't have a telephone number; they don't even have an unlisted number, at least not in the names we have. Which is unusual, but keep in mind these two aren't exactly your run-of-the-mill couple to begin with. Second, from the little bit of research we've had time to run since last night, we've come up empty on both of them. Even the NCIC computer draws a complete blank on these people, which doesn't surprise me all that much. If we had time, we'd go to Lloyds for information on Harcourt, but we don't want to risk it now. Third, they live in a loft apartment, top floor of a five-story building, which makes for problems. Manhattan lofts have become very "in" places over the past ten years or so, quite scarce and extremely expensive to buy as well as rent. Sizes and layouts vary widely, of course, but most lofts have a few things in common. They're relatively old buildings, they were once used for storage of some kind, so their structures are unconventional, and the apartments are usually floor-throughs. This often means you can't gain access to the roof except by going through the top-floor apartment. It also means the absence of conventional hallways. If there's an elevator, it opens at an individual apartment and the most you can expect is a small foyer of some kind right in front of the door. Some I've seen have security devices such as a key to open the elevator and a separate key to make the elevator stop at a given floor only.

From the street, 12 Carmine looks like an average Manhattan loft, a narrow gray building with just three windows per floor. Its sides are flush with adjoining old apartment houses, one the same height, five stories, the other only four. Most of the other buildings in the row are five floors or lower. Tent could easily escape from the roof, keep running over adjoining roofs for a considerable distance, and climb down any one of a number of fire escapes that are undoubtedly in back. If we can't get to the roof through the building, we'll have to get around to the back somehow, position one man there, have another man climb a fire escape on an adjoining building and walk across the roofs.

One big advantage we have is the element of surprise. Tent hasn't budged from the apartment so far today, which is understandable because he works nights. Wouldn't surprise me if he's still asleep.

Just before two o'clock, I decide it's about time to go in and give the place a quick look. I walk on the same side as the building. Carmine is a tree-lined, shady little street, not much traffic. It's a sunny afternoon, not too humid, temperature in the mid-seventies maybe. People are shopping at a small grocery store and a pastry shop on the opposite side of the street; on my side there's a colorful open-air fruit and vegetable market that Kazanski mentioned. I'm dressed casually, sport shirt worn outside because of my service revolver holstered in the small of my back, but I want to appear as relaxed as possible, so I stop at the market and buy an apple. Would you believe thirty-five cents for a lousy apple? Have to put it on the expense account, part of my cover. Love to see the chief's face when he reads that: " 'Undercover *apple*'!? Rawlings, what the f-f-fuck's *this* shit?"

Anyway, now I'm chewing away, I turn nonchalantly and walk in the front door. Dim and cool in the little lobby. Apartment door to the right, five mailboxes in the wall to the left. Above them, five doorbells arranged vertically, names and apartment numbers alongside. Top one reads "H. Harcourt 5." About fifteen feet away to the left, small elevator, steel door painted red. Looks like a conventional elevator, standard button at the side. Above the button is a little plastic window and the floor indicator reads "L." I press the button, door rolls to the right, I step in. Display panel has six buttons; bottom one reads "B." I push that one, door closes quietly, down I go. Door opens to a fluorescent-lit, clean-looking basement. I step out, take a bite of my apple, glance around. Area ahead is a small, cement-floored laundry room, neat and tidy. Two coin-operated washers and driers, lids open. On the wall to the right, five circular glass-faced Con Edison meters. Next to them, a rectangular window holding a fire hose. Next to that, a flat gray box with telephone connections. Ceiling is dotted with sprinklers.

Narrow hall to the left leads to a rear fire door painted red. I munch on the apple, walk over and check it out. No knob, big Medico deadbolt lock with a heavy slide-bolt above it. I click open the Medico, slide the bolt, push the heavy door open. Strong sunlight. Small flight of cement steps leading up to the backyard. I hold the door open with one hand, glance straight up. Standard fire escape, weighted ladder, small landing on every floor. Stops at a window on the top floor; no access to the roof. I want to take a quick look at the fire escapes on the adjoining buildings, but I have to go halfway up the steps to do it and the door has no outside knob. I glance around for something to jam the door. Nothing. I take a final bite of the apple, place it on the floor between door and frame. It holds. I take several steps up. All the adjoining buildings in the row have rear fire escapes and I can see several that extend up to the roofs, as escapes on many conventional apartments often do. I step down, retrieve my apple, go back in, lock and bolt the door. When I get back to the elevator, it's still on my floor. I push the button, step in, press "3." Up I go, holding my half-eaten, slightly dirty apple. Elevator's not exactly a speed demon, but at least it's quiet.

Door finally opens to a very small, brightly lighted foyer, no furniture, high ceiling, bare wood floor. Apartment door is no more than five feet away, highly polished dark wood, two gleaming locks. Peephole, big brass "3" below it, doorbell below that. My only possible cover would be the elevator itself. I press "L" and descend, research accomplished.

Walking back to the car, I can't help thinking about Penny Tent and Hamilton Harcourt and what goes on behind closed doors in a relationship like this. Penny Tent, with a figure that can't possibly be faked in a string-bikini, except for the falsies (or silicone), who's psychologically and emotionally committed to living as a female. Hamilton Harcourt, an attractive, clean-cut executive type, flat-chested, impeccably dressed, who's psychologically and emotionally committed to living as a male. Now, in NYC in June 1981, there's no law against impersonating members of the opposite sex or wearing attire obviously associated with the opposite sex. Whatever turns you on. There's no longer a law on the books here against sodomy between consenting adults, but we're not dealing with sodomy in this relationship. What we're dealing with here is a bit more complicated: Young male and female transvestites living together as lovers or maybe common-law marital partners. And, with variations according to individual tastes, it's logical to assume that this couple probably engages in more or less conventional intercourse, except for the psychological role reversals. All of which is no crime, no way, no how, no time.

I realize the good folks out in Moral Majority City consider such permutations not only outrageous, disgusting, and immoral, but downright sick, not to mention sinful. Fine and dandy. The whole gay scene is extremely touchy to those who demand insulation from reality. Trouble is, they want to shove that artificial insulation down everybody else's throat. I wonder if the good people out there who've crowned themselves the Moral Majority realize that by logical extension that makes all the rest of us the Immoral Minority. Most of us don't have the dubious luxury of artificial insulation against reality, cops least of all. For cops, the reality of the gay scene has to be placed in logical and legal perspective, regardless of personal opinion. Logically, the gay scene in NYC in June 1981 is just part of life, no more, no less, just as it always has been, just as it always will be. No more, no less. Legally, what goes on behind closed doors between consenting adults is not only their private business but their constitutional right. That's not opinion, that's the law. Personal opinion is the pablum that built Moral Majority City.

The reason I can't help thinking about this as I walk back to the car is that within ten or fifteen minutes I have to go back in that building with a bulletproof vest and a twenty-gauge shotgun, stand face-to-face with Penny Tent, and serve him with a search warrant, knowing and understanding that he may very possibly be *innocent* of any crime whatsoever. I want to have my head on straight when I do that. Look at the facts. All we've really got on this guy is his known association with Harcourt. That's it. All we've got on Harcourt is his known employment as an insurance agent with Lloyds of London and his knowledge of the contents of Nancy Kramer's safe-deposit boxes. Unless our search of that apartment turns up something positively incriminating that will stand up in a court of law, we've got nothing. What we're doing in fact, all quite legally, is invading this couple's privacy, to which they're constitutionally entitled, on our *suspicion* that they may have committed a crime. Suspicion based on instinct based on experience. It's legal, but it ain't exactly ethical, depending on where your head is.

Of course, the macho rebuttal to this line of reasoning is obvious: People like this are used to harassment, they bought it with their lifestyle. I don't buy that. I'm no bleeding-heart civil-liberties buff by any stretch of the imagination, never have been, but I wouldn't feel comfortable in a Marlboro ad either. Horses are hard on the ass of a city boy.

Besides, I'm a cigar man. Proud of it.

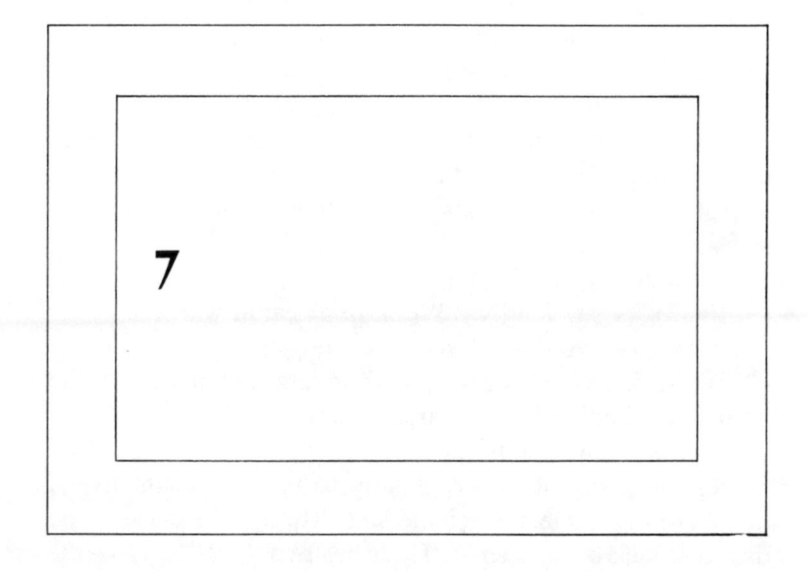

7

CODE GREEN COMES AT 2:37. Barnhart and Kazanski swing around the corner, double park in front, walk in at 2:39. We stay put, give them three minutes to grab the elevator to the basement and get out back, allow Barnhart two more minutes to scale the fence and start up one of the fire escapes. At 2:44, we pull up in front, get out, Thalheimer covers the front, Big John and Telfian accompany me in. Couple of passers-by spot me in the white vest with the shotgun and stop dead. We go in the lobby and the elevator's waiting. Telfian stays, Big John goes up with me. I'm adjusting the vest, trying to get comfortable, he's clipping his badge to his breast pocket. Now he draws his service revolver, holds it to his side, looks at me. Our faces are sweating. It's always like this, no matter how many times you've done shit like this. Elevator stops at five, door opens, Big John holds it with the button. I walk straight ahead, gun barrel down, stand in front of the peephole, give the bell three or four fast rings. Silence. I turn, check

Big John's position. As usual, Art Mitchell's words stick in my mind: "Never underestimate the hitter, no matter who it is." Big John's got good cover; I'm wide open, but I can pivot and flatten myself against the wall next to the door.

I ring the bell again. It's one of those chime deals, ding-dong, ding-dong, fairly loud. Now I hear footsteps, slap-slap, slap-slap, like thong sandals, coming toward me. Rapid, short steps.

A feminine voice: "Who is it?"

"Police," I say loudly. "We have a search warrant."

Peephole slides open. "What do you want?"

"We have a search warrant authorizing examination of the premises occupied by H. Harcourt and P. Tent."

Peephole slides shut. Silence. Then, suddenly: CLICK! Scares the crap out of me, I jump to the side instinctively, don't even remember to pivot. Shit, it's just the click of the deadbolt lock being opened. Door has two. CLICK! Now the door opens a crack, there's a chain-lock across the opening. Can't see anybody.

"Show me the warrant," the soft voice tells me, but it has a slight shake in it.

I reach my left hand up to the left armhole of the vest, pull out the warrant, hold it up near the crack in the door.

Silence. Door closes a fraction. Click. Chain is unhooked. Door opens. Penny Tent stands there, eyes wide as he takes in the full vest and shotgun. He's got long dark hair and he's wearing a white terrycloth bathrobe. Up close, this kid looks very much like Brooke Shields, maybe a few years older, thick dark brows and lashes, innocent hazel eyes, naturally sensuous features. No trace of stubble at first glance, but his tan is relatively dark. His eyes dart to Big John who's walking toward us.

"Your name Tent?" I ask. "Penny Tent?"

"Yes."

I hand him the search warrant, he steps back, holds it with both hands. We walk in, close the door. We're in a little vestibule just outside the living room. High ceiling, bare wood floor, white walls, several tables with lighted lamps, a grandfather's clock in one corner.

"You alone in here?" Big John asks.

"Yes."

Big John holsters his revolver. "Hands against the wall, assume the position."

"Is that in the search warrant?"

"Against the wall! Move it!"

Tent glares at him, assumes the position slowly. Big John's face colors slightly as he goes through the routine frisk.

"Okay, you can turn around."

He glares again as he turns. "Am I under arrest?"

"No," I tell him. "Nobody said anything about arrest. We're here to search the apartment."

"I'd like to call my attorney."

"Sure," Big John says. "Tell me his name and address, I'll look him up in the book and dial the number for you."

"That won't be necessary."

"It's absolutely necessary," Big John says.

Slap-slap, Tent goes to a table with mail on it, grabs an envelope and a ballpoint pen. "I want your names and precincts."

"Daniels, Nineteenth."

"Rawlings, same. It's all in the warrant."

He jots them down anyway, glances at Big John. "My attorney's name is Douché Bagette, One-nineteen West Fifty-seventh. You can look it up inside, I want to speak to her immediately." He turns, slap-slaps into the living room. Douché Bagette?

You expect lofts to have lots of open space, but you could play basketball in this joint. One glance says easily 3,500 square feet, with only two separation walls, far front and rear. Theme décor of the living and dining areas is blond wood—floor, tables, couches, chairs, bookcases, cabinets, stereo speakers, even lamps. Very high white ceiling with black sprinklers (no skylights), track lighting across the whole length of the longest wall, but no paintings, pictures, nothing.

Stark bare white walls. Ultramodern kitchen has a butcher-block theme, separated from the huge dining area by a long rectangular "island" counter with butcher-block top and matching stools. Kitchen walls and floor are the only exceptions, pale gray one-inch tiles. If I had to summarize the décor I'd call it classy-weird.

Tent slaps across to a blond wood table with a blond phone, grabs the Manhattan directory, tosses it on the blond wood coffee table. Big John picks it up, sits on the blond cushions of the blond wood couch, looks up the attorney's number. I place the shotgun on the bare blond wood floor, start to take off the heavy vest.

"Exactly *what* are you looking for?" Tent asks me.

"If you read the warrant, you'll find out."

He flips the warrant open, frowns as he scans the long list of stolen property I've copied verbatim from the robbery résumé. "This is ridiculous, y'know. This is utterly ridiculous."

Big John's dialing the number now.

"This is just utterly—*insane!* How could *I* possibly steal all this shit?" He goes over and accepts the receiver from Big John. As he waits for an answer, the hand holding the warrant is shaking. "Carol, Penny, is she there? Yeah, well, tell her it's an emergency. Right."

Big John gives me a mysterious look as he walks over: Pat Moynihan with pursed lips holding a secret that's difficult to contain.

"Douché, Penny, you won't *believe* this! I got two *cops* here in the apartment, they got *shotguns,* they got *pistols*—"

Big John turns me away. "This kid ain't no fag."

"—they got bulletproof *vests!* They stand me against—"

"You sure?" I ask him.

"—the *wall,* they *frisk* me, they *feel* me, the whole God-damn *routine!*"

"Positive."

"They got a *search* warrant, for Christ's sake, you *believe* this? They got a whole list of stolen—! Gladly, wait a minute."

She holds the receiver out. "My attorney wants to speak to one of you."

Big John takes it. "Sergeant Daniels here. There's no need —there's no—there's no need to yell, ma'am. No, ma'am, she's not under arrest. We simply served her with a court order to search the apartment. No, no, ordered by the chief of detectives. That's correct. Don't call him that, lady, that's not nice. Same to you, ma'am. Fine, come on over, we'll be here." He hangs up, shakes his head. "Foul-mouthed little lady."

Tent's somehow reassured by the call. She sits on the couch now, crosses her legs, lights a cigarette. "I don't want anything touched until my attorney arrives, is that understood?"

Big John ignores her, removes the walkie-talkie from his belt. "Able One to Able Two, acknowledge, over."

Static, then Kazanski: "Able Two here, over."

"Able Two, proceed with operating plan, over and out."

"*What* operating plan?" Tent asks. "Who was *that?*"

We ignore her. I carry the shotgun and vest out to the vestibule, stash them in a corner. When I come back, Big John is on the phone to headquarters. Tent's curled up on the couch now, blowing smoke at the ceiling. I find I'm looking at this kid in an entirely new way now. She's got equipment that won't quit. She notices I'm taking it all in.

"What'd you say your name was?" she asks softly.

"Rawlings."

"Detective Rawlings, I don't want a thing touched until my attorney gets here. I know my rights."

"You don't know shit," I tell her.

"How *dare* you talk to me like that!"

"Save it. We caught your act at the Vamp last night."

She tosses her hair back with a jerk of her head. "So what? Nothing illegal about it."

"You're running a pretty good con there."

"It's a living."

Big John's just lit a cigar but he's already chewing on it now.

Somebody's giving him an earful. "Holy shit. They up there now? You got the number?" He takes his pad and pen out of his jacket pocket, jots it down. "Thanks, Mat, see you." He presses the disconnect button, gives me a fast glance, rolls his eyes, dials the number.

"What's happening?" I ask.

He gets a busy signal, hangs up, ushers me out to the vestibule without a word. Now he leans against the wall, puffs on the cigar, looks worried.

"Ferragamo didn't show," he says quietly.

"Oh, shit."

"It gets worse. Staucet and Lanifero were on him till one-thirty. Outside the apartment, right? One-thirty, relief team of Arnsen and Jarvis get positioned at Broadway and Tenth, set for the exchange at two. I figure, no sense risking a tail from his apartment to the bank. Too critical a time, not worth it. Meantime, McCabe throws us a curve that drops off the table. We're so worried about him calling Ferragamo, we don't pick up on the obvious. Ferragamo's expecting him to call after he does the deal with the fence."

"It figures, yeah."

"No call means trouble. Ferragamo waits, probably tries to get McCabe—hotel room, office, home, whatever. No McCabe. Something's very wrong. Boom, he takes off."

"Gone? You sure?"

"When he doesn't show at the bank by ten past two, chief's team scrambles up to his apartment, shotgun operation. No response. Ready for this? Chief's so fuckin' mad, he *blasts* the door open! *Believe* this guy? 'Stand back, men!' Blam-blam-blam!"

I'm laughing softly, I can see the chief doing it.

"Five double-O shells on a wood door. They get inside, no Ferragamo. It's now about two thirty-five. Chief grabs the phone, calls Mat, tells him to give us Code Green fast. They're searching the apartment right now."

"Anything?"

"Don't know yet."

"He wouldn't leave anything, not him."

We head back to the living room. Ding-dong, ding-dong. I go back, open the door. Thalheimer, Telfian, and Kazanski file in smiling.

"Barnhart's coming," Kazanski says. "He's climbing down."

"You remember to jam the door?" I ask.

He gives me his fag look.

All five of us march into the living room. Tent's not on the couch anymore. We hear her voice coming from the far left. She's on the kitchen phone, her back to us.

"Get off that *phone!*" Big John shouts.

She turns, hair swirling. "Go to *hell!* It's *my* apartment, it's *my* phone, I have every *right* to use it!" Now she speaks quietly into the receiver: "Please hurry, honey. Right, she's on her way now. Right, see you." She hangs up, takes a happy drag on the cigarette. "Mr. Harcourt. On his way! Absolutely furious!"

"Good," Big John says. "Like to talk to him."

Barnhart walks in, hands black from the fire escape. "Mind if I use your sink, lady?"

"Be my guest," she tells him.

Big John turns to us. "All right, let's go to work. Gene, Rick, take the bedrooms in back; Ted, you and Vic might as well start on the kitchen; we'll take the room up front."

We fan out and get to it. The separation wall up front doesn't have a door. We walk in, we see immediately it's an artist's workroom. Shafts of sunlight slant down from the three curtainless windows to pick up two partly finished oil paintings on easels and a dozen or so finished canvases leaning against bare white walls. To the right, a long rectangular butcher-block workbench with palettes, oils, brushes, spatulas, jars and other supplies, all neatly arranged. Whole room has a pleasant smell of paint. We walk around, look at the paintings. A few abstracts, one still-life of wine bottles, all the rest are portraits. Every single portrait is unmistakably Penny, ranging from head-and-shoulders to full-length, nude to fully clothed. All are extremely well done, imaginative, obviously the work of a gifted artist. Finished canvases all have the signature "H. Harcourt" and the year, mostly 1980 and 1981.

We see Penny in the doorway now, arms crossed over her chest, holding herself like she's cold. In direct sunlight, the resemblance to Brooke Shields is surprisingly close. Her voice is so soft we can hardly hear her: "Please don't touch those."

"We won't," I tell her.

"Some are still wet, y'know?"

I nod. "You got a talented boyfriend."

"Yes. He's studied very hard."

"Where?" I ask.

"England and France."

"He's British, right?"

"Yes, but he has his green card. He sells insurance."

Big John goes to the workbench, inspects some jars. "Pretty expensive apartment for an insurance agent, isn't it?"

"We rent," she says quietly. "We can afford it, we both work."

"Yeah, we know," he says. "We saw you last night."

"It's honest work, man. It's not hurting anybody."

He looks at her. "You call impersonating an impersonator honest work?"

"It's entertainment. I'm an entertainer."

Big John's going through the tubes of paint now.

"Please don't touch those. He has those carefully arranged."

"Look, lady," he says. "We have to touch some of this stuff, okay? That's why we're here."

"We're not thieves," she tells him. "We work hard."

I walk toward her. "Nobody's calling you a thief. Look, why not go inside and relax till your attorney gets here? We'll be very careful, that's a promise."

She holds my gaze, nods, slaps back to the living room.

If Penny Tent can be described as a relatively intriguing combination of personalities and moods, her attorney turns out to be a veritable genius of geniality. Big John and I are searching the living room when Ms. Bagette throws open the door without ringing and pounds through the vestibule. From that moment on, we realize that introductions of even the most cursory nature seem somehow unnecessary. You feel the floor shake and hear the gravel-throated "*Daniels!*" and it's like a nostalgic class reunion. This little charmer was a Silent Generation Youth. Brings tears to your eyes to see how she's blossomed. Late forties now, short, heavyset, straight-cut bangs, Steinem glasses on a Durante schnoz in an Abzug face. Abrasive, belligerent, obnoxious, and intuitively rude, in no particular order. Voice like Leo the Lip, accent born and bred in Brooklyn, lovingly nurtured by a dazzling decade of hollering home Dem Bums at a long-gone legendary shrine called Ebbets Field. This kid didn't give umpires the Bronx Cheer, this kid *was* the Bronx Cheer, long and loud and staccato. Today, that's all behind her, she's shown 'em, she's done real good, she's an atoynee awready. My dawtah the lawyah. Today we ain't tawkin cawfee an Daynish heah, we're tawkin Bella an Lugosi an Powah an Glooryah an Big Bucks heah.

"*Daniels!*"

Big John's standing by the bookcase; he hesitates, blinks, momentarily incapable of responding to such poetry in motion. "Ms. Bagette, I presume."

"So lemme see the caught awedah!"

"Your client has the, uh, caught awedah."

She turns, polka-dot outfit swirling, saddlebag purse swinging, sees Penny on a stool at the kitchen counter. "Penny, so what kinda garbage they pullin' on ya, sweetheart, ya awright?"

"I'm fine."

Bagette clomps over, bracelets jangling, gives her client a big kiss and hug, whispers something in her ear, gives her another kiss. Penny hands her the search warrant. Now Bagette slings the heavy purse on the counter, hoists herself up on a stool, flings the warrant open with all the panache of an irritated F. Lee Bailey. "Penny, be an angel and brew me up a cup a cawfee, hah?"

"Sure. How you like it?"

"Reglah."

Big John and I go back to work, grateful for the respite, however brief. Her reading's punctuated by astute legal comments like "Ha!" and "Oy!" and "What's this, the crown jewels awready?" Finally, she yells out: "So who's this schmuck J. Rawlings?"

"Detective John Rawlings," I mutter. "At your service."

"So you write this piece a shit?"

"Guilty as charged."

"Rawlings, y'gotta be kiddin' heah. Y'got everything in this piece a shit but the Alpo ya ate last night."

While I'm considering an appropriate rejoinder, we hear the front door open and close, quick footsteps in the vestibule, and Hamilton Harcourt hurries in, slim in a gray European-cut three-piece, long-brown hair disheveled, face sweating, somewhat out of breath. The dark eyes take in Big John and me with a flicker of recognition, then flash directly to Penny. "You all right?"

"Yes."

"What's going on?"

"Everything's under control," Bagette assures. "They got a warrant, it's all legal. Just don't say nothin', I'll do all the tawkin' needs to be done."

Harcourt glances at me. "I believe we've met before."

"Tuesday, office of Alistair Rodger. Detective Rawlings, and this is Sergeant Daniels."

"Oh, yes, of course." Harcourt steps over, shakes my hand, nods to Big John. "Mrs. Kramer's jewels."

"Right," Big John says.

Boom, Bagette's on her feet now. "Ham, just don't say nothin', leave this to me, huh?"

Harcourt gives me a smile. "May I assume you're looking for Mrs. Kramer's stolen jewels then?"

"Everything's detailed in the warrant."

"Ham, leave this to me, will ya!"

"Not to worry, Douché, we have absolutely nothing to hide here. These gentlemen are welcome to look all they like. They won't find anything that doesn't belong to us."

Strange how the mind locks in on first impressions and builds on them. Our line of work, it pays to study faces, voices, mannerisms, clothes, and I do it almost automatically when I'm on the job. Three days ago we meet Harcourt and I pick up subtle effeminate suggestions. These are unconsciously reinforced in the all-too-persuasive atmosphere of the Vamp last night. But now, knowing what we know about Tent, I can't help reevaluating, I need to take a much closer look at Harcourt.

In my experience, men are easier to figure than women. Normally, a man's standard repertory includes your run-of-the-mill medium-to-hard fastball, a fair-to-middling curve, maybe a changeup now and again to keep you off balance. I'm not talking twenty-game winners, I'm talking journeymen throwers. Women? Now you're in a much more sophisticated league, playing by more complicated rules. More often than not, you're facing somebody who can't reach back for the high hard one, so she's throwing junk, she's got a bag of tricks out there. She depends on control, nicks the corners, pinpoint stuff. Starts you off with maybe a soft roundhouse teaser, breaks low outside, ball one. Next, a rinky-dink jiveass changeup, high inside, ball two. Now you figure she's got to come across, you start digging in. *Zaaap!* What the hell's *that?* Screwball, dummy, breaks opposite from a curve, don't see many of them babies in your twilight league back home. Okay, two and one, what's this garbage coming up now? Dipsy-doodle knuckler dances up there, like trying to hit a butterfly, but you bite, you go in the bucket and try to tomahawk the sucker. Embarrassing. Now you're two and two, you're hanging tough. Next? *Splaaat!* Spitball, strictly illegal, and that's not tobacco juice on there, that's Aliage body moisturizer by Estée Lauder, a squeeze too much, high outside. Full count. Money pitch coming. Now she's got you guessing up there, total suicide. Forkball? Slider? Palmball? Choke way up, maybe you'll get a piece. She's into her motion, you're choked, crouched, crowding the plate, meaner than a junkyard dog. *Ziiiiing!* The high-hard fastball she wasn't supposed to have, straight down the pipe, Sandy Koufax/Nolan Ryan, 98 mph., the aspirin tablet, forget it, go sit down. Am I right or am I right?

What I'm getting at, I'll feel a lot more comfortable if I can figure out exactly what this Harcourt kid is, male or female. I don't really give a shit one way or the other, just so I know for a fact what I'm dealing with. I like stuff like this nailed down, my radar works better this way. Penny Tent I feel okay about now. I got a handle on her, I think I know where she's coming from. Of course, appearances are even more deceiving than usual in Harcourt's case because he or she happens to be British and an artist to boot, living with—and probably in love with—a woman who makes a living impersonating a man who impersonates a woman for a living. Gets a little fuzzy in there, radar blips a UFO. I know enough about the British to realize that their definition of effeminate is a little different from ours, particularly when you're talking about artists, so I try to stay flexible on that score.

One thing I'll say for Harcourt, the kid's got moxie, he or she doesn't seem the least bit intimidated by the presence of six cops searching the apartment. You have to like that attitude: Go to it. Also, Harcourt manages to politely ignore the admonitions of our genial Ms. Bagette, so you got to figure Bagette must be Penny's pal, a holdover from pre-Harcourt days, somebody who provided a much-needed security blanket in return for maybe the vicarious trip of being a foxy-proxy mommie. Or more, although I choke at the thought.

We're about an hour-and-a-half into the search, we've covered all the main areas once, now Big John follows his standard search strategy of switching the two-man teams to areas covered by another team so we can go over everything fresh on the second try. He starts on the bedroom in back (turned out to be one large room with a king-size bed) and I take the big adjoining bathroom which is also connected to the kitchen. As in most lofts, the whole kitchen and bathroom section was installed new, and in this case the accoutrements are about as modern as you can get. For example, there's a pale gray sunken bathtub surrounded by a matching ledge wide enough to seat three or four guests if you want company, and the ledge holds a variety of exotic plants, *objets d'art,* and a pale gray telephone that almost matches the uniform pale gray one-inch tiles of the walls and floor. Following the classy-weird décor maybe to the point of absurdity, maybe not, there's a pale gray French bidet not far from the matching ultramodern toilet that has a pale gray foam-rubber lid and seat. I pull up the lid and look at this thing, it's a wicked temptation, I'm fighting it. What the hell, you only live once, I sit down on this mother. Not bare-ass, I'm not into method acting here, and I'm certainly not looking to dump in anything this classy, I just want to luxuriate for a brief moment on what must be the ultimate dump-machine in the history of Western civilization. I sit down carefully. Foam-rubber seat goes: *Shhhhheeeeet!* Swear to God. Like the longest, smoothest, classiest, most discreet and perfectly controlled fart ever expelled by man or beast. Wouldn't surprise me if maybe it's scientifically engineered to trigger a sympathetic physiological reaction.

Think that's the *pièce de résistance?* No way. Just before I get off, I glance up. I'm sitting there now, I can't believe this next thing. Facing me on a pale gray ledge directly above the door to the bedroom is a pale gray Sony TV set. Specifically positioned to be watched on the can. Too high to be controlled by hand, must have a remote-control device. This is creative dumping. Click on the set, light up a cigar and watch "Good Morning America" while the peons continue to grunt and strain in solitary animal drudgery. I get up fast now, I'm afraid somebody might walk in on me and get the wrong idea. Seat goes: *Teeeeehhhhhs!* Incredible, like a long one in reverse, only much louder. I flush the thing to cover the sound. Deep-blue colored water swirls in silently, chemicals to clean, coat, and deodorize, a final touch of class. I hesitate before closing the lid, half expecting it to go down automatically. It doesn't. I'm relieved.

Back to work. Although I'm sure Telfian and Thalheimer have already examined the toilet tank, I lift the pale gray porcelain top, place it on the seat lid, take a look inside. Can't see much because of the blue water. I flush it again, get a better look as the water level drops. Down on the right-hand side is a small glass jar of Blu-Boy Automatic Toilet Bowl Cleaner with Hygienic Action.

A soft voice: "Be glad to remove the jar for you."

I turn. Harcourt's standing in the doorway to the bedroom. I turn back to the tank. "No, that's okay."

"Must say, that'd be a marvelous spot to hide gems."

"Not really."

"No?"

"Too obvious." I replace the procelain top carefully.

"Even with the colored water?"

"One of the first places we look." I kneel down, inspect the underside of the tank.

"If you need any tools, I have a toolbox in the kitchen."

"No, thanks. I have a screwdriver and pliers, that's usually all I need." I get up, go to the bidet, look it over carefully.

"I'll leave you alone then. Just wanted to see if I could be of any help."

"Stay if you want. Doesn't bother me."

"Mind if I ask a question?"

"Shoot."

"I've read the search warrant. I assume I must be a suspect in the Champs-Elysées robbery, is that correct?"

"No comment." I walk to the large pale gray sink, kneel down, and look at the underside.

"I suppose I should be flattered in a way. Biggest hotel robbery in American history and all that."

Sink has two narrow aluminum legs. I rap my knuckles on one. Hollow. I examine the top, see it's held in place by a tension housing, turn the leg to the left several times. Tension diminishes. Now I unscrew the leg quickly, remove it, look through the cylinder. Empty. I screw it back on, start on the other.

"Penny tells me you saw her sketch at the Vamp last night."

"Right."

"You saw us both then?"

"Yeah."

"So I assume we've both been under surveillance since the robbery."

"Not necessarily." Other leg's empty too; I screw it back.

"Let me pose a hypothetical question: When your search uncovers nothing here today, will the surveillance continue?"

I stand up, open both mirrored doors of the large medicine cabinet. "I believe you said 'when' the search uncovers nothing. That's not a hypothetical question, that's drawing a conclusion before the fact."

"All right then, *if.* Will the surveillance continue?"

"I try to make it a rule not to answer hypothetical questions." Left side of the cabinet is packed with women's stuff, including a Lady Gillette razor and shaving cream. Right side is obviously men's stuff, including a Trac II razor and cream, plus various products named "Chanel for Men"—cologne, after shave, after shave balm, after shave moisturizer. Doesn't necessarily prove anything except you can spend a shitload of money to smell like a man. I ignore the small medicine bottles and examine the larger containers.

"Realistic question then," Harcourt says. "Why do you obviously dislike Penny and me? We haven't done anything to you."

"What makes you think I dislike you?"

"Your whole attitude. The way you're talking to me now, your tone of voice."

I keep looking through the cabinet. "I don't dislike you, Mr. Harcourt. Why should I? Matter of fact, I saw your paintings in the front room, I think they're terrific. I envy you your talent, I wish I had it."

"Do you paint?"

"No."

"Do you want to?"

"Not any more, no."

"Why not?"

"Wasn't any good at it."

"Did you *enjoy* it?"

I take the cap off a large container of Tylenol, look at the red and white capsules. "Yeah, I guess so. Didn't have the patience for oil. Couldn't wait for the paints to dry."

"What sort of things did you paint?"

"Portraits mostly."

"May I ask of whom?"

I open a tin box of Band-Aids. "I'd rather not get into that."

"I understand."

Now I close the cabinet doors, glance at Harcourt's reflection, move to the three glass shelves on the wall to the right. Top two hold neatly folded pale gray towels. Bottom shelf has an array of perfume bottles and a thick-stemmed crystal dish holding maybe a dozen miniature bars of guest soap.

"The only important thing is that you enjoyed it."

I examine the soap. "I guess you're right."

"That's what art is all about, isn't it?"

"I wouldn't know."

"Oh, I think you would. Somehow I think you would. But then, painting, I suppose painting isn't considered an especially macho thing to do, is it?"

"Depends on who's doing it." Some of the bars are in little plastic containers with names like Lanvin and Gucci and Lancôme. I open them, look at the decorative, colorful, finely crafted soap, wonder vaguely if any guest would ever actually use these things.

"Feel free to break them open."

"I would, if I could see any reason."

"I might've used an Exacto knife. Sliced them carefully open, lengthwise, hollowed precise little cavities in each, inserted the gems, pasted the halves together again, smoothed away all traces. Don't forget, I'm an artist. We're crafty little devils."

I don't respond, but I wonder why the kid's obviously decided to bait me now. Could I be getting warm? I continue to examine the bars of soap. Harcourt watches in silence. Directly below the glass shelves is a long towel rack. Small guest towels of embroidered white linen over larger pale gray cotton towels. Next, I move to the sunken bathtub and take a look at the tropical plants on the big ledge.

"May I make a suggestion?" Harcourt asks.

"Sure."

"Rather than removing the plants from their planters, why not use your screwdriver to probe the soil? Just as effective."

"I'll consider it."

"If you want me, I'll be in the kitchen. Care for a cup of coffee or anything?"

"No, thanks."

Harcourt leaves by the door to the kitchen. Instead of probing with my screwdriver, which would certainly damage the root structures, I use it to loosen the soil around the sides of each plant, hold it carefully upside down over the bathtub, slide the pot off, look over the inside and the soil, replace the pot. Bathtub winds up with loose soil which I scoop up and replace. Lastly, I run water in the tub, clean up the residue.

The bottom line, I come up empty, so does Big John in the bedroom, so do the others. About 5:45 we decide to call it quits. Needless to say, the lovely Ms. Bagette is drooling vengeful venom now. She's already called the chief twice, he's not back at the office yet, so she's read Murphy the riot act in several languages. She's got all of our badge numbers, of course, she's going to make a written complaint to the Civil

Liberties Union, she's going to "raise such a stink they'll smell it all the way to Albany." Durocher would love this lady. She come to play.

Big John calls Murphy just before we leave, tells him the bad news, gets an update on Ferragamo: Chief's team came up empty on his apartment. McCabe's long-since booked, still being questioned at the precinct. Well, at least we got something. Harcourt invites us to wash up in the kitchen, then politely escorts us to the door. Bagette and Tent are having a drink in the living room.

I'm picking up my vest and shotgun in the vestibule when I glance at the grandfather's clock in the corner.

"Rick, Gene, you check the clock?" I ask.

"Didn't even come out here," Rick says.

"Ted, Vic?"

"Nope," Vic says.

It's a tall, dark mahogany job, glass-faced cowl, face with gold numerals, separate dials for seconds and days of the week, even phases of the moon at the top. Below the cowl is a long glass-faced door showing the pendulum and two highly polished cylindrical brass weights. We have a somewhat similar clock at home that was actually my grandfather's. When I was a kid, my parents used to hide Christmas presents in the big bottom, below the glass door, where the weights descend.

I glance at Harcourt. "Sorry, but we'll have to check it."

"Please be especially careful."

There's an old key in the door of the cowl. I take it out, unlock the bottom door, swing it open. The brass weights are about halfway down, but there's enough room to reach in.

"Anybody got a flashlight?" I ask.

Telfian hands me a penlight. I get down on one knee, reach in and play the light around the bottom. Empty. Thick with dust. I hand Telfian the penlight, reach my right hand all the way down to the bottom, push hard on all four corners, then rap my knuckles in the center. True bottom. I get up, close the door, lock it, replace the key in the cowl door. My right hand is black with dust.

"That's it," I tell Harcourt. "Can I use your sink?"

"Surely."

Big John picks up the vest and shotgun. "We'll hold the elevator."

As I walk back to the kitchen, I hear the voices of the guys as they file out to the foyer. I wash my hands quickly, grab a paper towel, dry them. Then a thought occurs to me.

The door to the bathroom is open. I go in, switch on the light, look at the wide towel rack below the glass shelves. I push the towels to one side. Rack is just a polished aluminum cylinder held by side brackets screwed into the wall. I remove the towels, place them in the sink. I take out my small screwdriver, quickly remove the two screws in the left bracket, pull the bracket off, place it on the floor with the screws. Now I slide the cylinder out of the other bracket, look into one end. Something white just inside. I stick two fingers in and pull. Out comes a big cotton wad. I tip the cylinder carefully toward the towels in the sink. Nothing comes out. I rap my knuckles on the cylinder. Nothing. Finally I tap the cylinder against the edge of the sink.

Swoooooosh! Out they pour like crushed ice, tumbling into the pale gray towels: Diamonds, sapphires, emeralds, rubies, pearls, hundreds of them, brilliance, luster, color, fire, all sizes, all shapes, dazzling, breathtaking, a cool $1 million easy. I'm standing there stunned, flabbergasted, I'm squirting my pants, I can't believe this. From the corner of my eye I see something move at the door to the kitchen. I glance up fast.

Douché Bagette's standing there bug-eyed, starting to sway, legs turning to spaghetti. Now she clutches at the doorframe, fingernails screeching as she slides down slowly, Steinem glasses dancing at the end of her nose.

"Oy!" she says. "The crown jewels awready!"

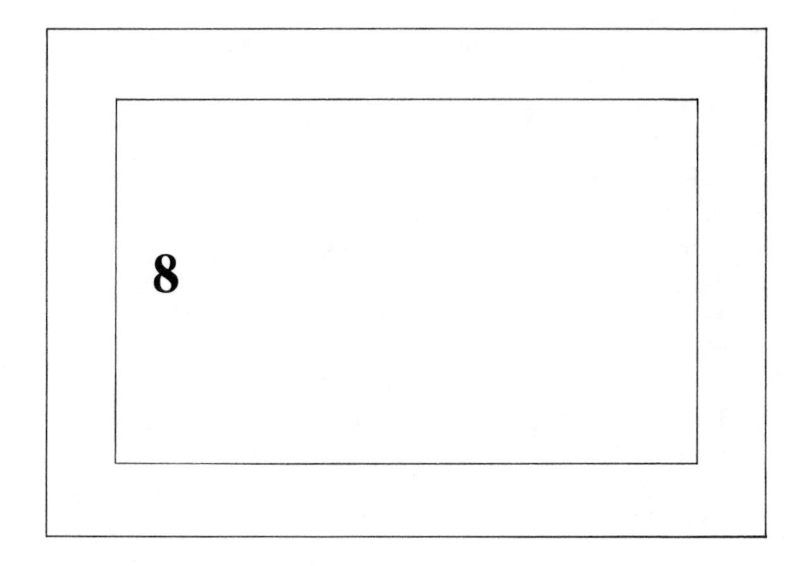

8

LIGHTS, CAMERA, ACTION! Next hour turns out to be the all-time classic documentary on the Mickey Mouse/Machiavellian machinations of police press relations. Conceived, produced, written, directed, and performed by the one and only genuine original chief of chicanery, the fella with the polydontoid oral façade, Walter "Smiley" Vadney, playing Edgar Hoover in what's got to be a blockbuster shoo-in Academy Award tour de force, a *coup de théâtre,* a creative mass-media event that nobody in the Archie Bunker NYC public out there in June 1981 is ever likely to forget. Most remarkable thing of all is how he manages to pull it off so fast. Big John calls headquarters at 5:55, I remember because by now we're both thinking like the chief will be thinking: Can we make the hour-long six o'clock news shows live by at least 6:30 so the boys and girls will have enough time to edit the best segments for the network news shows at seven? Cutting it awful close but, yeah, it's certainly possible. Big John talks with Murphy, tells him we hit the jackpot, finds out the chief got back from the Nineteenth Precinct just a few minutes ago. Chief gets on the line now, he's ecstatic, he's going nuts, tells Big John not to move a muscle till he arrives, this thing's got to be "a carefully planned, coordinated, time-synchronized operation, systematically orchestrated for maximum effect, the department's got to look its best." We know what that means.

Barnhart and Kazanski are sent downstairs to meet him. Carmine Street's no more than a ten-minute drive from headquarters, maybe fifteen in rush-hour conditions. Chief makes it in eight minutes flat. We hear a bunch of sirens screaming outside, I look out the front window, he's got a four-man motorcycle escort. I have visions of what's coming. He squeals to a chassis-rocking stop, jumps out, leaves the door open, motor running, emergency lights flashing. Barnhart and Kazanski lead him in fast. Meantime, everybody's ready for instant fame: Tent's changed from her bathrobe and thongs to a smart Lilly Pulitzer flowered print and classy Capezios; Harcourt remains quietly elegant in the gray three-piece; they're both cuffed; all the gems are in one large plastic evidence envelope, signed, sealed, and dated. Bagette, who recovered quickly enough to preside over the reading of their rights, begins to sound like a recorded message now, reminding them every couple of minutes: "Just don't say nothin', I'll do all the tawkin' needs to be done heah," but that's all she says. I know why. She's saving it for Vadney.

I know something else, finally, once and for all. Soon as Harcourt's placed under arrest and read the rights, I make it a point to personally do the honors on the standard frisk. Kid's not only a man, he's hung like a mule. For a second there, I wonder if he might be concealing a bagful of loot or something. Unbelievable. Just goes to show you about these Brits, right? Might not look tough, but they hang loose. Predictably enough, soon as we arrest Penny, Harcourt gets very protective, swears up and down she didn't know anything about the gems, she's totally innocent of any wrongdoing, the whole shot. We don't buy it, of course, but in any event it's academic, she's got to be booked on the prima facie evidence, which is more than sufficient to presume conspiracy under the law. Bagette gives us lip about it, which we expect in front of her clients, then she shuts up like a clam. Saves it for the chief. Clash of the titans. Bella Abzug gets her shot at Duke Wayne. Lib versus Lob. Meeting was arranged before they were born. I'm looking forward to this, I'm lighting a cigar.

Door opens, chief struts in, badge clipped to his breast pocket, followed by Kazanski and Barnhart. Everybody stands. You see the Duke sashay in to take charge, you stand. Bagette, she goes him one better, she leaps up, clomps straight at him in the Brooklyn "street walk," shoulders hunched, head down, arms swinging, chutzpa hissing.

"*Vadney!*"

He's oblivious to her, keeps walking. "Daniels, call the Nineteenth, get Barnett, see if they're set up for us."

It happens so fast, nobody's sure what's going on, but Bagette and the chief damn near collide at full stride, try to avoid each other at the last split second, both zig when they should've zagged, and somehow—crunch!—the chief stomps one of his size-fourteen cordovan clodhoppers on one of her size-ten open-toed flatboats.

"*Aaaaaeeeee! Ow!—Ow!—Ow!*" She's yelping at the moon now, hopping around, cat on a hot tin roof. "Ya fuckin' *ass-hole!* Ya filthy disgustin' *scrote,* ya! Ya rotten lousy *pigfucka!*"

Chief watches her like she's from another planet. "Daniels, who the hell's *this* bitch?"

"Their attorney."

She's hobbling to the couch now. "Call *me* a bitch, will ya! I got ya for as-*sawlt,* mistah, I got witnesses heah!"

"Blow it out your ass!" He turns to Big John. "What're you gawking at? Call Barnett, let's get this show on the road!"

Bagette plunks down on the couch. "I'll get ya for this, Vadney, so help me Gawd, I'm gonna nail ya for this, ya ignorant tub a puke!" She crosses her legs, grabs her left foot. "Oh, my *Gawd,* I knew it, I got a *frackcha* heah! Ya slimebag motherfucka, I'm gonna—"

"Hey, *you!*" the chief snaps. "You keep a civil tongue in your fat ugly face or I'm gonna collar you for obstructing justice!"

"Go ahead, ya pervert cocksucka, I'm pressin' *charges* heah!"

Telfian and Thalheimer start laughing through their noses now, turning away, they can't hold it in; spreads instantly to Barnhart and Kazanski.

"*Stop* it!" Tent screams. "For God's *sake,* the woman's in *pain,* can't you *see* that!"

"Hold it *down!*" Big John shouts. He's on the phone, hand cupped over the receiver.

"Everybody *shut up!*" the chief says. Now he takes me aside, speaks very quietly as he ushers me into the kitchen. "John, I want to congratulate you on this collar. Fantastic job, I'm gonna write a letter of commendation for your file first thing tomorrow morning. Excellent work, first class all the way."

"Appreciate it, chief."

"You deserve it, you've earned it, one of the most important collars of the year. Now, you guys up to speed on McCabe and all?"

"He's still at the precinct?"

"Right. Stopped off there myself before I went back to the office. His lawyer's there, he's making a stink about the delay between collar and book, now he says we're going slo-mo on the paperwork, wants to get McCabe down to Criminal Courts, get moving on the arraignment. Now, John, here's what we're facing next, this gets a little complicated. Talked to the commissioner just before I left the office, told him what you came up with here. He's delighted, of course, but now he wants to make absolutely certain we touch all the bases for the media people. You know Reilly, he's a nut on this kind of shit. Now, here's the thing. Between you and me, he's plenty pissed-off because I didn't call an immediate press conference on the McCabe collar. Fact is, I decided to hold off on the announcement, I told everybody up at the Nineteenth to play it D and D."

"Why's that?"

Left eyebrow goes up, then down with the left-sided Duke grin. "Knew I'd catch flack on it from Reilly, but I'm a giant step ahead of him in the psychology department. Back up a little. Had to delay the booking till two o'clock, as you know. Didn't tell Reilly because I knew damn well he'd be on the phone in a shot, turn it into a media circus and blow the rest of our operation. Couldn't risk it. Him being a civilian, he doesn't really grasp the big picture, so I gotta play these crappy little games with him, try to keep him from getting in the way. So, the upshot, McCabe gets booked without a single reporter present. Still couldn't tell Reilly yet. Why? You know why. Ferragamo doesn't show at the bank. I grab my team, tear up to his apartment. Boom, he's split. Now it's about two thirty-five. I call Mat first thing, tell him to give you guys Code Green fast. Next, I call Barnett, give him two orders: One, get a diamond expert from one of the insurance companies that's involved to get his ass up there pronto. If we can get positive identification on only one single stone, we got it made. Two, go slo-mo on McCabe's paperwork—anything, screw up the fingerprints, get the wrong numbers on the mug shots. We're buying time. Expensive time as far as the media's concerned. Told Barnett we're buying time till we get positive ID on one of the diamonds; that's all he needs to know. Truth is, that's only half the reason."

I nod, puff on my cigar, wait for the other half. Chief's leaning back against one of the butcher-block counters, eyes narrowed at the living room, trying to hear what Big John's saying on the phone.

"So what's the other half?" I ask finally.

"*They got problems?*" he shouts at Big John.

"*No press yet!*"

"*For Christ sake, give 'em time!*" Chief grins, glances at me, then his watch. "First call I made after talking with Daniels,

Grady in Press Relations, exactly five fifty-seven. Just eight past six now and Barnett's looking for a traffic jam already. He'll get one, all right. This thing's liable to be a three-ring circus."

"What's the other half of the reason?"

"Other half of what reason?"

"Buying time."

"Oh, yeah. Other half is good press relations, John. Took a course in it, actually, 'Psychology of Effective Press Relations,' FBI course, Matt took it with me. Fantastic course. Had to do with maximum utilization of time and space within given parameters of minimum lead times necessary for meeting deadlines in both broadcast and print journalism. Practical application? If I'd called a press conference to announce the collar of McCabe at, say, three o'clock, somewhere in there, all the TV crews, newspaper, magazine, wire services, they all flock up to the Nineteenth. Bottom line, what've we got? One perpetrator. Who looks like a middle-management trainee at IBM, yet. One out of four. That's a two-fifty batting average, John. But now, wait a minute here. What if we play a long shot, wait maybe three, four hours longer? And what if we luck out? What I'm saying, John, I placed all my chips on you guys. Gambled on the long shot. All the time keeping in mind the psychology of effective press relations. So what've we got now? I'll tell you what we got now. Now we got three out of four, John. Thanks to your investigative expertise and my psychological perspective. Three out of four, we're hitting seven-fifty now. Point-seven-five-oh, that's more than heavy hitting, that's slugging. Powerhouse slugging in anybody's league. Maximum utilization of time and space within given parameters."

"How's space figure in?"

"Good question. Back up a little. Before I left old Nineteen this afternoon, the diamond guy from Prudential's made a positive ID on not one but four of the largest stones. So we know we got a solid lock on McCabe. But, hey, if we follow standard operating procedure and take him and the fence down to Criminal Courts for arraignment, and then, boom, you guys hit paydirt on the other two here, what've we got? I'll tell you what we got. We got a counterproductive time-space situation from the standpoint of media staging. We gotta take your two collars all the way up to Sixty-seventh to be booked, but McCabe's all the way down to Centre Street now. Counterproductive media staging, John. Translates into bad press relations. Waste of valuable time and energy. Staging's critical to the whole psychology of effective—" He glances up as Big John walks toward us. "They set?"

Big John keeps his voice low. "Barnett's following it to the letter, no sweat. He'll have McCabe, the fence, and their attorneys ready in the lobby when you pull up. Crowd-control procedures just like you ordered: Ten mounted police from Central Park Precinct arrived a couple of minutes ago, he'll give them instructions himself. Wooden police lines set up from curb to steps. Preferential step positions go to TV crews and press photographers with proper credentials. Fifteen uniformed cops in front of the lines. He figures, this time of day, street's liable to be jammed solid with gawkers. Soon as people see the TV cameras, horses, cops, reporters, photographers, forget it. So he's decided to close off the street to traffic starting six-fifteen. They open it to us, period."

Chief checks his watch. "I got nine past six now. Carmine's about even with Third Street, so we got sixty-four blocks to cover. You two in my car with the perpetrators. Rawlings, you're wheel-man. Sixth Avenue straight to Fifty-ninth, over to Third, up to Sixty-seventh. We got a four-cycle escort, full sirens, we should make it by six-thirty easy. Prime time for live coverage. Let's go to work."

"What about their attorney?" I ask.

"Tell bitch-face to grab a cab. Let's go."

Down we go. Elevator's only big enough to hold five, so the big shits go first, chief and Big John, Harcourt and Tent, me last with the vest and shotgun. Considerable crowd outside the building. I talk to the motorcycle cops, tell them the route, full sirens, the works. We pile in, Big John next to me, chief in back with Harcourt and Tent.

We take off, two cycles in front, two in back, five sirens, appointment with destiny. Carmine through Bleecker and pick up speed on Sixth. We're still in what's euphemistically called the rush "hour" that lasts from roughly four to seven, so we're snaking through relatively heavy traffic. Cycle cops up front set the pace, of course, and it's just my luck to have a couple of young jocks who've been watching "CHiPs" since puberty. Now they're jumping lights at maybe sixty per, cars and trucks and bicycles still shooting across, of course, go ahead, hit us, we dare you, serenely confident of victory over death. Lots of kicks streaking through the bigger intersections like Fourteenth, Twenty-third, Thirty-fourth, and Forty-second, wondering what it feels like to be broadsided by a good buddy in an eighteen-wheeler with his stereo blasting C&W too loud to hear us. Every time I take a fast glance in the rear-view mirror, Harcourt and Tent look like unwed expectant parents being rushed to the hospital by a wild-eyed father with a Boris Karloff grin.

When we finally hang a right on Fifty-ninth and head for Third, the chief leans forward, head between us, raises his voice over the sirens. "Don't suppose I have to tell you men what's waiting for us up there."

"Front-page fever," Big John says.

"Eyes of the world," I add.

Chief leans his elbows on the backrest, mouth close to our ears. "Maybe not the eyes of the world, but sure as hell the eyes and ears of the city of New York. Know what those citizens out there really want? They want what this city can't ever give them again. They want safety and security again. They want law and order. Can't give it to 'em. Not in this city. No way. Impossible in this day and age. At this point in time, all we can do is hold our fingers in the dikes. Most of 'em don't really understand that yet, thank God. They like to think we're just going through a rougher period than normal, that things'll settle down. They won't, men. You know that, I know that. They're gonna get worse. Much worse. Hell, we've long-since run out of jails, everybody knows that. No place to warehouse 'em anymore, gotta send 'em back on the street now. Statistics are unbelievable. Frightening. Know what some criminologists say? If the crime rate in this city continues to accelerate at the present rate, before the end of this decade we'll see a form of anarchy in the streets. People taking the law into their own hands, vigilante groups. Confusion, disorder, chaos. Complete breakdown of society as we know it. Like Paddy Chayefsky said in *Network,* remember that? People're gonna get mad as hell. They're gonna start yelling 'I'm mad as hell and I'm not gonna take this anymore.' And they're not. That's the truth. We gotta live with that truth, those of us who know. We gotta keep it to ourselves. We gotta pretend we got our shit together, that the crime rate's not out of control, even though we know in our gut it's getting progressively worse every day. Truth is, there's no plateau in sight. We don't have the manpower or money to make a dent in it. As I see it, there's only one logical alternative left to us."

We're weaving through traffic on Fifty-ninth, waiting to hear the one logical alternative. Chief sinks back in his seat now. I exchange a fast glance with Big John. I see Harcourt exchange a fast glance with Tent. Now we hang a rubber-burning, siren-shrieking, horn-blasting left turn into Third Avenue, scattering pedestrians like spray.

Big John turns around calmly. "What's the alternative, chief?"

"What we're doing right now, of course."

"Huh?"

Chief snaps forward again, voice loud in our ears. "Setting an isolated example to give the *illusion* we're still in control. That's right. Only intelligent, logical alternative left to us. Is that so farfetched? Consider the psychology of the illusion we're creating in this case: If we can outsmart even the boldest, smartest, most sophisticated gang of crooks this city's ever faced, we *must* have our shit together. You kidding? One major collar like this every couple of months, we got it made, providing we set up and maintain effective press relations, give the media what they want. That so farfetched?"

Big John shrugs. "Guess not."

I shrug, keep my mouth shut.

No comment from Harcourt and Tent.

Chief continues, right in our ears. "Think of it in terms of real people. Think of it in terms of a seventy-five-year-old widow in the Bronx living on a fixed income in a senior citizens' low-income housing project. Maybe hundreds of thousands like her. Been mugged by teenage punks for her grocery money three times so far this year. She's literally afraid to go out in the street, day or night. She's sitting in front of her TV tonight, watching the news, suffering in the heat, afraid to open her windows even. What's she see, lead story, live coverage at six-thirty? 'Cops Capture Smartest Crooks,' that's what she sees. There they are in handcuffs, heads down, being hustled into an old neighborhood precinct just like hers. Outwitted. Caught. Collared. Jailed. The old widow watches every detail, listens carefully. Now, finally, look at that. What's she doing?"

Big John shrugs. "Don't know, chief."

From the corner of my eye I can see the chief looking straight ahead through the windshield. He pauses and I know damn well he's really visualizing the old dame in the Bronx. Me, I'm getting flashes of her too, despite myself, I'm wondering what the hell she's doing now.

"There," the chief says, softer now. "You can see her face in the glow from the TV. She's—yeah, she's smiling now. Not a big smile, not a real happy smile, she's long past that. Just the corners of her mouth. And her eyes. Look at those eyes. Those eyes hold the wisdom and kindness and pain of two lifetimes, men. Two lifetimes in the Bronx. They've seen it all. Now there's just a quick little spark in there, a glimmer.

Windows of the soul, the eyes. What's the spark? Not happiness, not joy, nothing that grand. No, it's something much deeper in there. Understanding. That's right. That special street-smart understanding you get deep in your bones when you grow up in the Bronx and you're an adult by the time you're twelve. Now what's she do? She gets up, she pours herself a little glass of sherry from a bottle her deadbeat son gave her last Christmas. Think she sips that sherry? Not tonight. Tonight she chugs it, God bless her heart, bottoms up. Feels the fire down in her old loins. And she says to herself, out loud, she says, 'Thank God they nailed them fuckin' schlepps.' She goes to bed with a feeling of quiet satisfaction tonight. Not joy. Just nice, quiet, vindictive satisfaction. Tomorrow morning she'll rush out to buy the tabloids first thing. Now *that's* what I'm talking about here. The *illusion* that we're still in control. Not farfetched at all. Only intelligent, logical alternative left to us."

This may come as a surprise to you, it did to me, although it didn't really sink in at the time: Part of what the chief was saying in those few minutes got to me. Really got to me. Delayed reaction, I suppose, but in retrospect it touched a raw nerve somewhere inside me. I'm not talking about the old widow in the Bronx, that's just typical Duke Wayne cornball, the chief gets carried away sometimes. I'm talking about his idea, his philosophy, if that's the word, of setting isolated examples to give the illusion we're in control, because it's the only logical alternative left to us. Stung my ass, I'm serious. Now, I don't know the chief as well as Big John, in fact this special assignment is the first time I've worked directly with him. No question he's a complicated case, a split personality maybe, but the man has a way with words, you got to give him that, and he's been around long enough to have a very realistic handle on what enforcement in this city is all about. So, what I'm saying, if this is really his handle after twenty-seven, twenty-eight years in the department, that we're now finally reduced to giving the illusion we're in control, then something's seriously wrong somewhere. One thing I know for sure, it's not *my* handle, never has been, never will be, God willing. And I'm not exactly a rookie after twenty-six years. Granted, I don't have the advantage of the day-to-day departmental overview he has, I'm not anywhere near the rarefied atmosphere of the celestial hierarchy down at headquarters. Never wanted that kind of responsibility, but that's another story altogether. Question is, has Vadney been exposed to some dipshit fundamental philosophical truth from his perch up in the catbird's seat that I've somehow missed after all these years of getting my hands dirty down in the street? Maybe. Maybe he has. Got to admit it's a possibility; I'm not privy to the kind of long-range statistical prognostications the top brass has at its fingertips. Still, the whole idea burns my ass. No, it does more than that, much more, if I'm honest. Hurts. Hurts deep down. Touches a very, very sensitive nerve somewhere. Surprises me.

Back to the action, we're now approaching Sixty-seventh, we're a block away. Cycle cops slow, signal for the left turn. I do the same, check my watch; about 6:25, not bad at all. Not much of a crowd at the corner, maybe a couple dozen people standing near the blue wooden horses that block the street to traffic. Two uniformed cops from the precinct, Conners and Phelps, move one of the horses to the side. Big John and I wave to them as we drive in behind the cycles, sirens still wailing.

Scene up ahead is totally unreal, goes far beyond anything I could've imagined, you'd absolutely have to see this shit to believe it: Press cars, vans and trucks double parked on both sides, a positively gigantic crowd floods the whole area in front of the precinct, at least a thousand people, no exaggeration, mounted police are lost in a sea of faces, all turned to us now, TV cameras on the tops of two trucks are already shooting, precinct steps are jammed with shoulder-mounted TV cameras, *paparazzi* are running all over the place. Cycle cops slow to a crawl, mounted cops clear a path fast, we're moving through the crowd now, all kinds of curious faces staring in at us, hands on the windows, cameras clicking, people being shoved against the fenders and doors.

Chief's voice sounds amazingly calm: "When we pull in front, I want you guys to stay put. Don't want your faces seen. I'll escort these two in alone."

"In *this* mob?" Big John asks.

"No problem. Don't want your faces seen, goes without saying. Wherever Ferragamo's holed-up in this city, you can bet your ass he'll be watching TV news."

I'm just about to remind him that Ferragamo's known my face for at least eight years now, but I decide against it.

Big John grabs the bulletproof vest on the seat between us. "Chief, do us all a favor and put this thing on before you get out."

"You kidding? Don't need that."

"*Kidding?*" Big John says. "For Christ's *sake,* Walt, *look* at this fuckin' mob! *Nobody's* safe plowing through a mob like this, you know that as well as I do! Don't try to be a hero—*protect* yourself!"

Chief hesitates. "Maybe you're right, John. Gimme that thing." He yanks the vest in back, starts putting it on fast.

Big John turns around, kneels on the seat, helps him with the straps. "You're nuts to go out there alone, you know that?"

"Comes with the job, John. Now do like I said and stay put till I'm inside. From here on out, you guys got just one assignment, like everybody else: Find Ferragamo. Fast."

Cycle cops pull up in front; I stop right behind them. Uniformed cops are lined up shoulder-to-shoulder, both sides of a clearing from the curb to the steps. All cameras are rolling, all reporters are into their live commentaries, millions of New Yorkers are poised in front of their sets. A uniformed cop is trying to open the back door; now he knocks on the window. Big John adjusts the last strap on the vest, pulls up the door lock. Chief grabs the upper arms of Harcourt and Tent as the door swings open. All three duck heads and slide out to a deafening roar. Door slams shut, Big John hits the lock, turns around, sinks back in his seat, watches the spectacle. Can't see his face, but I know he's wearing the impish grin of a delighted Daniel Patrick M.

Chief gives in to the impassioned shouting of newsmen, pauses briefly on the steps now, flanked by the expensively dressed, attractive young masterminds of the greatest hotel robbery in American history, heads down in shame, hands cuffed behind their backs, arms held firmly by the Duke who dwarfs them, head held high. His white vest is almost luminous in the soft sun of a long spring twilight. Can't see his face, but we'll catch it in the edited segments of the seven o'clock network news in the bar just up the street.

Are you watching, Jimmy Ferragamo?

Are you eating your heart out, Vinnie Casandra?

Are you smiling, old widow in the Bronx?

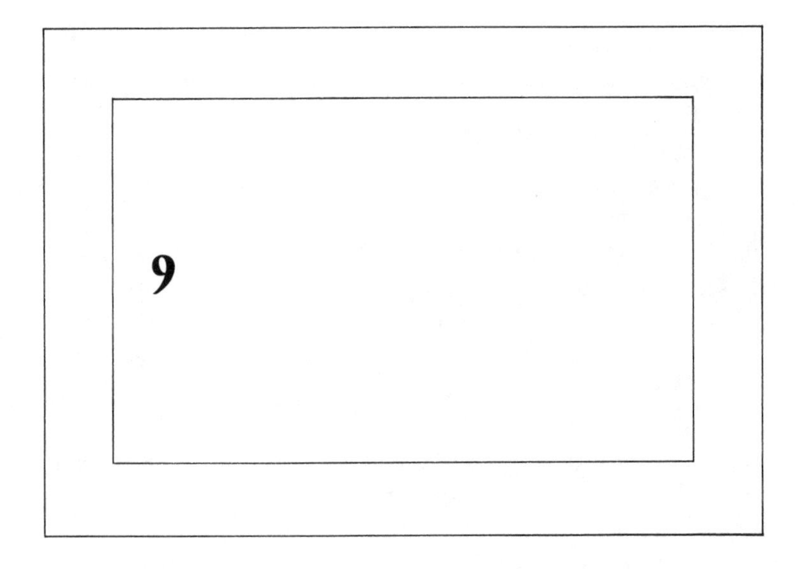

WE'RE CELEBRATING TONIGHT, we figure we deserve it in spades, Friday night, case just one week old, three out of four collars already, seven-five-oh, chief's famous. We're happily ensconced in soft armchair stools at Hal Kendig's Speak Easy Saloon, Sixty-seventh and Madison, favorite hangout of the Nineteenth Detective Squad, you'd love this joint. Small, softly lighted, tastefully furnished, twenty-one-inch Sony Trinitron, bowls of peanuts, variety of hors d'oeuvres, superb menu reasonably priced and you can chow down right at the bar if you want, napkin stuck rakishly in your collar, nobody knows a thing about it. Sit here after a long day, sip a very dry Beefeater martini on the rocks, smoke a cigar, got the world by the dork on a downhill drag. Kendig tends bar himself, big distinguished animal of a man, terrific sense of humor, should've been a cop. Born in Dodge City, Kansas, had his horns capped by wife Regi, classy little blonde from Tarrytown, N.Y., doubles as maître d' and cashier, kid's a real pisser. On the wall behind the bar is a glass case holding an old nickel-plated Colt .45 Single Action Army, the famed

"Peacemaker," the gun that won the West. Still works perfectly, Kendig's got a permit for it. Claims it belonged to his grandfather Tyson Kendig who was once a deputy sheriff under Bat Masterson in Dodge City. Of course, we only have Hal's word for that. Regi says, "Deputy sheriff, my ass, his grandpa weren't even housebroke." Directly below the gun is a big wooden plaque with the elaborately handpainted Old West inscription:

SPEAK EASY

Or Forever Hold Your Piece

Hal comes over now, wiping his hands on a towel. He's graying at the temples these days, nice touch. "You guys in on the Hollywood action down there?"

Big John jerks a thumb at me. "Blue Eyes here was the star."

"No shit."

"Made two out of three collars," Big John says.

Hal sticks out his big ham of a hand, keeps his deep voice low. "Congratulations, John, beautiful. Saw it on the news. Everybody in here was watching."

"Pretty good show?" I ask.

"Gave it a full five minutes. Listen, drinks on me, naturally, both of you. In fact, dinner on the house tonight." He turns, motions Regi to come over.

Big John glances at the TV, then at his watch. "Maybe we'll catch some of it on national news."

"Regi!" Hal yells.

"Yeah?" Vivacious Regi with the ultrafeminine-voice and figure to match comes quickly, over smiling, short blonde hair bouncing.

Hal lowers his voice. "Little John made two of the three collars."

"No shit!" She gives me a big kiss on the cheek. "Wow, a real live hero!"

"Film at seven," I tell her in my soft hero's voice.

As it turns out, we have to wait till about 7:20, next-to-last story on NBC. By now Regi's after Hal to switch channels, but he sticks to his guns because he's a fan of John Chancellor and Roger Mudd. Finally it's billboarded to come up next after the commercial break. We watch to see how an antifungal spray liquid kills athlete's foot on contact, even in the most stubborn cases, relieves burning, itching, and speeds healing. Next, we're exposed to the wonders of a medicated spray powder for jock itch and told, without benefit of an actual demonstration, how the environmentally safe propellant relieves excessive perspiration, itching, chafing, rash, and irritation in the groin area. Throwaway line at the end tells us it helps reduce odor too. Nice to know. Wonder how many families are watching this over dinner. Screen-filling can of jock itch spray powder fades into the sober, if slightly flushed face of John Chancellor. Everybody at the bar goes, *"Shhhhh!"*

"One week ago today," Chancellor says, "the famed Hotel Champs-Elysées in New York was the scene of a bizarre holdup said to be the biggest of its kind in American history. Today, three suspects were arrested. Gabe Pressman has the story in Manhattan."

We're looking at a high-angle long shot of the motorcycle escort leading our car up Sixty-seventh Street, surrounded by a crowd that seems even larger than I thought. Pressman speaks voice-over, obviously recorded in the studio: "Today, New York City detectives arrested three suspects in the three-point-four-million-dollar Hotel Champs-Elysées robbery and recovered an estimated one-and-a-quarter million dollars in stolen jewels." Cut to a closer angle as our car pulls up to the curb and stops. "Unexpectedly, one of the suspects is a young woman." Cut to three-shot of the chief escorting Harcourt and Tent to the steps. "Identified by police as Penny Tent, nineteen, a Greenwich Village nightclub entertainer, she is said to be the live-in girlfriend of Hamilton Harcourt, twenty-six, who police say is an insurance agent with Lloyds of London." Cut to side-angle medium shot of the three as they pause on the steps; chief's white vest and stern expression give him the distinct aura of a modern-day knight in shining armor. "Both were booked at East Side Manhattan's Nineteenth Precinct along with the third suspect . . ." Cut to medium two-shot of McCabe and the chief in the lobby: ". . . identified as William McCabe, thirty-two, said by police to be an executive with National Airlines. Chief of Detectives Walter Vadney answered questions." Cut to medium shot of Vadney outside now, surrounded by reporters; he frowns as he listens to the last few words of a shouted question, and his voice is calm but loud enough to command the attention of all: "Question is—question is, do we have any leads on the fourth member of the gang. For obvious reasons I won't comment on that, other than to say that we've had all four under twenty-four-hour surveillance for several days now and we expect an apprehension of the final suspect relatively soon." Cut to medium shot of Pressman with the jammed press conference still in progress behind him: "Two young men and one attractive young woman in custody one week to the day after the biggest hotel robbery in American history. One suspect still at large. Gabe Pressman, NBC News, New York."

Hal and Regi treat us like real celebrities that evening. We have one of the big corner tables in back, a large carafe of chilled Gallo Chablis Blanc, bluepoint oysters on the half-shell, and my all-time favorite entrée, Maine lobster, served by Regi herself. All on the house, of course. Big John and me are sitting there in candlelight, sipping wine, pigging-out on all this stuff, we're feeling no pain at all. Finally, Hal comes over with a couple of brandy glasses and pours us doubles of Courvoisier cognac. We light up cigars, sit back, start to philosophize. After we've got most of the city, state, national, and world problems tucked away, we talk about our friend Jimmy Ferragamo. Where might he be, we wonder. Big John's of the opinion that he's long-gone out of the city. I know Jimmy a little better and I'm betting he's holed up somewhere with one of his girlfriends; the guy's an unbelievable ass-man, attracts them like flies. Can't help thinking about the bellydancer he used to date down at the Sirocco, they were pretty tight for a while. It's a long shot and it's been a long day, but the club's down on Twenty-ninth and we've both got to grab trains home on the Long Island from Penn Station, so we decide to stop off on our way and talk to the bellydancer, name of Uta Tabor. We figure it's worth a shot, what the hell, might even catch part of her act. Before we leave, I call Catherine, tell her I'll try to make the 10:40, gets me in at 11:27, if it's on time for a change. I tell her to catch the chief's act on the eleven o'clock news; she says she already saw the whole thing live at 6:30. Says she thinks the chief's come a long way, he's ready for "Hill Street Blues," a natural actor, even scratched his groin on camera.

We don't have a car, of course, Telfian and Thalheimer drove it back to the station, checked it in for us, so we grab a cab down to Twenty-ninth and Park. Twenty-ninth has a variety of other restaurants, L'Italianissimo, Shalimar, Suehiro, Weathervane Inn, but the Sirocco's in a class by itself, clean white stone façade, stately pillars flanking a white semicircular canopy with the name, even a spotless green carpet from curb to steps. Couple of long black limos double-parked outside, chauffeurs talking to each other.

When we arrive about 9:45, the first show's in progress in the big dining area, the Greek band's giving out with something exotic, and a bellydancer who may or may not be Uta Tabor is doing her thing in the colored lights. We sit at the far end of the bar, wait for our eyes to adjust. Bar area is clean white stucco, separated from the big room, but we can see the show fairly well.

Bartender comes over. "Good evening, gentlemen."

Big John shows him the gold shield. "Like to talk to somebody in charge."

"The owner is Mr. San," he says with a Greek accent. "He is busy right now."

"Appreciate it if you'd call him," Big John says. "Tell him we only need a minute of his time."

"Mr. San is the bandleader, sir." He points to the bandstand. "The one playing the bouzouki, can you see?"

Big John takes a look, nods like he knows what a bouzouki is. "How long's the show last?"

"It started at nine-thirty." He squints at his watch. "About ten minutes to go. Would you care for a drink while you wait?"

"Yeah. Yeah, I'd like a cognac straight up."

He looks at me. "And you, sir?"

"Make mine an ouzo. Straight up."

Big John waits till the bartender's gone, then gives me a look. "A *what?*"

"An ouzo, you ignoramus. Greek drink. When in Rome, y'know?"

"A Greek drink when in *Rome?*"

I ignore him, take out a cigar, bite off the end. "Read somewhere that Aristotle Onassis liked ouzos. Matter of fact, it was his favorite drink. You wouldn't know shit like that, you're not a connoisseur of the finer things in life."

"What's in it?"

I light the cigar. "To fully appreciate something like an ouzo, you have to savor the subtle delicacies of the aromatic spirits first, of course, and your taste buds and palate have to be educated to anticipate the aesthetic sublime."

"What's in it?"

"Don't have a clue."

Whoever the bellydancer is, she's giving the supersonic set their money's worth. Rhythmic, supple, sensuous movements, reminds me a little of a darkly mysterious Bo Derek. Outfit consists of a red-orange bra with a dash of spangles and a matching long skirt worn dangerously low on undulating hips. Bracelets, bangles, and beads, plus little cymbals on her thumbs and forefingers. She's whirling around gracefully, arms over her head now, working the ringside tables. You should see the faces of the men, sweat rolling down, wide eyes darting up and down. Notice most have their legs crossed. Can't say I blame them. Kid like this, moving around like that, brings out the primal instincts in a chap. Kid's just a tantalizing little bundle of biological urges. I'm sitting there, chewing on my cigar, wishing the guy would hurry up with my ouzo, and for some reason the words of the Bard come to mind, *The Tempest,* I think it was, when he said that immortal line about tempestuous broads are such stuff as dreams are made on. Remember that? The Bard knew where it was at. We'd call them erotic fantasies today, anything goes, but he had the right idea, he just had more class.

Bartender finally comes over with our drinks. I pick mine up, turn to Big John. He's like hypnotized by the bellydancer, moving his head and shoulders to the music, forget it. I can't wait to taste the ouzo, find out why Onassis was so crazy about it, so I toast to myself, take a sip. Can't believe it, I take another one. Now I understand. Now I know why Onassis always had such baleful eyes. Stuff tastes like sweet licorice. Dreadful shit.

When the show ends, the lights come up, the bellydancer takes her bows to a terrific ovation. Room's just like I remembered it, décor of a modern luxury cruise ship, authentic nautical appointments, panoramic view of the sea through the big portholes, except I never saw the ceiling because the houselights weren't up. Ceiling turns out to be a turquoise blue sky with fluffy realistic clouds. Room's on the top deck. Up near the ceiling is an enormous wraparound railing with a series of blue-and-white life preservers, real lifeboats with the name *Sirocco,* and, behind the bandstand, a triple-decked ship's bridge.

Houselights dim to normal now, bellydancer exits gracefully, goes into an unmarked door to the right of the bar area. Shortly after that, three musicians come into the bar, talking, lighting cigarettes. Bartender motions to one of them, whispers something, points us out. Man walks over to us quickly, dark suit and tie, good-looking, I'd say about forty, average height and build, brown hair, light brown eyes.

He sticks his hand out to me. "I'm Aris San, the owner, may I help you?" Just the trace of a Greek accent.

I shake hands, show him my gold. "Detective John Rawlings."

Big John shakes hands. "Sergeant John Daniels."

"What can I do for you?" he asks.

I keep my voice low. "Do you have a dancer named Uta Tabor?"

"Yes, she just performed. Is there some trouble?"

"No," I tell him. "She's not in any trouble at all. We'd just like to ask her some routine questions about an acquaintance of hers."

"Only take a few minutes," Big John says.

"No problem. Follow me." He leads us past the bar to the unmarked door we saw Uta Tabor enter. He knocks, glances at me. "She's probably changing now."

Voice from inside: "Yes?"

"It's all right, it's me."

Lock snaps, door opens, we see Tabor's face.

"Some gentlemen want to speak to you in private," he says.

Her dark eyes dart to us. "All right."

We follow San in, he remembers our names, does the introductions. "You're not in any trouble," he assures her. "They have questions about someone you know, that's all. I'll be right outside if you need me."

Tabor's eyes look a little frightened as she watches him leave. She's changed from her outfit and now wears a white silk dressing gown that accentuates her dark features. Up close she looks like a very young Sophia Loren, early twenties, long dark hair worn loose, high cheekbones, rather heavy mascara. Although she displayed an absolutely flamboyant professional confidence on the dance floor, the first impression I get now is disarming, intriguing, as if that part of her personality is peeled off with her costume, revealing a young lady who's rather tired of being stared at. She makes a conscious effort to avoid our eyes as she turns, and her voice is soft and almost lyrical with an accent that's difficult to place: "I'm dressing for dinner now, will this take long?"

"Just a few minutes," I tell her.

"Good. Go ahead and sit down." She goes behind a large Oriental screen and we hear the rattle of clothes hangers.

We take chairs nearby, close to the mirrored dressing table. All we can see of Tabor is the top of her head and her feet. Room is relatively small, windowless, looks like a converted cloakroom; two of the white stucco walls still hold long coat-racks, empty now except for a few dozen hangers. In the center of the room, dominating everything, is a black wrought-iron circular stairway to the next floor.

"Ask away," Tabor says.

I clear my throat. "You still date a gentleman by the name of James Ferragamo?"

"No, I don't, and the man's no gentleman, I assure you."

"When'd you stop dating him?"

She drapes the white dressing gown over the screen. "I'd say —about six months ago."

"You know he was in the club here Tuesday night?"

"I saw him in the audience, yes."

"He didn't see you after the show?"

She hesitates; one bare foot rests on the other for a moment. "He tried. He came to the door with another man, wanted to come in and talk. I told him I didn't want to see him, period. He called me a name. I slammed the door. That was it, that's the truth."

"I understand you dated him for about a year, is that correct?"

"Absolutely not. Three, four months at the most."

"Where was he living then?"

"Two thirty-six West One Hundred Sixth."

"Know of any other places he lived, rooms, hotels, apartments?"

"The guy's in trouble, right?"

"No, but we'd like to talk to him."

Her arms go above the screen as she slips into a dress. "He

took me to one other place, I don't think it was his. Well, it might've been, I don't know. Took me to a place in the Bronx one time. Don't know the address, that's the truth. An apartment in the Bronx, and I had to take the subway home. He wouldn't drive me home. Wouldn't even give me cab fare."

"You know the general neighborhood?"

"No. Honest, I don't know the Bronx at all."

"Could you see Yankee Stadium from there?"

She hesitates again, then walks around the screen, adjusting the sash on an expensive-looking white silk dress with flower designs. "As a matter of fact, I did. Saw Yankee Stadium from the subway platform." She picks up a pack of Winston's from the dressing table, takes one out, frowning, lights it with a slender gold Dunhill, inhales deeply, blows smoke toward the mirror, watches it hit and curl upward. "Had to wait a long time for the train, it was late at night. I remember I could see the apartment house from there too. No, not the apartment, the end of the street it was on. This was autumn, late autumn, and it was cold and I didn't have a coat. And I looked at that street for a long time and thought what a bum he was for not driving me home."

"Jerome Avenue line," Big John says.

"Sounds like it. Miss Tabor, one more question. Would you be willing to help us try and locate that apartment?"

"How could I do that?"

"Tomorrow afternoon," I tell her, "at your convenience, we could pick you up at your home, drive you up to the Bronx, escort you around to various elevated subway platforms along the Jerome Avenue line. Up in the general vicinity of Yankee Stadium. Just three or four platforms is all, wouldn't take more than an hour. You take a look from each platform, see where Yankee Stadium is, get your bearings."

She sits on the edge of the dressing table now, crosses her legs, blows smoke at the ceiling. "Let me ask you a question. Why should I? What's in it for me?"

I try to avoid staring at her smooth brown legs, but it's hard.

"All right, up front. Ferragamo's in big trouble. We want him. We want him bad. We want to put this guy away for a long time."

Her dark eyes glance at me. "I see. May I ask what he's done?"

"Armed robbery."

"Uh-huh." She begins swinging her ankle. "A big robbery?"

"Very big."

She nods, catches me taking in her legs, smiles just a fraction. "If I agreed to try—*if*—that would have to be the end of it. Period."

"Absolutely."

"I won't sign anything, I won't say anything else, I won't do anything else. I don't want my name involved in any way whatsoever."

"It won't be," I tell her. "We'll guarantee absolute confidentiality. That's a promise. You can have it in writing if you want."

"That won't be necessary. As long as I have your word."

"You've got it."

She swings her ankle, looks at it, hair covering her profile. "You see, I'm not a citizen of your country, I was born in Greece, I grew up in Israel. I'm an Israeli citizen. So I'm not what you call 'public spirited' about things like this, because I don't want to get into any trouble. But I'll tell you something. This man, he *belongs* in prison. He really does. The man is an animal. I don't want to say any more, you understand?"

"Certainly."

"I hope you find him and put him in prison where he belongs." She looks at me from the corner of her eye. "So, yes, I agree to cooperate, subject to what I said."

"We appreciate it."

"Understand, I'm not at all sure I *can* help. I really don't know the Bronx at all. But I'll try."

"Anything you can do," Big John says. "We'll make it as easy as possible. Is tomorrow afternoon convenient for you?"

She takes a drag on the cigarette, nods. "I work very late

here, I sleep late. This will have to be—I usually sleep until four-thirty or five in the afternoon. Would six-thirty be all right?"

"Absolutely," I say.

"All right, six-thirty then. Tomorrow afternoon. I live at One-fifteen West Thirty-first. I'll be in the lobby at six-thirty sharp."

We take a cab over to Penn Station, agree to meet at the precinct six o'clock tomorrow afternoon. I'm in plenty of time for the 10:40, so I buy the late city edition of the *Post.* Front page has a terrific candid shot of the chief, head up, flanked by Harcourt and Tent, heads down. Big headline above it reads:

**NAB 3 BIGS
IN GREATEST
HOTEL HEIST**

Porno Dancer Stashed $1M Gems!

I take my time walking to Gate 18, glance at the inside pages. Leave it to the *Post,* they managed to dig up two Village Vamp publicity shots of Penny, one in her white string-bikini dancing up a storm on the runway, the other on her hobbyhorse spanking the hell out of Tanya Hide. Since the reporters obviously don't have any juicy background material on Harcourt and McCabe, at least not yet, they make Penny the star by default, playing up the pure porn angle of a voluptuous nineteen-year-old girl who makes a living by impersonating a male transvestite who makes a living by impersonating a voluptuous nineteen-year-old girl in a tawdry sadomasochistic relationship with a male transvestite impersonator of Joan Crawford, while the poor girl's British boyfriend slaves away at Lloyds of London and dreams of winning her love by conspiring to steal a fortune in gems like those he insures every day. Well, it ain't the *Enquirer,* but it's getting there.

10

SATURDAY EVENING, we're driving Uta Tabor up to the Bronx and Big John's being real nice, giving her a little background history on the place. I grew up in this city, I worked here all my life, I don't know half the stuff he's telling her. Says the Bronx was named after Johannes Bronck, a Scandinavian, first guy to settle beyond the Harlem River, 1639. Area started to develop after 1850 around the village of Morrisania, roughly Third Avenue and 161st Street. Not too far from where Yankee Stadium is today, 161st and River Avenue. Uta's in the back seat taking all this in, asking questions in her Greek-Israeli accent. She's wearing a thin white turtleneck sweater tucked into tight Calvin Klein jeans, and without makeup she looks like a college kid, an exotic exchange student. Our first stop, we park at Jerome Avenue and 170th Street, take her up on the elevated subway platform, let her walk around. It's almost seven o'clock now, fairly crowded, people heading into Manhattan. You can see Yankee Stadium from here, but it's a long way off. Next stop, 167th Street platform. Stadium's closer, of course, but the area just doesn't look familiar to her at all.

Now we're up on the platform at 161st Street, which is the famous subway stop for the stadium itself. Brings back a lot of memories. There's no game tonight, the Yankees are in Boston, but again there's a small crowd because it's Saturday evening. Uta strolls north on the cement platform in the strong twilight, gets a few penetrating glances from the neighborhood rapists. Rows of modern lamp posts to the right are covered with layers of graffiti as high up as punks can reach. Low steel fence to the left was originally painted blue, now it's any color you can name with streaks of bright orange dominating. Beyond is the enormous stadium itself, "the house that Ruth built" in 1923, except it's just not the same house now with its modern façade. Across the street to the north is a wide green stretch of public park, ragged baseball diamond at one end, football field with goalposts at the other. Park is bordered by tall trees with full green crowns and surrounded by rows of old apartment buildings, most ten-to-twelve stories, TV antennas spread across the sky.

Uta takes a long look at these buildings, changes her position several times, keeps glancing left to the stadium. In the distance, a subway train rattles south toward us.

"This is the one," she tells me.

"You sure?"

"Yes." She points toward the row of old apartment buildings. "See that light-colored building, the tall one?"

"The newer one, yeah."

"All right, now look, the dark one to its left there, the one on the corner, see it?"

"The dark narrow one?" Big John asks.

She nods and says something, but we can't hear because the train booms in now, screeches to a stop. Every car is layered with graffiti, including the windows. Doors open, crowd pushes in.

Uta keeps her eyes on the buildings. "The dark narrow one, yes. I think that's the one on his corner. I think—I'm almost sure Jimmy's building is one or two doors in from the corner."

Big John and I study the location of the dark narrow building in relation to the others. From that distance it can be deceptive, so we're trying to bracket with surrounding landmarks we can recognize up close.

"The street's on a hill," Uta says. "That's right, I remember now. It was on a steep hill going down to the park."

We go down now, get in the car, drive over there. Turns out to be Anderson Avenue. It's on a fairly steep hill, all right, one-way south, wrong way for us. We drive to the next one-way street, hang a right, scoot up the hill, hang another right, then another. Anderson looks like it was once a nice neighborhood. Today, like so many other streets in the South Bronx, it's a disaster area. What happened is common knowledge. Landlords weren't allowed to raise rents high enough to cover operating costs, primarily fuel, taxes, and maintenance. Couldn't break even, couldn't find buyers. So they simply abandoned the buildings. At least half the apartments along Anderson are empty now, windows boarded up, left to the rats. Once it starts, it's like an epidemic.

We drive down the hill very slowly. Uta's watching the left side of the street. Cars are parked bumper to bumper, both sides.

"Wait," she says softly. "That's it, right there."

We pull over, double park on the opposite side, take a look. It's 11 Anderson, an attractive five-story red-brick building. Four tall windows across each floor, widely spaced. Black wrought-iron fire escape extends down the front with landings at each of the two center windows. Ground floor has a fairly clean gray stone façade, garbage cans lined up neatly to the left. Narrow alley to the right.

"You certain that's it?" Big John asks.

"Yes. Third floor front, that far right window there with the blinds."

We crane our necks to see the window. The blinds are open. Big John's driving, he decides to move it. We continue down the hill, hang a right, another right, two more, double park about fifty yards up the hill from the house. Big John shuts off the engine. We're facing due south. It's about 7:25, the sun is quite low now, and the apartments to the east are bathed in a soft gold.

"Find a pay phone," Big John tells me. "Get through to the chief, tell him everything. Cover our asses."

I walk up the hill to the cross street, then three or four blocks east before I find a few stores. They're all closed for the night. Another two blocks, I find an open deli with a pay phone in back. I call the chief's private number. Mat answers.

"You sleep there?" I ask.

"Not funny, John, whadda you got?"

"Possible rathole on Jimmy F."

"Yeah? Where you at?"

"South Bronx. Chief in a good mood?"

"Practically passing out cigars. Just got back from the lineup at the D.A.'s office, been there all afternoon."

"Positives on all three?"

"After five-and-a-half hours, yeah. Real circus, apparently. Had the whole night crew of the hotel down there. Hold on." Click.

Click. Chief's voice: "Yeah, Rawlings, whadda you got?"

"Possible address on Ferragamo, chief. South Bronx. Haven't gone in yet."

"Reliable source?"

"Very."

"Worth my while humping up there?"

I hesitate. "Could be nothing, chief. You know how these things—"

"Who's the source?"

"Former girlfriend."

"I like it. I like it, Rawlings. Yeah, in fact, I love it. What's the address?"

"Eleven Anderson Avenue. Third floor front."

"Former girlfriend. Love it. Crazy about it. Wait'll I get a piece of paper here. Okay, what's the address?"

"Eleven Anderson Avenue. Third floor front."

"Where the hell's Anderson Avenue?"

"South Bronx."

"Christ, I know *that,* Rawlings, you just *told* me that."

"Due north of Yankee Stadium, across the public park, parallel to Jerome Avenue."

"I'll find it. All right, now listen. Goes without saying, these other three clowns, they're one thing, Ferragamo's something else. We're talking about a hardened criminal here, Rawlings, we can't play games with this asshole. Accordingly, he should be considered armed and dangerous. You guys sit tight up there, I gotta get a warrant, I gotta get my team together. We'll get up there just as fast as we can. Meantime, you sit tight on the little bastard. Don't make a move till we get there, understood?"

"Understood."

"Rawlings, one more thing."

"Yeah, chief."

"I'm the warrant-man on Ferragamo. He's mine."

"You got him. By the way, congratulations on—"

He hangs up.

I continue anyway: "—on the lineup, asshole. Absolutely great work. By the way, I'm personally nominating you for the Asshole of the Year Award. Which you richly deserve." I hang up on the asshole.

Walking back to the car, I'm visualizing what that lineup must've been like, I can't help smiling. Harcourt, Tent, and McCabe, separately, lined up with five "look-alikes," probably wearing variations of all the disguises, viewed by each member of the hotel's night crew separately. I can see the chief orchestrating. I can see the lovely Douché Bagette exercising her gentle windpipes, fore and aft. Hope she's not on crutches. I can see her reacting to the spit-cific vernacular of James Cagney. Hope she brought a handkerchief. Sorry I missed the show. Ordinarily, the arresting officer is present in the viewing room, together with the assistant D.A. and the attorney for the accused. That's by the book. Of course, this case being special, certain police procedures depart from the book. Chief listed himself as the arresting officer of Harcourt and Tent for reasons of undercover security. Pinch hitter after the fact. You look in the box score next morning and find out you didn't play.

I get back to the car now, I tell Big John what's going down. Uta says she's not going to be around for this shit, thank you. Well, we promised her, so Big John does the honors, escorts her back up the hill in hopes of finding a cab. I tell him where the deli is just in case he has to call for one. Turns out he does. Cabs don't get too much action around this particular neighborhood. Ten minutes later, he's back. Slides in, closes the door quietly, adjusts his tie, clears his throat.

"Little lady was appreciative?" I ask.

"Well, now, you might say that, lad."

"How—? *How* appreciative was she?"

"Bite your tongue, lad. No, I wouldn't think of revealing the physiological details of such a—such an outrageously wild, passionate, erotic assignation."

"Didn't want a blow by blow."

"No way, my lips are sealed."

"Unfortunate."

He takes out a cigar, bites off the end, spits it disdainfully out the window. "Virility is such a wretched affliction."

"That mean you couldn't get it up?"

He lights the cigar, puffs, thinks about it. "Problem is, lad, I have a great deal of difficulty getting it *down.* Takes hours, usually. Beastly uncomfortable. Embarrassing sometimes."

"Tried tying it down?"

"Tried everything. Problem is, they don't make extra-heavy-duty jocks the way they did in the old days. Elastic's not worth a damn."

"Tried a cup, I suppose."

"Tried 'em all. Steel, aluminum, magnesium. Never found

one strong enough to contain the sheer brute force. Crack like eggshells."

"Frightening, the power of passion."

He nods, studies the glow of his cigar. "Certain young ladies, outspoken creatures they were, have actually compared my orgasmic power to that of various wild and exotic jungle beasts. Like sleek young—"

"Like chimps, huh?"

"Don't give yourself away, lad."

It goes on like this, but we never lose sight of the front door of the apartment. What happens next is hard to believe, but it's often like that on the job. Just when you have the happy illusion you might be dealing with genuinely sophisticated crooks for a change, they turn around and pull stunts so incredibly dumb you wonder if they're playing with a full deck.

So now Big John pauses in mid-sentence and we both watch this next thing with our mouths open. Boom, Jimmy Ferragamo comes out the front door, big as life, bald head glistening in the twilight, and he's holding a handful of tools. Steps over the garbage cans, tosses the stuff in. We can see this stuff clearly, it's not even bagged—heavy crowbar, big hammer, chisel, metal punch—we can't believe our eyes.

We jump out, sprint toward him, weapons drawn, we're yelling, "Hold it right there, Jimmy!" Words to that effect.

He freezes over the garbage can, Telly Savalas in a robin's-egg blue T-shirt and designer jeans. Now he looks at me running up to him and he says, "Oh, shit." Believe it? That's all he can think to say at such a dramatic moment, "Oh, shit." Forty of New York's finest detectives working unlimited overtime seven days a week to track down and apprehend the final illustrious fugitive in the greatest hotel robbery in American history, now we catch him redhanded with his tools of the trade, frozen over his garbage can in the gritty reality of the South Bronx twilight, material worthy of Cagney and Bogart, Newman and Redford, Brando and DeNiro, made to order for the long pause, the shake of the head, the expression in the eyes that transcends dialogue. And this clown looks at me and says, "Oh, shit."

"Up against the wall!" I tell him.

He assumes the position slowly, speaks in his usual soft voice. "Rawlings, I'm clean, I swear to God. What's goin' on here?"

I holster my revolver, give him a quick toss. He's clean. Big John leans deep in the garbage can, makes a face as he fishes out the crowbar and chisel. Slob who used the can before must've dumped a load of Chinese food in there; either that or somebody barfed. Hard to tell, looks the same. Big John's shaking rice and slimy shit off the tools.

"Let *him* do that," I say.

He plops the tools back in the can, shakes his hands. "Jimmy, what the hell you been eating here, maggot pie?"

"That shit ain't mine!"

I pull him to the can. "Get your tools, Jimmy."

"Get 'em yourself. I ain't diggin' in that shit."

"As it happens, you're a lucky man," I tell him. "I know cops who'd make you go in there with your teeth."

He knows it's all too true, reaches in without further ado. As he's digging around the bottom, Big John does an awful thing; not like him at all. Wipes his hands on the back of the guy's T-shirt, inside and out.

Jimmy's voice sounds like it's coming from the bottom of a well: "You stink, Daniels, y'know that?"

"What's that? Can't hear you."

"I said you stink!"

Big John grabs him by the hips. "Ever stand on your head in a pile of chop suey?"

Silence from within. Then: "Ey, gimme a break, huh?"

Now Big John brings his knee up slowly, applies pressure to his ass, forces him lower in the can. Jimmy braces both hands on the bottom.

"Tell me something, Jimmy. Do you really and truly think

I stink, or is that just metaphorically speaking?"

"Daniels, come on, huh? I'm up to my elbows in this crap."

"Answer the question. Do you really think I stink?"

Jimmy hesitates. "Naw."

"What's that, lad? Can't hear you in there."

"I says *naw.*"

"Naw? Naw *what?*"

"Naw, you don't *stink!*"

Big John applies still more pressure with his knee. "Now, Jimmy, one final question. This is important, so listen carefully. Then I want you to answer thoughtfully and honestly. Do you understand me, lad?"

"Yeah, right."

"Good. All right, here's the question. Who do you think *really* stinks around here, Jimmy?"

"Awright, awright. *I* do."

"Do what?"

"Stink."

"I see. And how bad do you stink?"

"I—oh, man. Real bad, okay?"

"How bad's real bad?"

"Daniels, come on, huh? Lemme outa this thing!"

"How bad's real bad?"

"Awright, I stink like *shit!* Satisfied?"

"What *kind* of shit, lad?"

"What *kind?* Daniels, gimme a break, will ya!"

"What *kind* of shit? Human or animal?"

"Animal!"

"What kind of animal?"

"Oh, Jesus, what kind? A *dog?*"

Big John calmly kicks Jimmy's legs apart, grabs under his thighs, lifts, gives him a swift knee in the ass. Splat, Jimmy's down on his elbows now, legs in the air, new yellow Adidas kicking.

"I happen to love dogs," Big John says quietly.

Jimmy's voice is muffled: "Christ, Daniels, whaddaya *want* from me?"

"Name another animal, one that's on your level of shit-stink."

"A rat, okay? *Rat*shit!"

"I've no frame of reference. Never smelled ratshit."

Jimmy's squirming now. "Daniels, you're a sick man! Sick!"

"Sick of skunks like you. That's it! *Skunks!* Say it, lad!"

"I stink like *skunk*shit! Lemme outa here!"

Big John grabs his belt, yanks him out. Wish I had a camera. Top of Jimmy's bald head is plastered with multicolored Chinese goo—tiny bits of meat, chicken, onions, bean sprouts, green peppers, mushrooms, lots of rice, and soy sauce. He stands there catching his breath, hands on hips, looking up at us, feels the stuff begin to ooze down his face. Now he crosses his chop-suey arms, pulls the robin's-egg blue T-shirt off over his head. We wait a few seconds while he wipes the stuff off.

"We still need your tools," I tell him.

"I know, I know." He takes a deep breath, grabs the can rim with his left hand, reaches in with his right. As he retrieves each tool, he drops it on the sidewalk.

"Okay," Big John says. "Pick 'em up and let's go upstairs."

Jimmy unlocks the inside vestibule door. Old stairway to the right, no elevator. We walk up to the third floor, he goes to his apartment door, takes out his key.

"Got anybody in there?" I ask.

"Naw."

"Struck out on a Saturday night?"

"Yeah." He unlocks the door.

"You're slipping, Jimmy."

"Yeah, ain't we all."

We escort him in cautiously. Place is a real bachelor's dump. One fairly large room with a small windowless kitchen, food all over the place, dirty dishes stacked in the sink, small bathroom with a shower. Bare wood floor, old Castro convertible against the longest wall, overstuffed chair in front of a new-looking Zenith TV on a stand, wooden table with four collapsible chairs. Big John and I look at the table, we blink, we glance at each other, we can't believe the stupidity of this guy. He's got a high-intensity lamp there, it's off, but it's poised over three ring settings with no center stones, about a dozen bracelets, count 'em, some of them diamond, one of which is in the process of having its stones removed by the ingenious means of a screwdriver and small pliers.

"Needless to say, you're under arrest," Big John says.

"Yeah."

"Know your rights by heart, Jimmy?"

"By heart. Listen, Daniels, before the cuffs, let me wash up and change clothes, huh?"

"By all means."

"Actually, I'd like to take a shower, if that's okay."

"Go to it."

Big John follows him to the bathroom. I start looking around, starting with the two small closets. It's obvious he left his other apartment in a big hurry, because the first closet contains two open suitcases, neither completely unpacked, and the other closet has only three suits, a blue blazer, a few casual trousers, some shirts, ties, and two pairs of shoes. I go through the luggage first. Underwear, socks, sport shirts, sweaters, belts, like that. First thing of interest, an expensive-looking dark brown hairpiece, which doesn't surprise me, he's always had a few, but I put it aside for evidence; we'll want him to wear it during the lineup. Second suitcase is much more interesting. Mark Cross leather passport holder with his passport, plus a considerable amount of cash, mostly large bills. I count it carefully, $4,180, put it aside with the wig. Next thing, a leather Dunhill tobacco pouch. I unzip it. Four ladies' wristwatches dripping with diamonds; seventeen rings with stones still intact; twenty-three fairly large loose stones, probably from rings—diamonds, emeralds, and sapphires dominating. Zip up the pouch, lay it aside. Here's a large manila envelope. Open it up, bingo, the negotiable bonds, twenty-seven of them, all in $5,000 denominations, adds up to $135,-000, exactly right to complete the deal with Bo, shame he couldn't get down there. Put the envelope aside, that's it for the luggage.

Now I go to the other closet, search the suits. Alligator wallet, fat with cash, in the inside breast pocket of a classy dark gray Cardin. Count it out, mostly $100s and $50s, comes to $1,520. Put it back, flip through the plastic credit card holders, he's got a nice assortment, all in his own name, don't leave home without me: American Express, Visa, Master Charge, Diners Club International, must have an excellent credit rating; cards for airport clubs: American's Admirals, United's Red Carpet, Pan Am's Clipper; New York State driver's license; Social Security card; Ma Bell telephone credit card. In the little leather pockets, various slips of paper with names, addresses, phone numbers, and—what's this?—a small steel key, very thin, number stamped on it, 576, looks for all the world like a key to a safe-deposit box. Now we're getting somewhere. Exactly what a seasoned professional crook would do, stash the bulk of his share in a safe place like a bank; can't be too careful these days, burglaries increasing at an alarming rate. Put the wallet aside. Nothing much in the other two suits, the blazer, casual trousers, shoes. I'm about to close the closet door, I glance up at the single shelf. Two pillows up there, some sheets and blankets for the Castro. I reach up, pull down the pillows, examine them. Reach up for the sheets, start to pull them down, feel a slight resistance, stop immediately. Now I pat the sheets carefully, locate an object under the folds. Lift the top fold, slide my hand in. Cold steel.

You never know if a gun is cocked until you see it, so I touch gingerly with the tips of my fingers, find the grips, lift the weapon out. I'm genuinely surprised at this. Jimmy's got himself a piece that even an out-and-out handgun aficionado would be delighted to own, the classic Beretta 9mm Parabellum Model 1951, which used to be James Bond's standard issue before this year's version when 007 switched to the lesser-known but equally powerful Walther .380 PPK. Personally, I prefer the Beretta, has a nice feel and balance, 4.51-inch barrel, before this year's version when 007 switched to the lesser-known but equally powerful Walther .380 PPK. Personally, I prefer the Beretta, has a nice feel and balance, 4.51-inch barrel, 8-inch overall length, 1.93-pound overall weight. Manufactured by Pietro Beretta of Gardone Val Trompia Brescia, an ancient Italian firm with a worldwide reputation for quality arms. This particular model is sold commercially as the "Brigadier," and it's far-and-away the finest high-powered semiautomatic to come out of Italy. In fact, it's the standard service arm of Italy, Israel, and the UAR. Jimmy's got the safety on, a wedge-type locking device at the top rear of the grip. I remove the magazine, see it's fully loaded, eight slugs. Now I draw the slide to the rear; out pops the single slug in the chamber. I pocket it, temporarily, along with the magazine, place the gun on the floor next to the wig, passport holder, tobacco pouch, manila envelope, and wallet.

I'm searching the Castro when Jimmy comes out of the bathroom wearing a towel and pads over to the closet with the suitcases. He sees the stuff I've positioned on the floor, gives me a quick glance.

Big John's behind him. "Give the gun a wide birth, Jimmy."

"It's unloaded," I tell them. "Jimmy, how'd you get your mitts on such a classy piece?"

"I'm a classy guy."

"Lift it?"

"Bought it."

"Harlem?"

"Never deal in Harlem; dangerous place."

"Bet it set you back a bundle."

"Believe it." He's climbing into his shorts, wish you could see this guy's tool, you'd understand his reputation as a ladies' man. This clown's got a sausage here that could choke Linda Lovelace.

While he's putting on his Sunday finest, I go down to the car, get some plastic evidence envelopes. Now I start thinking about the chief. Wouldn't have done any good to call from can't be helped, at least he'll be in on the action that really counts—two media events in two days. I glance at my watch and I'm surprised, it's already 8:22. Obviously counterproductive time-space situation from the standpoint of media staging. Translates into bad press relations, but you can't win 'em all. On the bright side, we'll be in time for the eleven o'clock news, lots of people watch the late news on Saturday night, and we're a shoo-in to make the front pages of the Sunday papers, which have the highest readership of all. Now I'm walking back to the apartment, I stop dead in my tracks and I think: What the hell's happening to me here? What's going wrong with my head?

Swear to God, before this case I never really gave much thought to shit like effective press relations, media staging, setting isolated examples to give the illusion we're in control. The plain, simple truth is, *I don't buy any of that crap.* I don't buy any of it, I never will, so why am I beginning to think in those terms? Because of the chief? Because I'm afraid of rubbing him the wrong way? I'm forty-seven years old, for Christ's sake. I've been a cop virtually all my adult life, twenty-six years I've given to this department. That's a lot of years. That's a whole career. What's he going to do, fire me? Suspend me, demote me, reprimand me for doing my job and doing it right? What's wrong with my head these days? I didn't get into this line of work to play psychological games with politicians and media people. As deadly corny as I know it sounds, I got into this line of work because I wanted to help people. I also wanted the perks, of course, the challenge, the fun, the danger, the satisfactions, the power, the security, the benefits, the pension, all that, goes without saying. But I also wanted to help people. Why? Because I just did, that's all, and I still do. That's the best way I know to explain it, I'm no psychiatrist. When I was twenty-one years old, I was an idealist, and so were a lot of my friends, and that was nothing to be ashamed about. It was a different country, a different world, what can I tell you? Now I look around, I see guys like the chief, the commissioner, even cops on the beat straight out of the Academy, and I can't believe these people. They don't seem to want to give anything of themselves, they want to take the line of least resistance. I see uniformed cops around town, they dress like slobs, they have contempt for the public, they just don't seem to give a shit. Not the majority, I'm not saying that, but a lot of them. And their numbers are growing.

When I started out, here I was, I just barely made the height requirement of five-foot-eight (there is none today), so I figured I had to compensate for that somehow. What'd I do? Made up my mind that I'd be the most polished, professional cop in the department, bar none. As a patrolman, before I left home every day, I looked spit-polish sharp, head to toe. My visor was shined, my uniform was clean and freshly pressed —this is no shit, I'm serious—I bought more expensive shirts than required, got my badge silver-plated, every piece of my equipment was maintained like new, my shoes were shined, and let me tell you, I *looked* like a good cop, I *felt* like one, I *acted* like one, and I was *respected* like one. Paperwork? On time, factual, accurate, comprehensive, every word spelled right, every sentence punctuated correctly, everything typed neat and clean. Same thing when I became a detective, dress, attitude, discipline, work habits, I wanted to be the most polished, professional detective in the department, bar none.

The difference is, I still feel that way, and I don't know what the hell's happened to a lot of others in the department. I've mellowed some, I see things in a different perspective now, I know I've got a much better sense of humor, but I've never lost my feeling of genuine pride in my work. How can I word this without sounding like a sanctimonious asshole? Straight out: When I finally have to hang it up, when I reach mandatory retirement age, or get injured or whatever, God forbid, I want to go out with no recriminations or regrets. Know what I mean? It's been my whole life and I'm proud of it. Is that so corny, to be proud of your life?

So I'm standing there on Anderson Avenue with a streetlight behind me, I can see my shadow on the cracked sidewalk, I'm looking down the hill toward the dark public park, a sudden calm comes over me and I think: Fuck the chief and the commissioner and the new kids in the department who don't understand what pride is. I do. I understand it. I know what it means.

Boom, as soon as I've formed the thought in my mind, I hear tires squeal at the bottom of the hill, headlights swerve side to side, and here comes a car tearing up the hill toward me, wrong way on a one-way street. Now everything happens so fast, it's hard to believe. Incredibly, somebody opens the door of a parked car. *Wham!* Wrong-way car takes the door right off, keeps on going. Skids to a stop in front of 11 Anderson, four men jump out, leave all the doors open, Hawaii Five-O. Lead guy has a shotgun and white bulletproof vest.

"*Rawlings!*" he shouts. "*Cover the front! We're going in!*"

"*Chief,*" I tell him, "the guy's standing there in the street with his *door!*"

"*Fuck* him!" he says. "He shoulda *looked!*"

11

CHIEF SCRAMBLES IN THE DOOR, two teammates on his heels, another splits for the alley. I start yelling "He's collared!" over and over, nobody gives me a backward glance. Inside vestibule door is open, I unlocked it on the way out, so now they're rushing for the stairs. I'm standing there with my plastic evidence envelopes, I can't believe this shit. I look down the street, here's this little man hiding behind his car now, probably thinks we're Mafia hit men. I shrug, go inside for the show, take two stairs at a time. They're pounding up the last flight—walking at this point—and I'm almost up to them as they thump down the hall. Chief slams his shotgun butt against Jimmy's hardwood door, *wham!—wham!—wham!* "Police! Open up!" His two teammates, Arnsen and Jarvis, are flat against opposite walls, revolvers drawn, badges gleaming, adrenaline pumping. Obviously, somebody could get killed around here, so I step forward and make bold to repeat myself in a reasonably calm tone of voice: "Chief, the man's collared."

Click! Deadbolt lock snaps open. Knob turns slowly. Chief

pivots, flattens himself against the wall, motions for me to hit the deck. I crouch instinctively, I'm on my hands and knees, for Christ's sake. Door slides open a crack. White handkerchief appears, starts waving. I feel an almost irresistible urge to laugh; Big John thinks it was me slamming on the door, playing games, doing my imitation of the chief. Before I can shout a warning, out comes his favorite imitation of a jiveass faggot black pimp he once busted for flashing:

"Aw *rite,* my man, I gives *up!* Momma ain't fixin' to mess wif *no* patty-honky *buck*shot in m'ass, understan' what I mean?"

Frowning, flabbergasted, chief steps forward, shotgun ready, kicks the door wide open, instantly assumes the combat position. Big John's standing there with the handkerchief in his hand, bug-eyed, face coloring fast. God, I'll never forget the expression on his face, like somebody just kicked open the bathroom door and caught him jerking off. What do you say? What do you do? Hi, there, ever think of knocking?

He tries a crooked smile. "Hello, chief, I was just—y'know how it is, we were just—"

"Daniels! What the fuck—? Where's—? What's goin' *on* here!"

Big John wipes his face with the handkerchief, glances at me, still crouched on the floor like an asshole, tries the crooked smile again. Now he shrugs, wipes his hands on the handkerchief. "Suspect's inside, everything's under control."

Chief's voice drops to almost a whisper. "Daniels, step aside, huh? You feelin' all right?"

"Never better. Little tired, little punchy, y'know?"

"You been workin' pretty hard, John, we all have, I know that. Step aside, huh?"

Big John steps aside. Chief looks him up and down, walks in, shotgun belt-high now, not knowing exactly what to expect under the circumstances. Arnsen and Jarvis follow, two veterans I've known for years, they're smiling broadly, shaking their heads. As I pass Big John, his eyes are sparkling and his lips are drawn into a delightfully impish grin. Have to admit the guy's a consummate actor, I believed the whole bit, I bought it all the way. We walk in together, take out our cigars. Job has its perks, no question about it.

Inside, Jimmy's sitting at the table, hands cuffed behind his back, wearing a smart navy-blue pinstriped Paul Stuart three-piece, bald head freshly washed and sparkling. Big John's taken pains to arrange all the evidence on the table, neat and tidy, ready for the envelopes: crowbar, hammer, chisel, metal punch, ring settings, bracelets, screwdriver, pliers, dark brown hairpiece, passport holder fat with cash, tobacco pouch bulging with gems, manila envelope thick with negotiable bonds, alligator wallet swollen with all kinds of goodies, and the handsome Beretta 9mm Parabellum. Jimmy's staring down at this shit, licking his lips, looks like a layout in a museum, This Is Your Life.

Chief's not amused by all this. Confused is the right word, an expression of thoughtful, patient, paternal, cautiously optimistic confusion, but he's not such a bad actor himself, if you happen to like *True Grit* or *Rio Lobo* or like that. Left eyebrow goes up, holds a beat, lowers quickly, forehead goes flat-out wrinkle-free with the honest left-sided grin, sky-blue eyes narrow to dark slits. Sends something of a chill down the spine, despite yourself, recalls the cool dark theaters of youth. Voice holds the trace of a laugh, underplayed, not bad at all: "Rawlings, I got a—got a little problem here. Wonder if you could help me out?"

"Sure try, chief." I bite off the end of my cigar.

He fingers the thick ridges in the vest. "I had a—seems to me I had a conversation with you earlier this evening. Phone conversation? You, uh, you recall that?"

"Sure do." I spit the end on the floor.

"Yeah? Well, that's a—that's a comfort. That's a comfort to me, maybe I'm not going senile after all. Now, correct me if I'm wrong, sometimes I experience lapses of memory. Didn't you indicate to me that you had this apartment under surveillance, but you hadn't gone in yet? That sound basically correct to you?"

"Absolutely correct." Now I light the cigar.

He nods, grins, shakes his head as he walks to the overstuffed chair in front of the TV, places the shotgun down carefully. "Now, correct me if I'm wrong, but I seem to recall giving you explicit instructions to sit tight on this guy, to wait till I got a new warrant on him and got my—" His eyes dart to Arnsen and Jarvis, who stop smiling immediately. "Orrie, Roy, do me a favor, huh? Do us all a favor? Holster them fuckin' peashooters before one of 'em goes off and scares us all to death, will ya? I believe the man's in custody?"

"Sure, chief."

"Sorry, chief."

His eyes roll to the heavens, the ineptitude he's got to put up with. Now he has a good scratch at his balls, he turns back to me, snaps the words out: "Point I'm getting at, Rawlings, bottom line, you just couldn't sit tight like you were told, could you?"

"Circumstances made that—"

"Couldn't obey a direct order!"

"Circumstances made that impossible, chief."

"You make two out of three arrests, you just can't resist playing hero again, making it three out of four."

I puff on the cigar, gaze at him through the smoke. "That's an incorrect assumption."

"*What?*"

"You care to examine the facts, you'll find that's an incorrect assumption."

"Know what I call that attitude, mister?"

"No, sir."

"I call that insubordination!"

"Walt!" Big John says. "It's the God's honest truth! Skinhead here comes out of the building, dumps his fuckin' burglar tools in the garbage can right in front of our eyes! We jump out—"

"You didn't have a *search* warrant!"

"Didn't *need* one!" Big John says. "He *gave* us the evidence, right on the *street,* dumped it right in our *laps!* Ten to one the lab'll find scrapes from the safe-deposit boxes on every tool he used."

Now Ferragamo stands up. "Chief Vadney, I think there's something you should know here. I didn't give these guys *shit!* They harassed me, they—brutalized me, they incarcerated me in the garbage can!"

"They—*what?*" the chief asks.

"They subjected me to degrading physical and psychological torture before I was arrested and informed of my rights."

"Jimmy," Big John says, "save it for the judge, huh?"

Chief's very interested in this. "Ferragamo, you have the legal right to remain silent, you understand that?"

"Yeah, but I think you should know a few things here about what's going on behind your back."

"What things?"

"Things like this officer here forcibly incarcerated me upside down in a garbage can full of putrid, foul shit, and made me say a whole series of lewd and obscene statements about myself before he'd release me. Obviously, that's a severe violation of my civil rights and I think you should know I intend to press charges against him."

Chief looks shocked. "Sergeant *Daniels* did that to you?"

"Yes, sir, fuckin'-A right."

"Would you mind being specific?" the chief asks. "This is a serious allegation, you understand that?"

"Of course. Specifically, he forced me to state that I stink like shit, all like that."

Chief shakes his head. "What else? All like what?"

"Made me state I—this is embarrassing to me, to all of us. Man obviously suffers from some kind of deep scatological fixation."

Chief nods, then frowns. "Some kind of what?"

"Scatological fixation. Abnormal preoccupation with excrement. In this case, animal excrement."

"*Animal* excrement?" Chief looks at me. "What the hell's he talking about, Rawlings?"

"Beats the shit out of me."

"What I'm talking about," Jimmy says softly, "is typical of the kind of sickness that's allowed to go unchallenged and untreated in police work today. If you want it spelled out, this officer forced me to say that I stink like *dog*shit, *rat*shit, and *skunk*shit."

"That true, Daniels?"

"At the time, yeah. He's had a shower since."

"Don't get smart with me, mister. You make him say those things?"

"Yeah. Had provocation."

"Provocation? For *that* kind of—unorthodox behavior?"

"It'll be in the report."

"I'd like to know right now, John."

Big John puffs on his cigar, takes it out, studies the white ash. "In the presence of fellow officer Rawlings, who will testify as a trained professional to the accuracy of the allegation I'm about to enunciate, the alleged perpetrator did verbally and with malice aforethought accuse me of emitting a strong, constant, nasally offensive substance of a substantially gaseous nature from an unspecified, and therefore legally and scientifically invalid, area of my corporeal habitation."

"Yeah," Jimmy says, "but you wiped shit on my T-shirt *first!*"

Chief's standing there in his bulletproof vest, he's looking at the two of them, eyes darting back and forth with the uneasy expression of a first-time visitor to a nuthouse. "Where's the telephone?"

"Kitchen," Jimmy says.

"Rawlings, get this stuff in the envelopes fast—itemize, time and date 'em, seal 'em, both of you sign 'em, everything legal."

While we're doing that, he's on the phone for a solid fifteen minutes: Press Relations first, then the Nineteenth Precinct, then he calls the assistant night manager of the Champs-

Elysées at home, then the assistant D.A. at home, finally the commissioner at home. It's now 8:49, he figures we'll arrive at the precinct between 9:30 and 9:45, allowing for Saturday night traffic. Naturally, he wants the same media staging as yesterday, street blocked off, crowd-control procedures, mounted cops, police lines, preferential step positions to TV crews and press photographers with proper credentials. Press briefing immediately after Jimmy's booked, give the boys and girls what they want, send them happily on their way, then a lineup at 10:30 with every member of the hotel's night crew in attendance, second time today, plus Jimmy's attorney and the assistant D.A. Wants a TV in the lineup room so he can catch the eleven o'clock news. Hopes to wrap the whole thing before midnight.

We go down, get in the cars, no sign of the little guy who had his door taken off. Chief takes a quick look at his smashed right front headlight and fender. "Dumb son of a bitch didn't even have the common decency to leave his name and address," he tells us. "South Bronx is a jungle, men, *Fort Apache* was a whitewash. Where's Murray?"

Jarvis looks around.

Arnsen looks around. "Still out back, I guess."

"Still out *back!*" the chief says. "He's been standing out *back* all this time? Jesus Christ, didn't anybody have the common decency to *tell* him?"

"Guess we forgot," Jarvis says.

"Well, go *get* him, Jarvis, let's *go!* Arnsen, you guys take the other car, lead the way, full siren; Daniels, give him the key. Rawlings, you guys in my car, you're wheel-man, get the flasher out, let's go! He hands me the keys, gets in back with Ferragamo, keeps the shotgun on his lap. Bulletproof vest balloons out, looks like the underside of a turtle.

I attach the portable emergency light to the roof, turn around on the narrow street, wait for the lead car to pass, Eddie Murray at the wheel, expression like a mad dog. Off we go, lights flashing, sirens screaming, down Anderson, west to

Jerome, south to 161st, east past the stadium, south on Grand Concourse, across the Harlem River, then south on Park all the way back to civilization as we know it. Actually, the traffic's not that bad, just past nine o'clock, too early for the gridlock exodus from theaters, movies, restaurants, bars, parties, whatever, so the timing's on our side for a change. Little hairy jumping the light at 125th, heart of Heroin City, but we draw green at 116th. It's a pleasant spring evening, sidewalks crowded with strollers, the Big Apple at its seasonal best, although autumn has more juice.

Now Murray jumps the light at 110th, Spanish Harlem, narrowly misses two gypsy cabs, one beat-to-shit VW bug, a kid on rollerskates with stereo headphones, and a handful of senior aliens who remain leisurely oblivious to gringo-honky sirens, flashing lights, screeching tires, and blasting horns—*„¿Cómo dice, señor?"* Chief leans forward, elbows on the backrest, head between us, raises his voice to a tolerable holler: "Big John and Little John, helluva *team! Helluva* team! Proud as hell of you guys, goes without saying, you're both gettin' letters of commendation outa this. Just realized something. You realize, between the three of us here, we got—let's see, twenty, forty, sixty, add six, eight, seven, that's—twenty-one, carry the two, that's—eighty-one years of police work we got between us, between the three of us! *Eighty-one* years of police intelligence in this car at this minute! *Think* of that! Eighty-one fuckin' *years!*"

"Lot of fuckin' years," Big John admits.

"I was just tellin' the wife," chief says. "Just the other day, I was tellin' the wife, I says, 'Sam,' I says—I call her Sam, her name's Samantha, y'know, former policewoman, that's how I met her. Weren't too many of 'em back then weren't bull-dykes, remember that? It's interesting, met her at the old Academy shooting range. I'm shootin' away, minding my business, I hear this incredibly fast rapid-fire sequence from the next booth. I look in there, here's this broad in the combat position, two-hand rapid-fire, ass on her like a coupla fuckin' watermelons. Turns around, sees me, we're both wearing the big regulation earmuffs, y'know, can't take 'em off in there, so I give her a smart salute, a wink, and a smile. That's all, swear to God, wasn't lookin' to hit on her, nothin' like that. This beautiful creature—she *was* back then, too, before she took to stuffin' her face with pasta and turned into a fuckin' real-life Miss Piggy—this broad, she looks me up and down like I'm a tub a turd, then she gives me the *finger!* Yeah! Not just your conventional, stationary finger, this kid gives me the *up-and-down* finger! Believe *that?* Up-and-fuckin'-*down!* I'm standin' there, I'm—this is like twenty-two, twenty-three years ago, long before *Ms. Magazine* and crud like that poisoned their minds, right? I'm standin' there, I'm—*Rawlings, watch out for that bike!* Holy jumpin' Jesus H. Kee-rist, y'*see* that little asshole wetback fucker! Doin' a *wheelie* right between two speeding official police vehicles? Kid's blown his doors, another teenage doper runnin' around loose, jeopardizing the lives of innocent spics here. Good driving, Little John, nice reflexes there, buddy. So, anyway, now where was I?"

"Miss Piggy gave you the finger," I remind him.

"Oh, yeah. So, anyway, I was tellin' the wife, just the other day, I says, 'Sam,' I says, 'I keep having this dream, this nightmare, that the whole city's been taken over by dirty, rotten, filthy, subhuman teenage doper slimebags. Millions of the fuckers I'm talkin', millions of 'em, streets crawlin' with 'em, armed to their slimy broken teeth with handguns, rifles, shotguns, teargas, everything *we* got, our whole fuckin' *arsenal!* Plus all of 'em are wearing filthy-dirty bulletproof vests and jeans and sneakers that stink like puke. Millions of these fuckers runnin' around in huge gangs, mobs of 'em, total occupation of the city of New York. Every manjack a virtual prisoner in his own home, scared pissless to go out!' I told her, I says, 'Dream's so real, I can *feel* 'em, I can *smell* 'em, I can *hear* 'em, practically every night, it's drivin' me totally nuts!' Know what I can *hear?*"

"What?"

"What?"

"The poundin', slammin', drivin', twangin', shitsplittin' roar a *rock-'n'-roll!* Hard rock, acid rock, punk rock, every pricklickin', cuntlappin', cornholin' rock group you can name, playin' every type a cocksuckin', muffdivin', pigfuckin' rock tune you ever heard—*simultaneously!* Twenty-four hours a day, seven days a week, never a break for a single, solitary, motherfuckin' minute! Know where it's comin' from?"

"Where?"

"Where?"

"From big portable transistor *radios,* that's where! *They all carry 'em! All* of 'em! Millions of the fuckers, they're never *without* 'em! They're on their *belts,* their *bikes,* their *cycles,* their *cars,* they *rob* with 'em blastin', they *assault* with 'em blastin', they *rape* with 'em blastin', they *crap* with 'em, they *sleep* with 'em, they *dope* with 'em, they *screw* with 'em! Earsplittin' rock, it's their *religion,* their *politics,* their whole *world!* They don't *know* anything else! They can't *read,* they can't *write,* they can't even speak a *language!* These fuckers are sub*human!* Know what's worst of all? I'll tell ya what's worst of all. I'm convinced this dream, this nightmare, it's not all that far from reality. *Future* reality, I'm talkin' here. *Future Shock,* men, you read that book?"

"No."

"No."

"Mind-blowin' book. You guys should read more books, y'know, keep up to speed on what the future holds. Fascinatin' shit. I was tellin' the wife, just the other day, I says, 'Sam,' I says, 'the city's already invaded by 'em, no question about it, it's like an epidemic here.' I says, 'You read those figures in the *Times* yesterday?' She says, 'No.' I says, 'No!?' I says, 'I cut it out for you, I left it in the bathroom there for you.' She says, 'Where?' I says, 'Where?!' I says, 'Where else, right there on the floor behind the toilet with all my magazines and that.' She says, 'Look, Walter.' Always calls me Walter instead of

Walt when she's pissed; dead giveaway. She says, 'Look, Walter,' she says, 'I'm not lookin' to get into no argument here,' she says, 'but I'm tellin' you, I'm gettin' sick and tired of you stashin' all them hard-core pornographic magazines and shit behind the toilet there.' I says, 'Hard-core pornographic magazines?' She says, 'Yeah.' I says, '*Playboy, Oui,* and *Penthouse* are hard-core pornographic magazines?' She says, 'Yeah, and don't forget *Playgirl,* mister, I seen *that* sandwiched in there, too.' I says, 'Sammy, come *on,*' I says. I says, 'Times have *changed,* y'know, in this day and age those are all highly respected magazines.' She says, 'Yeah, huh?' I says, 'By the way, how would *you* know what's in those magazines, Sammy; you wouldn't be *peekin'* in 'em, now would you?' She gives me this look, she says, 'Walter, I got just one word for you.' I says, 'Yeah?' She says, 'Yeah.' I says, 'And what might that word be?' She holds up a big fat finger, right in my face, and she says, '*Perch!*' Well, you men know how women are, what can I tell you, that's how the arguments start, right? I change the subject fast, I get back to that article in the *Times.* Figures were so extraordinary I'd already committed 'em to memory, I've always had something of a photogenic memory. Bottom line, over the past four years, people living in the city of New York have been the victims of—get this now, this is official—people here have been the victims of six hundred and seventy-five thousand reported burglaries; one hundred and fifty thousand reported assaults; and more than thirteen thousand reported rapes. Think about those figures carefully. Know what we do? Today, we tend to take figures like those with a shrug and a fart, y'know, so what else is new? Homicide? Same thing. Last year alone we had one thousand eight hundred and fourteen homicides committed in this city. Cop on the beat hears that figure, he says, 'Yeah, well, in a city of eight million people, whaddaya expect?' And, in a sense, I suppose he has a point."

"That's an incorrect figure," I tell him.

"What figure?"

"Eight million. Not even close."

"That a fact? What's it up to now?"

"In nineteen-seventy," I say calmly, "the official population of the city of New York was seven million, eight hundred ninety-five thousand, five hundred and sixty-three. In nineteen-eighty, the official figure was seven million, seventy-one thousand and thirty. People who continue to say we're a city of eight million are more than ten years behind the times and wrong by approximately one million heads."

Nobody says anything for a while, all we can hear are the sirens. I'm concentrating on the road, but when I glance to the right I can see the chief's profile out of the corner of my eye. He's staring straight ahead, no doubt trying to decide if he's been corrected or insulted.

"You sure about those stats?" he asks.

"Census Bureau figures."

"Yeah? Well, I guess figures don't lie."

"No, but they can be very misleading," I tell him. "Take that homicide figure you mentioned. What a lot of people don't know, that figure includes all deaths from motor vehicle accidents within the city limits, which add up to a substantial percentage of the total. People hear the word homicide, they immediately associate it with murder. Not true at all. Very misleading figure. Exactly the kind of figure media people love and politicians eat up and regurgitate, especially during an election year, so they can add fuel to their claim that serious crime is out of control."

Chief stares out the windshield, watches cars and pedestrians scatter as we whiz through the light at the Eighty-sixth Street intersection. At this point, he decides to choose his words very carefully: "That's true, Rawlings, you got a point there, a good point. By definition, the word homicide means the killing of a human being, not murder. But those other figures I quoted—burglary, assault, rape—those are hard-and-fast stats. Those are facts. Can't dispute 'em. Can't dispute facts. Example, excellent example: Last year alone, reported serious crime in this city increased by sixteen-point-one percent, while arrests declined by five-point-three percent. That sound to you like serious crime's under control?"

"Misleading figures."

"Misleading? Rawlings, those are fuckin' *facts!*"

"Misleading facts," I say calmly. "You know as well as I do that the overwhelming majority of robberies, burglaries, and rapes aren't even investigated today, because we don't have the manpower we once had. We take the call, we fill out the report, we turn it in. Some asshole feeds all the figures into a computer, another asshole reads the statistical analysis—which is worse than useless—and comes up with the brilliant conclusion that serious crime's out of control. The blind misleading the blind."

Chief leans closer now, he's got his mouth right next to my ear, so he lowers his voice just a tad. "I want to be sure I understand you, Rawlings, because you're getting awful close to touching on a subject that happens to be of critical importance to me. Let's call a spade a spade here, let's get down to it. Are you saying—correct me if I'm wrong now, I want you to feel perfectly free to do that. But are you saying, despite reams of top-level authoritative evidence to the contrary, are you saying you're not *convinced,* totally *convinced,* that serious crime in this city is finally, inevitably, out of control?"

"I know how important it is to you, chief, and I don't want to sound—well, impertinent, y'know? I realize you have access to much more sophisticated lines of intelligence than I have."

"True, buddy, but I'm interested in opinions on the subject, especially from rank-and-file guys like yourself, detectives on the street, the little guys. Strictly off the record, tell it straight like you believe. You been around long enough, you earned that right, I respect your right to say it."

I clear my little-guy throat, try to rise to the occasion. "Here's the long and short of it. Seems to me, based on my perspective from down in the street, limited as it is, that maybe you guys are putting the cart before the horse. Seems to me crime's not out of control, our criminal-justice system's out of control. Police, judiciary, courts, penal system. They're out of control because they haven't kept pace with change. They're outdated, inadequate, inefficient, underfunded, and understaffed. Emphasis on the last two."

"Get specific, huh?"

"Take our department. Past nine years, serious crime's increased dramatically, no question, unprecedented rate of increase. Same nine years, we're reduced from a force of thirty-one thousand officers all the way down to the present force of eighteen thousand, one hundred and ninety-five. Bottom line, we lost almost thirteen thousand police officers—more than forty percent of the department—at precisely the time we needed an increase in manpower to keep pace with the unprecedented increase in crime. I suggest that no police department in any major city in the country can afford to lose forty percent of its workforce and remain in control of serious crime. No way, not in this day and age. Same basic problem with the judiciary, the courts, the penal system. They just haven't kept pace with change. Understaffed, underfunded, outdated, overloaded. Criminal-justice system's out of control, completely inadequate to the task."

Chief's silent for a block or two, then: "We got a—I think we got a little problem with *semantics* here, Rawlings, that's all it really is. Gotta admit I agree with almost everything you just said, except you—somehow you got screwed up in your conclusion to the thing. Now, let's be logical here, let's attack the thing according to the rules of logic. If we can't control crime here, for *whatever* reason, then wouldn't you have to conclude that crime's out of control?"

"No, sir. Not in my opinion."

"Well, okay. I respect your right to that opinion, buddy-boy, weird as it is. Now, long as we're on the subject, what I want to know, exactly where you pointing the finger here?"

"Since money's the primary stumbling block, as usual, only

one place you can point. City government. Worst part is, city's coming in with a budget *surplus* this fiscal year."

"Didn't know that. You sure of that?"

"Don't forget it's an election year, chief. Koch says he'll report a budget surplus of five hundred and two million dollars this year."

"Five hun—? No. *This* city, *this* fiscal year? Think you got your commas in the wrong place, buddy."

"No, sir. Five-zero-two, comma, zero-zero-zero, comma, zero-zero-zero, decimal point, zero-zero. Five hundred and two million bucks. Half a billion. Check it out yourself. Think of the difference that kind of money could've made to—say, our department."

"*Difference?* Rawlings, an injection of half a billion bucks in the ass of the NYPD could put us back in the ball game for —hell, maybe twenty *years!*"

"Then all we'd need is an injection of at least another half billion to pull the judiciary and court system out of the eighteenth century, and at least another half billion to build just one modern prison to hold all the people we arrest, indict, try, convict, and sentence under our new, competently staffed, adequately funded, updated, streamlined criminal-justice system. I figure, conservatively speaking, an injection of one-point-five billion might possibly put us back in control for the next five, six years, considering the inflation factor."

He mulls that over for a while. "Tell you what, Rawlings, you just proved my point, buddy. Just proved it beyond any reasonable doubt whatsoever. Crime's not only out of control in this city *now,* it's gonna *remain* out of control! How long? I'm talkin' *forever* here, I'm talkin' future-*shock* reality, I'm talkin' transistor-*radio* reality here! Hell, I've known it for *years,* I've learned to *live* with it—why can't *you?* Coupla years back I looked down that long dark tunnel and saw a speck of light at the end. Last year I watched that circle of light get bigger and brighter. This year, to my horror, I suddenly realize that light's a headlight on the front car of a speedin', swayin', foul-smellin', out-of-control subway train that's comin' straight at *us!* Splattered with graffiti inside and out, reekin' with pot smoke, roarin' with rock, crawlin' with dirty, rotten, filthy, subhuman, teenage doper slimebags, millions of the fuckers, pissin' out the windows, screwin' on the seats, crappin' on the floors! No way to stop that train now, Rawlings, it's the wave of the future, a tidal wave of dope's already flooded a whole new generation of Americans, turned their brains to spaghetti. Know where most of it's comin' from today? From fuckin' *I-ran,* that's where! DEA knows that, FBI, Customs, Coast Guard, they all know it's comin' from Iran. That bearded fuckin' freak over there, what's his name?"

"The Ayatullah," I tell him.

"Yeah, the fuckin' Ayatullah Khomeini, he said it himself, he says, 'If you wanna control a country, first weaken its youth,' remember that? The Aya-fuckin'-tullah himself, right? That's what we're facin' here, a conspiracy to gnaw away and cripple the very foundations of the American way of life! No way to stop drugs, everybody admits that, we don't have the manpower or money to make a dent today, it's just overwhelming. Insidious, unstoppable, positively out of control. That's the bottom line on crime in this city, Rawlings, we all know that, we're one of the target cities, New York, Miami, and L.A. Know what I've done? I've seen the *future,* buddy. That's right. I've seen the future—and it's *stoned!*"

We're all the way down to Park and Sixty-sixth now, Murray hangs one of his hotdog left turns, skids sideways, fishtails, keeps blasting his horn above the siren as he shoots east toward Lex. Nobody in his right mind would drive like that in a nonemergency situation, not even an Irishman, so I figure he must have to piss so bad it's coming out his ears. I stay right on his tail, obviously courting imminent disaster, but I'm not looking to give another space cadet the chance to wheelie between us.

Suddenly, the chief slaps my shoulder. "But, hell, look at the *bright* side, Rawlings! That's what *I* try to do! Optimist sees the Big Apple, pessimist sees the medfly, right? Next decade or so, we can still make it *look* good, we can still create the *illusion* of control, right? That so farfetched? Look at us now! Just apprehended the final perpetrator in one of the most celebrated robberies in American history! Right? Did it in eight days flat! Caught 'em with their pants down—or panties, as the case may be—tons of evidence, positive lineup makes on all but this clown here, which we'll get before the evening's over, plus the return of at least several millions in *jewels!* What's so bad about *that?* Think of the media exposure on this case alone. Think of the coverage waitin' for us at the precinct right now. Think of the millions of dollars of favorable publicity for the department, think of the badly needed boost in morale for all the cops on the beat, the little guys who have to wade through all the shit of this sewer here. What's so bad about *that?* We couldn't buy that kinda press if we had fuckin' George *Stein*brenner runnin' this show! Think of the eight—oh, shit, *seven*—think of the seven million people out there, how most of 'em will feel when they see it on TV tonight and read about it in the Sunday papers. That's gotta be some kinda moral victory for every average, honest, hard-workin' man and woman caught in the jaws of this big, awful, beautiful, bloodthirsty city. Who, by the way, still make up the majority population here, will for the next decade or so, God willing, before the dopers finally claim what's left of this rathole and we all move to Boise. Meantime, what I'm sayin', we should look at the *bright* side! We did one helluva job, men, we should be very proud! Eighty-one fuckin' years of police experience in this car, goin' all the way back to the old days when the world was *sane,* and somehow we *survived!* We're still showin' 'em who's *boss,* still kickin' 'em in the *ass,* still bringin' home the *bacon!* Gimme high-*fives* here, you guys, come on, slap it to me! Hot *damn!* Hot-fuckin'-diddly-*damn!*"

What can I tell you, we're holding up our right hands, chief's slapping away like Reggie Jackson in October, Murray's just jumped the light at Third, he's hanging a hard left now, I'm on his tail, struggling to turn with one hand, cars and cabs are swerving, squealing, horns blasting, pedestrians standing there totally aghast at this shit. I can easily imagine what we look like to the average, honest, hard-working man and woman caught in the jaws of this big, awful, beautiful, bloodthirsty city. Cigar-chewing cabbie on my too-near left communicates the emotional and intellectual consensus opinion of all parties present with a single, absolutely beautiful metaphor, short, descriptive, right on the money, delivered with precisely the right amount of gravel and disdain.

"ASSHOLES!" he shouts.

I shout back: "Have a nice day!"

12

THAT SPECIAL CHEMISTRY that characterizes an exciting, fast-breaking, hard-news story depends for the most part on the interaction of a variety of largely unpredictable factors, not the least of which is timing. Call it unfortunate timing, call it conflicting press priorities, call it a combination of fortuitous circumstances, all I know is, when we turn west into Sixty-seventh past the barricades at about 9:35, there's no crowd to control, no double-parked press vehicles, no mounted cops, no TV cameras in sight, and only a handful of photographers up ahead on the precinct steps. Chief's leaning forward between us, he's speechless at first, he's like in shock. My guess, number one, TV news dispatchers simply don't rate our collar of the final gang member newsworthy enough to assign camera crews; can't argue with that. Number two, it's just too early to attract a crowd of gawkers; most people are still at theaters, movies, restaurants, what have you, which is par for a Saturday night. Number three, we find out later, ten mounted police from the Central Park Precinct are still en route; horses had long since been put in stalls for the night when the call came, now they're trotting all the way from the stable at 175 West Eighty-ninth, a considerable distance.

In any event, I pull up and stop behind Murray. He jumps out, leaves the door open, streaks across the sidewalk, takes the steps two at a time, emergency situation, hope he makes it. Uniformed cops assigned to crowd control quickly form two lines from curb to steps, shoulder to shoulder, they outnumber the crowd by a multitude. Scene comes close to being an embarrassment of overkill, I'm glad the TV boys aren't around for this. Chief unlocks his door, then hesitates. Every officer in both lines stands at attention and looks at us; three or four photographers stand poised on the steps, motor-drive Nikons, Honeywell strobes, battery-packs slung on belts, ready for the Pulitzer.

Chief sizes up the situation. "Rawlings, you're the arresting officer, right?"

"No, sir, Big John did the honors."

"Take him in and book him, John."

Big John's face colors fast. "I—uh—like I said, I'm a little punchy tonight, chief, know what I mean?"

"Come on, outside, get your picture in the papers for a change, you've earned it."

"Chief, I'd rather keep a low profile on this, if that's okay."

"Sergeant, it's your collar, it's your book, it's your lineup, now take him *in!* Come on, everybody's *waitin'! I* can't do it, *look* at me! Bulletproof vest, shotgun, I'd look like a fuckin' *asshole!* Vinnie Casandra got hold of a shot like this, he'd start a whole new cartoon series, 'Lone Ranger Nabs the Bald Midget!' I don't *need* shit like this, I got enough aggravation already! Now get *out* there!"

Swear to God, I'm really feeling for Big John now, this is very uncomfortable. He adjusts his badge, straightens his tie, clears his throat, gets out and slams the door with all the poker-faced but seething hatred he can muster, Pat Moynihan playing diplomatic courier for Yasir Arafat. Opens the back door, ushers Ferragamo out, holds him by the upper arm, towers above him as they walk toward the steps. Flash-click-whine! Flash-click-whine! Sights and sounds to that effect.

Suddenly, Jimmy stops dead, sits down fast on the sidewalk, starts yelling: "Police *brutality!* I was *tortured* and *imprisoned* before *arrest!*"

Now everything happens fast. Bunch of the uniformed cops break ranks and pounce on the little guy—flash-click-whine! —he's lifted bodily and hustled up the steps by Big John and at least three other cops—flash-click-whine!—legs running crazily in midair, bald head thrashing back and forth, voice still audible above all the shouting: "*Sadists! Bullies! Brutalizers!*"—flash-click-whine! Chief bolts out of the car, cussing like a madman, sprints up the steps, still holding his shotgun —flash-click-whine!

Whole thing happens in less than ten seconds, now almost everybody's inside, strobes still flashing, Jimmy still shouting. I'm alone in the car, I start laughing out loud, I can't help it. Little Jimmy Ferragamo in his best navy blue pinstriped three-piece, a ground-ball second-story man who never gets any respect his whole career, who's about to get aced-out of his long-awaited, well-deserved fifteen seconds of fame, finally manages to con a taste of it, despite everything, maybe even front page, who knows? Me, I'm happy for the little guy, I really am. Every dog should have his day, it's only meet and just.

After I get hold of myself, I grab the evidence envelopes and go inside. Photographers are having a field day now. From the looks of it, Jimmy's playing the passive-resistance rag-doll bit, refuses to stand up during the booking at the desk, so Big John's holding him up under one armpit, chief's got him under the other armpit. All four photographers have decided to shoot side-angle from the chief's side; logical, since he stands out so vividly in the white bulletproof vest and he also happens to be holding the shotgun in his other hand. Makes an interesting picture for another reason, too. Ferragamo, whose Guccis are now maybe a foot or more off the floor and whose pin-striped shoulders are up to his earlobes, gives the unexpected appearance of someone horribly deformed, hairless and neckless, hunchbacked maybe, wide eyes darting now to Big John, now to the chief, thin lips starting to twitch in a chilling grin, reminds me of Peter Lorre.

Before they take him upstairs, Jimmy decides to knock off the rag-doll routine, it's too uncomfortable. Photographers leave now, all smiles, they got lucky. Book goes routine from that point on, fingerprints, mug shots, he's allowed to call his attorney, finally we put him in the squadroom cage while Big John completes the paperwork.

Lineup starts a bit earlier than scheduled, about 10:15, all members of the hotel's night crew present: Four security guards, assistant night manager, room clerk, bellboy, two elevator operators, and the night auditor Adolph Reese, the only one who wasn't eventually blindfolded. From the standpoint of convenience, most lineups these days are held at the Manhattan District Attorney's office, 155 Leonard, just around the corner from the Criminal Courts Building, 100 Centre Street, but almost all precincts have their own small lineup room and ours isn't bad at all. Each witness stands in a little soundproofed viewing room with a one-way glass window and looks at potential suspects in the brightly lighted lineup room. In the viewing room with each individual witness are the arresting officer, an assistant D.A., and the suspect's attorney. In the lineup room, the actual suspect stands against a wall together with five others, often police officers, selected because of basic physical characteristics similar to that of the suspect. Each of these individuals wears a large number from one to six. A simple intercom system allows the arresting officer, the assistant D.A. or the attorney to speak to any of the six, calling him by number, asking him to say a few words, turn around, whatever. Before the next witness is allowed to enter the viewing room, the numbers on each of the six men are changed and frequently they're asked to subtly alter their general appearance via clothes, hairpieces, mustaches, glasses, what have you.

Ferragamo's attorney, tall dark-haired man by the name of Ian Cleghorn, speaks with just the trace of a British accent, advises Jimmy to stay in the three-piece suit to face the first witness. Chief selects always-well-dressed me to be in the lineup along with detectives Arnsen, Jarvis, Murray, and Nuzhat Idrissi, a detective from the Nineteenth, good buddy of mine. Only Jarvis, Idrissi, and me bear any resemblance at all to Ferragamo, and Idrissi's got a short mustache and wears glasses, but this time of night it's not easy to find a casting director.

Okay, first witness is Thomas Gallagher, the guard who opened the door for the first two tuxedo-clad gang members. He goes in the viewing room with Big John, Assistant D.A. Arnold Grossman, and attorney Cleghorn. Ferragamo files into the lineup room with us natty detectives. Chief waits outside alone, scratching his privates.

No matter how many times I appear in lineups, I can't seem to shake the weird feeling that it's some kind of screen test for an important role in a movie or TV drama. Always strikes me that way. Room's very bright, you try to appear casual as you walk in and stand against the white wall with the height measurements, you look straight ahead, what do you see? Yourself, in the mirror that's the other side of the one-way glass window. Like watching your own test on the studio monitor. Tonight, silence at first, as usual. I squint at my image, clear my throat, straighten my tie. I'm standing in about the middle of the line, Murray to my left, Ferragamo to my right. I stand as tall as I can, all five-eight of me, I'm at least two inches taller than Jimmy. Well, maybe not quite, but I'm a hell of a lot better looking. Not to mention better groomed. Still, he does look a lot like Kojak, I'll give him that.

Intercom clicks on and we hear the calm, authoritative voice of Assistant D.A. Grossman: "Number Four, will you step forward, please?"

Nuzhat Idrissi steps forward, about five-ten, maybe 175, dark receding hair, dark eyes behind glasses with steel frames, neatly trimmed mustache, wears a blue blazer, gray trousers. He's a Palestinian, about my age, became a naturalized citizen in his early twenties. Excellent undercover man. As usual, he's got a small string of white "worry-beads" in his closed left hand, fingers massaging slowly.

"Number Four, please repeat after me: 'You get to the Princess yet?' "

"You get to the Princess yet?" Still has a very slight accent.

Click. Pause. Click. "Number Four, will you please turn to your left, walk to the end of the room and return?" Click.

Nuzhat complies, walks with a spring in his step, rubber heels making soft sounds on the light-green linoleum floor.

Click. "Thank you, Number Four. Number Six, will you please step forward?" Click.

Shit, that's me. Believe this? Gallagher saw me interviewing people at the hotel only eight days ago! I step forward, I'm asked to repeat the question about the Princess, then I'm asked to walk straight up to the window and stand there. If this was a screen test, I wouldn't look so hot in a tight close-up. I reach up and rub my chin and cheek; slight growth of stubble. I glance at Ferragamo's reflection. He's standing at attention, stiff as a board, trying to act like he's never been in a lineup before. From that angle, I see that his bald head makes quite a difference, really separates him from the others. Grossman's voice thanks me, asks me to return to the line. We stand there for another thirty seconds while this clown tries to make up his mind.

Click. "Thank you, gentlemen. Before the next witness, will you kindly exchange numbers?" Click.

Goes like that. Next guy's Albert Sale, the room clerk. He singles out Jarvis and me. I'm beginning to think I'll get the part. We exchange numbers again. Next guy's Leo Langdon, my favorite chief of security, Jimmy Cagney on fast-forward, can't wait to see what a crack memory he's got. Five seconds after he's in the viewing room, boom, he picks yours truly. Me and me alone. I'm so happy, my eyes well up, I've got to bite my lip to hold it in. Man's got total recall, I'm asked to say realistic stuff like: "Awright, it's a stickup! One false move, you're a dead man! Grab his gat, pal, then cuff 'im and wrap his puss in tape!" This guy gets my vote for the Best Original Screen Test of 1981. Haven't heard lines that good since *Public Enemy,* makes me feel like a kid again. Wish I had a grapefruit to push in some moll's ugly puss.

Now we wait in silence for a full two minutes while he's obviously talking up a storm in there. Wish they left the mike on. "Oh, yeah, that's him, absolutely positively, punk we called Hitler's Kid, wore a phony little mustache, y'know, lock a hair over the forehead, quiet, smooth-talkin' little runt with them baby-blue killer eyes, God help me, I'll remember them eyes till the day I croak!"

So now we're standing there waiting, suddenly Ferragamo drops a soundless fart. Don't have to be a detective to know it's him, he's just inches away. God-awful stench, like rotten eggs and stale beer. Worst part, it's a long, space-shot blast, exhaust fumes billowing up fast, like his countdown's been on hold for hours, maybe days.

Arnsen, on his other side, bolts out of line holding his nose. "Sweet jumpin' *Jesus!* That stink ain't *human!*"

I walk away fast with the others. "Jimmy, that's a dumb thing to do in a room full of cops."

He frowns indignantly, looks me up and down. "Whaddya talkin'? I didn't do nothing. What I always say, rat smells his own cheese first."

Everybody vacates the room immediately, grunts and groans, it's the only possible choice. We file into the waiting room, take deep breaths. Chief's still there, he's got a little black-and-white TV set now, terrible picture, he's adjusting the bunny ears.

"What's goin' on?" he asks.

"Fresh-air break," I tell him.

"Yeah? How many witnesses so far?"

"Three." I walk back to him.

"They pickin' out our boy?"

"Not exactly."

"Not exactly! Who the fuck they *pickin'?*"

I smile, straighten my tie.

"Oh, shit! Okay, that's it, Rawlings, I'm pullin' you! Hell, we'll be here all *night!* I'll have to go in there *myself!*"

I hesitate. "Chief, you're about a foot taller than him, you probably outweigh him by fifty, sixty pounds."

"*I* can't help that! We gotta get this show on the *road!*"

"Jimmy's lawyer won't buy it, D.A.'s boy won't buy it. You're a household face, you got more exposure this week than Cheryl Tiegs."

Chief's not looking at me now, he's staring past me with an expression I can only describe as a combination of intense admiration, envy, pride, and patriotism. Mounted cop just swaggered in the door, heavyweight trooper-type from the elite Central Park Precinct, riot helmet, gloves, heavy gunbelt with covered holster, jodhpurs, boots, and spurs. Chief's left eyebrow jumps to an A-frame, ears jerk back a split-second before his forehead flattens in the wake of a left-sided molar-shower that wipes away twenty years.

"*Coop!*" the chief shouts.

"*Walt!*" the Coop shouts.

They sashay up to each other. Coop holds his gloved hands out, palms up, chief slaps down fast, flips his palms up, Coop slaps down fast. Now they're into high-fives, both hands, perfect rhythm.

"Y'old saddle-tramp!" chief says.

"Y'old sidewinder!" Coop says.

"Y'old sodbuster!"

"Y'old ballbreaker!"

"Ya horny-toad lizard, ya!"

"Got ten ornery critters out front, partner, been standin' out there close to an hour now, they dumpin' big balls a hot-ass shit on your nice clean street!"

My instinct for unbridled camaraderie tells me this is likely to continue for a while, so I go out, jog up the rickety stairs to the office of the property clerk where I checked the evidence envelopes. Irish cop on duty, Brendan Thomas, old buddy of mine, he's about six-foot-four, 220 pounds, talks with a real brogue, comes from Wicklow, Ireland. It's a slow night, he's leaning out the window, chuckling to himself.

"Brendan, me lad, 'tis I, meself again."

He keeps chuckling, turns to me. "Jesus, them Royal Mounties down there, Johnny, they're fit to be tied. Ten fuckin' Royal Mounties in all their regal splendor, wanderin' around for the better part of an hour now, droppin' royal manure. Street still blocked off, mind you, no crowd to speak of, nothin' to do, can't find the brass who ordered 'em over here."

"One of them just found the chief."

"Thank the good Lord for small favors. Now they have to turn around and trot all the way back again. Efficient use of police personnel. Efficient use of horses and horses' asses. Know what I did, John? Yelled down at 'em! Yeah! Couldn't help myself, must be a full moon!" He laughs like a kid now, sits down. "Ah, Jesus, I must be goin' buggy up here! I did, just before you come in, I lean out the window, I yell, '*Officers!*' Five or six of 'em look up at me fast. Now I yell, 'Officers, where's the *parade?*' They look up at me, they can't yell back, they're too royal, they give me the royal finger in their royal gloves." He starts giggling, cups his hands, acts it out: "Now I yell, 'Hey, she was only the stableman's daughter, but all the horsemen-knew-'er!' " He roars at that one. "Ah, Jesus, I'm tellin' ya, I must be goin' bughouse up here. What can I do for ya, Johnny?"

"Need Ferragamo's rug for the lineup."

"You got it." He stands up, still giggling, ambles over to one of the large blue file cabinets, unlocks a drawer, pulls it out, rummages through the envelopes. "Jimmy Ferragamo, lad's movin' up in the world."

"Prime of a long and singularly undistinguished career."

"As Red Smith would say, 'Although he was a very poor fielder, he was nevertheless a very poor hitter.' " He finds the envelope, removes the tape seal, pulls the wig out. "Looks like the real McCoy."

"Wouldn't doubt it."

He feels it, hands it over. "What do you suppose they get for these things today, John?"

"I'd say fifteen hundred, easy."

"That a fact?" He closes the drawer, locks it. "The likes of little Jimmy Ferragamo wearin' a fifteen-hundred-dollar rug. That I'd like to see for myself."

"Come on down, pay your respects."

"Well, I don't mind if I do, John. It's been a few years."

We go down together. Big John's in the waiting room now talking with the chief. As we walk in, they both pick up on the wig and their faces brighten up. Jimmy sees the wig and his face seems to pale a bit. Next witness happens to be Adolph Reese, the night auditor, only guy who had a good long look at all of them through the whole robbery, so now's the ideal time for Jimmy to put it on.

I take it over to him. "Put the wig on, Jimmy."

He lights a cigarette, eyes the wig nervously. "That ain't my toup."

"No? Funny, I found it in your suitcase."

"It ain't mine. I don't have to wear that ratty thing, I know my rights."

"Do yourself a favor," chief says. "Put the wig on, huh?"

"Blow it out your ass!"

Big John comes over smiling, takes the wig from me. "Know what I'm gonna do, Jimmy? I'm gonna pull this wig over your brainless skull. Lift a hand to stop me, I'll break your fuckin' face. You got that?"

Jimmy puffs on his cigarette, stares straight ahead. Big John starts fitting the hairpiece in place. Everybody gathers around. Hair's dark and thick, styled to a medium-long length, comes over his ears just a bit, leaves the lobes showing. Makes an absolutely amazing difference in Jimmy's whole appearance. Unbelievable. From certain angles, you wouldn't know it was the same guy. Kojak to Columbo in nothing flat.

Big John steps back to admire his creation. Everybody goes, "Wow!" and "Incredible!" and like that.

Jimmy pulls the wig off, throws it on the floor. Everybody goes, "Oh, shit!" and "You asshole!" and like that.

Big John stays cool, picks up the wig, tosses it in Jimmy's lap. "You know what's good for you, you'll put it on. Now. Fast."

Jimmy places his cigarette in the ashtray, picks up the hairpiece, examines it, grabs an edge, yanks a big rip across the top, throws it on the floor. Everybody goes, "Ya dumb fuck!" Expletives to that effect. Now he's Kojak again, drags on his cigarette, crosses his legs. Tough little guy, Jimmy. Real tough. Alone in a room with a total of seven cops, doesn't faze him in the least. Fearless Fosdick.

Nuzhat to the rescue. Picks the wig up, examines the damage, tells us he'll be right back. Goes out, slams the door. Now the six of us stand there, hands on hips, surrounding the chair where Jimmy sits comfortably, calmly puffing on his True, benignly indifferent. Taps his ash in the tray, glances at his watch. Then, with astonishing nonchalance, damn me if he doesn't haul off and drop another fart. Out loud this time. Long and leisurely, a real French horn, stench is unreal, ripe Camembert. We all scatter instantly, head for windows, walls, corners. Chief struggles to open a window, he's making sounds in his throat like he's going to barf. Jimmy's happily alone now. This is a new side of his personality, if that's the word, he never used to have such sophisticated defensive mechanisms at his command. Obviously, he's trained himself to fart at will, a physiological exercise practiced to perfection in many prisons. Self-protective measure to ward off potential predators. Enforced idleness sometimes produces explosive creativity in creatures great and small.

Nuzhat comes back with the wig, a large stapler, and a wide roll of surgical tape. He pauses at the door, sniffs the air like a cautious animal, eyes darting first to Ferragamo, then around to us. Selects a chair as far away from Jimmy as possible. Turns the wig inside out, applies the tape carefully, snaps in three or four staples. Presto.

"Good man, Idrissi." Chief strides over, looking somewhat refreshed, examines the wig. "First-class job." Wig in hand, he strides over to Ferragamo, braces one foot on a chair next to him, tries his down-home folksy approach: "Ey, paisano, tell ya what. Y'think like ya got us over a barrel here, right? Think we can't waltz ya into a lineup in handcuffs? Wrong. Know why? Shit-fire, I can just march all *six* a ya in there with your hands cuffed behind your backs. Ey, *cabish?* Witnesses won't know the difference then. Unorthodox, yeah, but I seen it done. Tell ya what, paisano, make it easy on yourself. I'm gonna put this fucker on your head now and I'm askin' ya to leave it on for the last time. *Cabish?*" Ever so gently, he fits the wig over Jimmy's light-brown egg. Now he steps back for a better view. "Y'know, paisano, I'm not one to give compliments, never have been. But I'll level with ya. Y'look mighty good in that fucker. Takes ten years off—"

Jimmy yanks the wig off, throws it across the room. Nobody says a word. Nobody moves.

Now a chair scrapes loudly. Brendan Thomas rises to his full six-four, clears his throat, his cordovans squeak as he hauls his 220 pounds across the room to retrieve the wig. Smiles, walks over to Nuzhat, takes the big staple machine, then continues to the chief and Ferragamo.

"Chief Vadney," he says softly. "Would ye be kind enough to hold this staple gun for just a minute?"

"Sure thing."

"Thank ye kindly." *Wham,* he grabs Jimmy by the tie, yanks him out of the chair, chuckles to himself as he pulls the wig down over the little guy's skull with finality. "Now, Jimmy, me boy, listen up, lad, I don't like to repeat meself."

He punctuates his message by stabbing a big forefinger rhythmically in Ferragamo's chest. "If ye take that wig off just one more time, I'm gonna *staple* it to your fuckin' *head!*"

Jimmy leaves the wig on. Back to the lineup.

Night auditor Adolph Reese makes an immediate positive identification. Ditto the assistant night manager, two elevator operators, a bellboy, and the two remaining security guards. Now we take it from the top again. Thomas Gallagher picks Jimmy instantly, asks Assistant D.A. Grossman why he wasn't in the first lineup. Room clerk Albert Sale apologetically changes his mind, pleads nearsightedness. Nine down, one to go, but Leo Langdon's stubborn to the end; he only has eyes for me. "Oh, yeah, Hitler's Kid, I'll take them baby-blue killer eyes to my *grave!*" Third try, I wear Nuzhat's glasses and blue blazer. Can't con an old pro like Leo. "I awready *told* ya, that's Hitler's Kid in them *glasses,* whaddya *want* from me!" Fourth try, we're getting slaphappy, I change suits with Jimmy, wear his wig, look like Pete Rose on a bummer; Jimmy wears Nuzhat's glasses and blazer. Bingo! "Hitler's Kid in the *glasses,* absolutely positively, whaddya tryin' to do, *confuse* me?!"

Next morning, Jimmy finally gets his chunk of fame, albeit only page three of the *News.* Not exactly the stuff of a guy's dreams, but Sunday morning circulation is the biggest of the week. Story itself is typical tawdry tabloid stuff, nothing to put in the scrapbook. However, we find out later, there's an unexpected, happy kicker, which is maybe a thousand times better than even the front page of the *News.* The accompanying photograph is so unusual, so attention-grabbing, so instantly good for a belly laugh, it's picked up by both the AP and UPI wire services and runs that Sunday in newspapers from coast to coast, possibly even in foreign countries, I don't know. Even made *The New York Times,* for Christ's sake. It's a crystal-clear head-and-shoulders shot of two men. A strangely deformed little guy, hairless, and apparently neckless, thin lips twisted into a fiendishly evil grin, crazed eyes staring left at his obvious captor, a ruggedly handsome, square-jawed dude with a left-sided winning molar display straight out of *Hondo.* Boldface lead-in to the caption reads:

THAT'S HOW THE WEST WAS WON, RIGHT?

13

HONOR AMONG THIEVES? Tell me about it. Take Jimmy F, he happens to have one of the most talked-about records in bush-league ball for holding out on his teammates, which is undoubtedly why he pulled the big one with relative rookies. He's absolutely notorious for it, holds out on everybody he ever works with, so he's got a lot of enemies. We have a few stories, we have one where he's out with this nineteen-year-old broad he's living with. Like I said, he's a real ladies' man, hung like a gorilla, drives the girls cockeyed. So he's out with this broad, they're having dinner at the St. Regis Hotel, and this Irish cuckoo named Boyle comes in, stickup man from Queens, big monster of a punk, six-seven, six-eight, somewhere in there. Couple of days before, they'd done a heist with two other clowns, Jimmy was swag-man, told them the take was $25,000, whacked it up four ways. Figures come out in the papers, turns out to be more like $45,000. So this nut Boyle goes gunning for Jimmy's ass. Strolls in the hotel, Jimmy's in the dining room having a steak dinner with his girl. He walks up to their table, pulls a gun, right out in the open, points it at Jimmy's head, he says, "You little fucker, you held out on us!" This is no shit, we got the story from various employees at the St. Regis. Now Jimmy, very nonchalantly, he wipes his mouth, he gets up, he says, "I want to talk to you." Takes Boyle out to the lobby, gun's put away now, he grabs him by both lapels, yanks him down to eye level, he says, "You over-grown adolescent asshole, you ever annoy me again when I'm having dinner with a lady, I'll blow your fuckin' brains out!" Apparently, Boyle has enough common sense to distinguish between balls and bluff. He leaves the hotel. Jimmy goes back to dinner. The way we figure it, knowing Boyle, his only intent was to throw a good scare into Jimmy, maybe embarrass him a little. Jimmy doesn't scare or embarrass easy.

So, what I'm saying, this is a tough little guy, Jimmy. We knew he'd been shot a few times, too. Didn't surprise us. Various people were seriously gunning for him because he held out, it was his nature.

The Champs-Elysées was no exception. From what we pieced together, Jimmy got to Nancy Kramer's two boxes first, broke them open, pocketed every last jewel she had. All four of them were working boxes on their own, throwing everything into the suitcases, just flinging the stuff in as fast as they could, and in that kind of scene it's easy to visualize him getting away with it. When the four of them opened the suitcases later on, there was no way to distinguish Nancy K's jewelry from any of the rest. It's possible Harcourt, Tent, and McCabe had the word on Jimmy, took it more or less for granted that he'd hold out on some of the cash or whatever, but there was plenty to go around, there was tons of it, so what the hell, let him play his little game. Chalk it up to a necessary business expense.

Which would've been fine and dandy, but this time Jimmy made a big mistake. He trusted somebody. Remember all those surveillance photographs we took of him after he met with Bo Grasso that first day? Eddie Goliat, remember him, owned a couple of restaurants in Detroit? We got this story from Goliat himself. Day after the robbery, Jimmy calls up Goliat in Detroit, he says, "I just came into a lot of money,

I'm thinking about buying a restaurant in New York." Says, "I need your advice." So he brings Goliat into New York, puts him up at the Grand Hyatt, wines and dines him, and they look at a total of seven restaurants Jimmy has in mind down in Little Italy. We didn't have a clue what they were doing at the time. Anyway, just as Goliat's leaving to go back to Detroit, Jimmy says, "Hey, do me a favor." Gives Goliat this shoe box all wrapped up like a fancy present. He says, "Hold on to this for me, will you, it's a birthday present for my mother." Jimmy's mother actually lives in Detroit, Goliat knows that, so he says, "Sure, glad to." Takes the shoe box back with him, puts it in a drawer, forgets about it.

Less than a week later, when we finally nab Jimmy, his face gets splashed in newspapers all over the country. Goliat sees it in Detroit, reads the caption, that's all he needs. Boom, he opens the shoe box quick. Nine yards of diamonds, shitloads of sapphires, emeralds, rubies, you name it, all out of their settings, of course. Now Goliat's really pissed, doesn't appreciate being used like this, bad for his reputation as a legit front for his pals with the bent noses. Decides to fix this bum. Goes to a fence, says, "What's it worth, what can you do?" Fence examines it carefully, throws it back at him, says, "Whaddya givin' me here? It's all junk, it's all *paste!*"

Goliat turns honest fast. Wraps up the shoe box nice and neat, goes straight to the Detroit office of the FBI, says he happened to see Jimmy's picture in the paper, da-da, da-da, tells them the whole innocent story, dumps the box in their lap. FBI takes a quick look, returns it to us. Now our property clerk down at headquarters examines it. Every piece is there, every piece matches its detailed description, every piece is fake. Extremely good fakes, by the way, very expensive fakes. But fakes. Okay, property clerk reports his findings to the chief. Now we got a very interesting little scam going here. The Princess, Nancy Kramer, is obviously trying to rip off Lloyds of London for a cool $800,000. Chief should really hand the whole thing over to the D.A., but he decides to hold off for a few days. He's got something in mind.

At this point, it's Wednesday, June 10. Jimmy's been out on bail since Monday morning; McCabe, Tent, and Harcourt were sprung Saturday afternoon. Jimmy's gone back to his apartment at 11 Anderson Avenue in the South Bronx. Chief's already had one of his electronics guys go in and bug the telephone in that apartment, plus the phone in his pad at 236 West 106th. Both strictly illegal bugs, of course. Apparently, the chief gets his rocks off once in a while pulling shit like this, cloak-and-dagger syndrome, probably would've gone far in the CIA. Truth is, nine out of ten *legal* bugs—which are incredibly difficult to obtain these days—are a total waste of time. Occasionally, you get lucky. Chief didn't bug McCabe or Harcourt/Tent. Why? Don't have the foggiest. Probably didn't have enough time.

In any event, during Jimmy's first two days back at 11 Anderson, he makes a total of thirty-two calls, receives nineteen. Couple of calls are important to us. Here's a verbatim transcription of the first, received at 8:17 P.M., Monday, June 8:

FERRAGAMO: Yeah?
GOLIAT: Jimmy?
FERRAGAMO: Hey, Eddie, how you doin'?
GOLIAT: Saw your picture in the paper yesterday.
FERRAGAMO: (Laughs) Yeah, well, what can I—
GOLIAT: You sell your friends pretty cheap, man.
FERRAGAMO: What?
GOLIAT: Your mother's birthday present, right?
FERRAGAMO: What, you opened it?
GOLIAT: You bet your fuckin' ass I opened it, man! Who the fuck you think you're—
FERRAGAMO: Okay, wait—
GOLIAT: —dealing with, some fuckin' *flunky!* That's all I'd need, to be caught with that shit! Don't you *know* that?
FERRAGAMO: Okay, wait a minute, cool it.
GOLIAT: That's all I'd fuckin' *need!*
FERRAGAMO: Eddie, will you calm down a minute? We can work—

GOLIAT: Calm down my *ass!*
FERRAGAMO: Listen, we can work something out here, right?
GOLIAT: Work *what* out?
FERRAGAMO: A third of it's yours. Is that a fair—
GOLIAT: A third of *what?* You fuckin' asshole, that stuff's garbage, it's fuckin' *paste!*
FERRAGAMO: What're you talking about?
GOLIAT: I took it to a *fence!* It's *junk!*
FERRAGAMO: Bullshit! That stuff's worth a fortune!
GOLIAT: You calling me a *liar?*
FERRAGAMO: Who's the fence?
GOLIAT: Chuck Leonardo! Don't call *me* a liar, you fuckin' liar! Call Chuck, you done business with him before, call him and ask him! And one more thing. Get this, asshole, memorize it. You ever fuck with me again, I'll hand you your cock on a plate!

Transcription ends at that point. Goliat obviously hangs up on him. Very next call Jimmy makes is to McCabe's apartment at 201 East Thirty-seventh, logged at 8:21 P.M., just minutes after Goliat hangs up:

MCCABE: Hello.
FERRAGAMO: Billy, I gotta see you, it's important.
MCCABE: I've got a guest here, Jimmy, we just sat down to dinner. Have to call you back, you home now?
FERRAGAMO: Look, it's important. Meet me at DiLillo's in about an hour, can you do that?
MCCABE: What the hell's going on?
FERRAGAMO: Just meet me there, it's important, huh?
MCCABE: Jimmy, for Christ's sake, we just sat down. Make it—okay, look. Make it nine-thirty, right?
FERRAGAMO: Nine-thirty, DiLillo's. See you.

Owing to the relatively limited transmission range of our bug, the two detectives recording these calls are in a van parked on Jerome Avenue, fairly close to Anderson. Chief's left instructions with these guys to call him at home, any hour, if they come up with something that might need immediate action. They play the tapes back, think about it, decide to call him; van's equipped with a telephone. He listens to the tapes himself. Keep in mind, this is taped Monday, we didn't receive the box of fake jewels from the FBI in Detroit until Wednesday, so this is the first time any of us are aware of the situation. Now the chief's very intrigued, calls Big John at home, gives him a quick rundown, tells him to get an undercover man into DiLillo's bar fast. Big John calls the Nineteenth Precinct, which happens to be the closest to DiLillo's, assigns a detective by the name of Roger Stephenson, bright kid in his mid-thirties.

DiLillo's is a little bar-restaurant up in Yorkville, East Eighty-fifth between Second and Third. Ferragamo used to hang out here a lot. Okay, Stephenson arrives early, takes a seat at the bar. Jimmy shows first, around 9:20, takes a table in the bar area. Billy McCabe gets there fashionably late, about 9:45. By this time the bar area's pretty crowded, so Stephenson can't pick up a hell of a lot, but he's an experienced undercover man, knows how to move around just enough, play the pinball machine, pass near their table on the way to the john, whatever. About an hour later the place starts to get really jammed and the noise level goes way up. You'd think that'd make it harder for Stephenson, but now Ferragamo and McCabe start raising their voices to hear each other. Also, they've had four or five drinks by now. Bottom line, Stephenson can't piece together much of what he hears, but he picks up one word maybe half a dozen times: Princess.

Princess. That single word gives us a reasonably sound foundation to make some educated guesses. Next morning, Big John and I sit in his office, drink our coffee, smoke our cigars, and block out a rough scenario based on intuition. The way we figure it, what went down at that meeting, Ferragamo has to admit holding out, giving the stuff to Eddie Goliat, then getting the bombshell call from Goliat that evening. Now, extortion's nothing new to Jimmy, in fact it's on his rap sheet (with no convictions), so we make the logical assumption that he's looking to put the arm on Nancy Kramer. Which isn't going to be all that easy. He can't really do it by telephone and he certainly can't waltz into the Champs-Elysées without being recognized by security guards. At least, that's what he thinks. You have to know Jimmy F, he's as paranoid as they come. Always has been.

On the other hand, here's the eloquent, sophisticated Billy McCabe, who's just about the diametric opposite of Jimmy, no previous arrest record, a veritable Snow White to Jimmy's Dopey. Of course, he's been suspended from his job at National Airlines pending the grand jury's investigation, and he's certain to be indicted, but that's maybe two weeks down the road, thanks to our supersonic judicial system. In the meantime, we're talking David Stockman City here, Oval Office diplomacy, Harvard Divinity out of Michigan State, what could be better? Ask and it shall be given you, seek and ye shall find, knock on the Princess's door and it shall be opened unto you.

Big John calls the chief later that morning, verbalizes our creative first-draft scenario, gets the expected enthusiastic response. Chief decides to place handpicked special surveillance teams on both men again, around the clock, three shifts. Big John and me are automatically disqualified for surveillance; although McCabe wouldn't recognize us, Ferragamo would spot us a mile away and there's the strong probability they'll be meeting frequently and traveling together. Instead, chief wants Big John to supervise the special teams, and I'm appointed assistant to the supervisor. Highest temporary unofficial rank I've ever held in the department. I accept the honor, shabby as it is. Big John and Little John—helluva *team! Helluvlluva* team!

Now, a first-draft scenario based on intuition is one thing; a final-draft shooting script based on factual reality is quite another. That's why, next afternoon, when we get the report that McCabe's just stepped out of a cab in front of the Champs-Elysées, it seems too good to be true. But it's happening. We'd alerted the security guards to the possibility, of course, and we had a man working undercover in the lobby. Okay, McCabe walks into the lobby at 2:47, impeccably dressed, goes directly to the house phones, asks for Suite 3827 (we got this from the hotel operator), says, "I'm here." Mrs. Kramer says, "Come up." So we know he set it up earlier by telephone. Now he takes the elevator up to the thirty-eighth floor.

At 4:54, McCabe comes down, walks out the Park Avenue entrance. Doorman flags him a cab, gets a buck tip. Surveillance team follows the cab to Grand Central, and now it's 5:09, height of the rush hour, but one man manages to stay on his tail. McCabe goes to a pay booth, makes a call.

Ferragamo's at a bar called Torrintino's on Astoria Boulevard in Jackson Heights with a very young, very attractive young lady. They're sitting right at the bar, drinking bourbon and eating peanuts, watching the Channel 4 news, "Live at Five." We have one undercover man sitting at the end of the bar. Telephone under the bar rings at 5:12. Bartender answers it, nods, plunks it down in front of Jimmy. All Jimmy does, according to our man, is listen, pop peanuts, and say stuff like, "Yeah?" and "Uh-huh" and "No shit" for about three minutes.

Next afternoon, Thursday, June 11, Billy McCabe arrives at the Champs-Elysées again. Goes up to the suite at 4:22, but he doesn't come down again all night. We don't know what the hell to think. Big John and I stay in the office until midnight, receive half-hourly reports from the new surveillance team, then call the chief at home every hour. Chief's really sweating it, thinks Nancy Kramer might be in danger or something. She's not in danger, she's sleeping with Billy

McCabe. He comes down at 11:45 next morning, clean-shaven, bright-eyed, looks like a born-again Christian.

Now some heavy things start happening. Friday night, June 12, Ferragamo has a late dinner at DiLillo's with the same young broad who was with him the other night. They come out at 11:35, start looking for a cab. Boom, five fast shots from a speeding car, Jimmy's hit in the stomach, goes down on the sidewalk. Happens so fast our surveillance team parked just a few doors away doesn't have much of a chance. One detective jumps out, runs toward Jimmy, other man takes off after the car, which by this time is way up Eighty-fifth, hanging a right on Third. Blue Datsun 280-ZX, but we can't catch the license number. Incredibly, the girl with Jimmy isn't hit, kid by the name of Viki Nardella, eighteen-year-old brunette from Jackson Heights. Nobody else was around the entrance. Somebody in the bar calls an ambulance fast. Jimmy's flat on his back, unconscious, bleeding badly, the girl's crying hysterically, draped over him, crowd gathers around them. Squad cars arrive first, uniformed cops push everybody back, rope off the immediate area, the usual.

Takes the ambulance seventeen minutes to get there. He's rushed to the Emergency Room at Lenox Hill Hospital, Seventy-seventh and Park, operated on immediately, they remove a single .38-caliber slug from his abdomen. He's placed in Intensive Care. First few hours, it's quite serious, he's on the critical list. Next morning, the *News* squeezes it for everything it's worth. Jimmy's getting to be a celebrity of sorts. Through the back door this time, as it were, but fame's fame. A drag-bunt looks as big as a line-drive in the box score.

Two days later, he's out of Intensive Care and in a semiprivate room. His first visitor is Billy McCabe, next his attorney Ian Cleghorn, next his girlfriend Viki Nardella, finally Harcourt and Tent.

Big John and I go up to see him on Monday evening, June 15. He's in Room W-345, Wollman Pavilion, fairly large double, very modern, second bed unoccupied. We walk in unannounced about 7:15, he's sitting up in the bed nearest the door, watching Dan Rather on TV. He glances at us, rolls his eyes. All things considered, he doesn't look too bad, a bit pale, seems to have lost weight, but he needed that; a plastic tube is taped to his left arm, intravenous feeding.

"How you feeling?" Big John asks.

"Lousy."

"Want to tell us who did it?" I ask.

He keeps watching TV. "When I find out, I'll invite you to his funeral."

"How many times you been shot now?" I ask. "John says this makes three, I say no, it's got to be five."

"Get the fuck outa here, will ya?"

Pleasant conversation being in short supply, I glance around the room. Light blue wall to the left, windows straight ahead overlook fashionable East Seventy-seventh, white wall to the right holds the TV, new Sylvania set, excellent reception. Seven big baskets of flowers positioned around the room, count 'em, the man's obviously loved. Telephone on his little bedside table has an interesting recent history. Talk about clandestine planning, get this one: Sunday evening, when the medicos decide that Jimmy's well enough to be transferred out of Intensive Care, chief's already established a line of communication with an old buddy in Lenox Hill security, ex-detective, who finds out not only which room Jimmy's going into but which bed he'll have in that room. Magically, an illegal bug finds its way into the phone on that very bedside table. Of course, Jimmy could've decided not to have the extra expense of a phone added to his bill, but one has to play the odds, doesn't one?

Dan Rather's voice fills the room. Big John waits for a commercial break, then: "Baseball strike started Friday, suppose you heard about that, huh?"

Jimmy watches the commercial. A middle-aged woman with arthritis is having trouble lifting a heavy frying pan with her left hand. "That really *hurts!*" she tells the off-camera visitor to her kitchen. "I can't lift that *pan!*"

"Think it'll last?" Big John asks.

"Naw," Jimmy says. "She'll take the extra-strength stuff."

He's right. Now she lifts the frying pan easily. "I couldn't lift that *pan!*" she tells the unseen visitor. "Now I can lift that *pan!*"

"I meant the strike," Big John says.

"What strike?"

"Baseball."

"Yeah, look, Daniels, I'm trying to watch the news here, huh? I'm a sick man, I'm in pain. Gimme a break and get the fuck outa here, will ya?"

"Sure, if that's the way you feel about it." Big John goes to the door, motions for me, gives his impish grin. "Some guys have all the luck. Here's poor Jimmy all alone in this miserable hospital, and his friend Billy's sleeping with the Princess up in the luxurious Champs-Elysées."

Jimmy keeps watching TV, but he blinks a couple of times, almost like a flinch.

"It's a shame," I tell Big John. "But when you got a lover who looks like Elizabeth Taylor in her prime, I guess you don't have time for your old buddies anymore."

Jimmy, he keeps watching TV, but that one sinks in. That one sinks deep. I can see it in his eyes.

Next morning, we get an interesting report on the telephone bug. At 11:26 P.M., same night as our visit, Jimmy dials a certain number, 860–3957. Phone rings fifteen times. No answer. At 12:44, same night, he dials the same number, lets it ring eleven times. No answer. Tries again at 2:21, lets it ring seventeen times. No answer. Persistent little guy. At 2:26, he dials the operator:

OPERATOR: Operator, may I help you?

FERRAGAMO: Yeah, I been dialing a local number, I think it's out of order.

OPERATOR: I'll check it for you. What's the number, please?

FERRAGAMO:	Eight-six-oh, three-nine-five-seven.
OPERATOR:	One moment, please. (Dials number; phone rings six times.) I'm sorry, sir, the number appears to be in order; the party doesn't answer. May I suggest you hang up and try again later?
FERRAGAMO:	Yeah, thanks.

He doesn't try again that night, but he dials the same number at 6:26 A.M., lets it ring twelve times before hanging up. We know who he's calling, but I look up the name in the Manhattan directory anyway, no reason it should be unlisted. It's not: McCabe William 201 E 37 . . . 860–3957.

We're in the catbird seat now, waiting for Ferragamo and McCabe to make their moves. We don't know exactly what went down, but we figure it has to be one of two possibilities: Either McCabe makes a deal with the Princess to split the $800,000 insurance ripoff with her, then goes out and hits Jimmy on his own (or in cahoots with her), or he's still partners with Jimmy in the extortion bit, just picking up a little nookie on the side, and some other clown actually goes and hits Jimmy, somebody he'd held out on in the past. And, looking at it logically, those are the only two alternatives Jimmy's got to wrestle with too. McCabe's the only one who knows for sure; McCabe and maybe the Princess.

Meantime, the grand jury's just starting its investigation, we don't even have any indictments yet, much less a trial date, which leaves them plenty of time to maneuver. Chief figures we got the hook in pretty good now and he wants to give them the illusion of open water. Reason? He's looking to nail these guys with much more than armed robbery. Realistically, if we get a conviction for that, they'll pull maybe seven-and-a-half years, which means they'll be back on the street in four and a half, something like that. Not good enough. Chief wants to put them away for a long, long time. The way he put it to us, he says, "Gentlemen, I want to nail these guys with so much time that when they get out Central Park will be a flat-ass parking lot." Line straight out of *Big Jake.* Big John says, "Put that man's brains in a thimble, they'd rattle like a BB in a boxcar."

A key element in this whole situation, of course, is Jimmy's guesswork about who actually knows the jewels are fake. All he knows for certain is that Eddie Goliat got the word from Chuck Leonardo, the fence in Detroit. Jimmy finally checked that out, by the way, he called Leonardo for verification before he sent McCabe in to see the Princess. Anyway, Goliat never did tell him what he did with the jewels, he was too pissed off, which was a break for us. Matter of fact, it was critical. So Jimmy's guessing that Goliat dumped them. And, if you look at it from his point of view, it's a logical assumption.

Bug in Jimmy's hospital phone turns out to be useless except for the fact that he calls McCabe's number on three consecutive nights, all very late, and gets no answer. He's in the hospital for a total of eleven days and we keep a surveillance man at the desk near his room to observe visitors. Only daily visitors turn out to be McCabe every afternoon and Viki Nardella every evening. Viki gets kicked out of the room one night by a nurse who catches her doing something. She brings in a big bag of buttered popcorn and makes a hole in the bottom and she's jerking Jimmy off.

You'd love the nurse who caught them, old Irish busybody type. She tells our surveillance guy, she says, "Officer, I'm thinkin' to myself all the while she's his daughter, y'know, she couldn't've been a day over eighteen. Lovely little Italian lass she was, jet-black hair and eyes, nicely dressed. And so polite she was, oh. So I'm thinkin' to myself what a sweet lass she is, goin' in with her bag of popcorn every single evenin', spendin' time with her poor father like that. And every time I looked in on 'em, there they was, sittin' quietly, watchin' the TV, and her eatin' the popcorn. Mind, he wasn't allowed, bein' on a special diet, y'see. Never gave me a moment's grief, the two of 'em. Well, the night it happened, I looked in and I thought the patient was havin' convulsions. I ran in, snapped on the overhead and—well, I seen what they was doin' then. The little hussy, she looked me right in the eye, bold as you please, and didn't miss a stroke. Popcorn flyin' all over, it was—well, I'm not easily shocked, but it's a scene I'll not soon forget, God help me. It was like a geyser shootin' up in the air. And them sittin' there laughin' at me. Herself splashed with it, mind you, and the dirty little baldheaded man sweatin' like a pig. It's a scene I'll not soon forget, God have mercy on us all."

Billy McCabe's not having too bad a time himself. He's got a nifty little routine going for him in those eleven days. Sees Jimmy during visiting hours in the late afternoon (so as not to conflict with Viki's popcorn hour), then hops over to the Champs-Elysées, and that's usually the last our surveillance teams see of him till nine or ten the next morning. He's got no reason to suspect Jimmy's wise to him, so he must be laying it on thick about the extortion scheme.

Well, after eleven days, there's absolutely no doubt in our minds what's going down, and we're sure there's no doubt in Jimmy's mind. Billy's not only shacked up with the Princess, he's finessed a deal with her that obviously doesn't include Jimmy. Our assumption is a fifty-fifty split on the insurance ripoff. Princess might not enjoy splitting it down the middle, but you can bet Jimmy's original deal was much less altruistic than that, probably seventy-thirty his favor, then whacked up in some "equitable" way with Billy.

But we're still wrestling with more basic questions: Why did Nancy Kramer have all fake jewels in her safe-deposit boxes in the first place? Was she connected with the robbery? In what way? We don't know, but at this point we're starting to make some educated guesses, and they all hang on the suspected pivotal involvement of Alistair Rodger.

Alistair Rodger? Of Alistair Rodger Rare Jewels? Yeah.

Scenario goes this way:

SCENE I: Kramer works out a sophisticated little gem of a scam with Alistair to have the original jewels fabricated through one of his connections. She deposits the real jewels in a safe place, probably out of the country, replaces them with the fakes. Alistair gets word out to the street that $800,000 in gems reside in two safe-deposit boxes at the Champs-Elysées under the name of Nancy Kramer. Now they wait. How long? Give it a year. Match-dissolve calendar pages. Fade to black.

SCENE 2: Dazzling hotel robbery finally takes place. Nancy requests duplication of jewels in underplayed meeting with Alistair, agent from Lloyds, two handsome detectives. Within thirty days, Lloyds will pay the insurance check to Nancy, who will promptly endorse it over to Alistair Rodger Rare Jewels. Astute businessman that he is, Alistair will follow through with his exacting duplication of Nancy's gems, authentic ones of course, eveything strictly aboveboard. Meanwhile, he'll sell the original jewels, almost certainly in another country, depending on the most advantageous exchange rate at the time. Lap-dissolve: Big Ben, Eiffel Tower, St. Peter's.

SCENE 3: Autumn in New York. Alistair is far too sophisticated to pay Nancy her half (we're guessing it's half) in cash; his accountants would dump their Sassoons. No, this money must be spotlessly laundered. He'll make a shrewd investment of roughly $400,000 in something solid. Real estate? Blue-chip securities? Gold? Then, in a magnanimous gesture (uncharacteristic for a Scotsman, but still), he'll make a gift of that investment to his dearest friend, confidant, and (who knows?) secret lay, Nancy K. Closeup on flickering candle. Pull back to reveal wine glasses clinking. Freeze frame. Music up: Kate Smith sings "God Bless America." Roll credits.

Next question: Who shot Jimmy?

We don't know, but we're guessing Billy. Not exactly the type, true, but don't forget David Stockman went to Harvard Divinity School.

Gives you pause.

Back to reality. Jimmy's released from Lenox Hill at 3:39 P.M., Monday, June 22, and Billy accompanies him in a cab, together with Viki, to the apartment at 11 Anderson. Billy stays for a couple of drinks, whatever, comes out at 5:03, takes a cab back to his place.

Now, we all know Jimmy's no dummy. Whatever he's planning, he's not using his telephone for anything important. Stays home with the lovely Viki that night, McCabe also stays put. Next evening, Jimmy takes Viki out to dinner at Le Perigord, 405 East Fifty-second, very classy joint, we figure they're celebrating. One of our men follows them in and sits at the bar. That night Jimmy uses the phone booth to make two calls. After the second call he sits in the booth and waits. Phone rings. He picks up and he's on the line exactly twenty-eight minutes.

At 1:22 next afternoon, Wednesday, June 24, a cab pulls up in front of Jimmy's apartment. Out he comes, alone, wearing a dark suit, carrying a raincoat and umbrella. Sky's overcast, rain's predicted. Cab takes off for Manhattan. Jimmy gets out at Lexington and Fifty-ninth, walks straight into Bloomingdale's. One of our surveillance guys jumps out, follows him in. Jimmy's not shopping, he's headed for the downstairs subway. Goes through the turnstile, jumps on a downtown local that just pulls in, our man barely makes it aboard before the doors shut. Jimmy gets off at Grand Central, goes upstairs to the telephone center, gets in a booth, and makes a quick call. Comes out, buys a newspaper at the stand nearby, goes back to the same phone booth, sits down, and reads the paper. It's now 2:47. Phone rings at 3:08. Jimmy picks up, talks only a few seconds, hangs up, lights a cigarette, continues to read the paper.

Phone doesn't ring again until 3:46. Jimmy's on the line for like two seconds, hangs up, leaves the booth, walks through Grand Central to Forty-second, grabs a cab. Our man can't get to his partner in the surveillance car fast enough, loses him. It's starting to rain.

Now Jimmy floors us all. At 4:09 he walks into the Champs-Elysées. Walks through the crowd in his classy raincoat, only reason our man in the lobby picks up on him is his bald head.

Jimmy goes straight to the elevators in a small crowd, our man gets on with him. At floor thirty-eight, Jimmy gets off, our man stays on, returns to the lobby, calls Big John at the precinct fast. Catch is, the Princess isn't in her apartment, she went out about 3:45. "What time?" Big John asks. The guy's certain, just about 3:45. Now we know Jimmy's got his own man (or woman) in the lobby. Big John calls the chief at headquarters; soon as he gets the word he's going totally nuts: "Send the guy up! Get up there with everybody you got, he's in the apartment!" Big John stays calm, tries to quiet him down: "You want to nail him on something big, right? All you got now is another B and E. Wait him out. Let him make his move." Chief agrees, tells us to get up there fast, keep him up to speed soon as we arrive.

Big John and I get up to the Champs-Elysées in a hurry, touch base with our lobby-surveillance guy, Larry Morway, tell him to stand by. Now we go into the manager's office and introduce ourselves. This guy's the actual manager, Harold Crenshaw, we haven't had much contact with him. Bears a strong resemblance to Dick Cavett, mid-forties, soft-spoken Yale-type guy, lots of charisma. Asks us to sit down, smoke if we like, congratulates the department for solving the case so quickly.

Big John lights a cigar. "Reason we're here, Mr. Crenshaw, we got a little problem, we'd appreciate your cooperation."

"Certainly, anything at all." Crenshaw sits behind his Louis XIV type desk, folds his arms, gives us his concerned Cavett expression.

"Problem is," Big John says calmly, "one of the four suspects is in the hotel right now, man by the name of James Ferragamo."

"Ferragamo? *Where* in the hotel?"

"He's in Mrs. Kramer's apartment."

Crenshaw unfolds his arms. "Mrs.—*Kramer*'s apartment?"

"Yeah. She's out right now."

"And he's in there right *now?*"

"Yeah."

"How'd he get *in?*"

"Probably jimmied the lock."

"How'd you find this out?"

"We had a tail on him."

Crenshaw sits forward fast. "You mean to sit there and tell me you *let* this person go into Mrs. Kramer's apartment?"

"No, sir," I tell him. "We didn't let him do anything, we just observed what he did."

While I'm talking, Crenshaw's secretary shows in our lobby guy Morway. "Mrs. Kramer just returned," he says. "She's on her way up to the apartment now."

Crenshaw grabs the phone, punches a couple of buttons: "I want all four of you in my office immediately."

"What's all that about?" I ask.

"Security guards," he snaps. "This has gone far enough, I'm taking immediate action."

"What kind of action?" I ask.

"Detective Rawlings, I have a responsibility to protect the residents of this hotel! I intend to do that!"

Big John stands up, cigar in hand, leans over the man's desk, looks him straight in the eye, speaks very softly. "Mr. Crenshaw, you want a homicide on your hands here?"

"A homicide? What're you talking about?"

"I'll tell you what I'm talking about. The man in that apartment up there, Jimmy Ferragamo, is a known killer with a record as long as your lobby."

Door opens again and three security guards file in, big heavyset clowns in dark three-piece suits, almost exact replicas of the intrepid night crew, I'm really impressed. Lead guy, who's absolutely got to be chief of the day shift, it's written all over him, he takes one look at us and unbuttons his suit coat, ready to grab his new squirt gun.

"Police officers!" I yell. "Relax!"

"It's all right, Clark," Crenshaw says. "They're police. Come in and close the door. Where's Harris?"

"Making rounds. What's going on?"

Big John introduces himself very politely, then Morway and me. Tells the guards only what they need to know: Jimmy's in Kramer's apartment, he should be considered armed and extremely dangerous, and any attempt to arrest him at this stage would seriously endanger the woman's life.

"Exactly what do you intend to do?" Crenshaw asks.

"Stay calm and wait him out."

"Wait him *out?*"

"That's what I said." Big John picks up the telephone on the desk, punches a number as he talks. "You have to know Ferragamo. He's not looking to hurt Mrs. Kramer. Not unless we force his hand." Into the phone: "Mat, it's me. Chief around? No, I'll hang on." Back to us: "Ferragamo's looking to hurt somebody else. He'll tell Mrs. Kramer to call a friend of hers, ask him to come over and see her as soon as possible. When this friend gets here, we let him go in."

"I can't allow that," Crenshaw says.

"Yes, you can," Big John says, then speaks into the phone: "Chief, we're at the hotel. Cockfight should begin in about an hour. Uh-huh. Right. Listen, my word of honor, you'll be the first one in!"

Finally time for the cavalry. Hot *damn!*

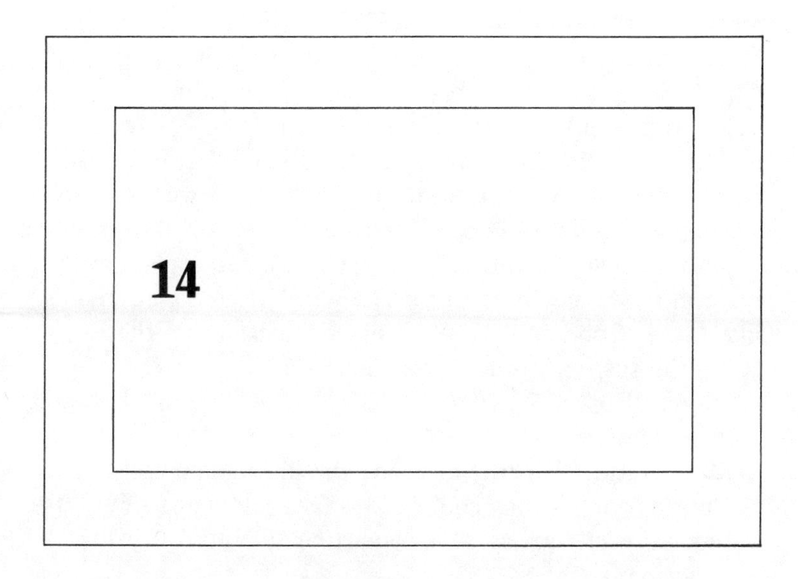

14

IT'S RAINING HARD when Billy McCabe arrives at the Champs-Elysées at 5:27. Chief's in the manager's office with us now and he's converted it into a command center. Radio gear, telephones, cables all over the place. He's been in contact with the surveillance car that tailed McCabe from his apartment, he switched the tail to our van at Fifty-ninth and Third, then he switched to walkie-talkie contact with one of three men he's got in the lobby. Soon as McCabe's in the elevator, beep, he alerts the woman detective who's posing as a maid in the linen room on the thirty-eighth floor. Beep, now he alerts our man in the fire-exit stairwell on thirty-eight. Beep, now he's calling the kitchen, where he's got a man in a room-service uniform who's taking a crash course in how to serve all kinds of shit from a cart. Crenshaw's sitting in the corner of the office popping Valium; his four crack security guards are playing pocket-pool, waiting in line to get in the john.

Chief walks around the desk now, goes to the window, lifts a slat in the blinds, looks out at the rain, then checks his Astronaut Moon Watch, frowns at it. Thing's got so many dials he can hardly see the time. Must say he looks the part here, shirtsleeves rolled up, tie pulled down, S&W stainless .38 Chief's Special holstered back on the right hip, black plastic-cased walkie-talkie on the left hip. Reliable sources swear up and down he can fast-draw with either hand, but eyewitness reports are few. At least, until tonight. Tonight we get lucky. Left hand: Slap-click-beep: "Tedesco."

Static. Then: "Tedesco." It's Carol Tedesco, playing the maid in the linen closet on thirty-eight, but her voice sounds like Lee J. Cobb and the resemblance doesn't end there.

"Is the suspect inside?" the chief asks.

Static. "Repeat?"

"Is he *inside?*"

More static. "Right, I'm inside the linen room."

Chief's trying to stay cool, but his face colors just a tad. "Is—the—*suspect*—inside—the—apartment!"

"Affirmative!"

"Commence Plan One. Repeat: Commence Plan One."

"Roger, out."

Big John and I exchange glances. Plan One calls for Tedesco to wheel her linen cart down the length of the hall, real slow, past Suite 3827, attempt to hear anything that might be going on, continue to the other end, and report to our guy Malzone who's waiting in the fire-exit stairwell. At 5:32 Malzone reports that Tedesco heard two male voices, apparently arguing, too muffled to be heard clearly. She's now headed back to the linen room and will report from there. At 5:36 Tedesco reports that she paused outside the apartment door for approximately one minute. Two male voices were arguing in relatively loud tones, but the only words she could distinguish clearly were obscenities. No female voice had been heard.

At 5:42, all hell breaks loose.

Static, then Tedesco's voice is shaking: "*Gunshots!* Series of fast—"

"*Emergency!*" Malzone shouts. "Five or six gunshots from the apartment!"

"Get in there!" the chief yells. "Use the *pass* key! Draw your weapons and get *in* there!"

Boom, everybody's shoving and pushing to get out of the manager's office. Chief's leading the way, followed by Big John and me, Crenshaw and his four security guards. Streak through the lobby, grab an elevator, shoot up to thirty-eight, sprint down the hall, weapons drawn. Door's wide open. Run down a white-carpeted hall. Smell of gunpowder is very, very strong.

Scene in that living room is frozen in my mind: Thin bands of smoke still rising above the low, graceful lines of the furniture, the soft color schemes, the track-lighted oil paintings, the blond mahogany piano. Jimmy Ferragamo is sitting on the floor in a widening pool of blood, legs spread, back propped against a long white couch, arms by his sides, head resting on the cushioned seat that's already drenched red. He's been shot in the chest, neck, and head; the bullet that entered his left temple has blown away a large section of the right side of his skull. Billy McCabe has fallen backward through the glass top of a large chrome coffee table. His legs are hanging over the square chrome frame. His eyes are open and both hands still grip his neck where one bullet entered at an upward angle and took away the back of his head. There are also wounds in his lower chest and stomach. His blood is being absorbed by the thick white carpet, and the shattered glass surrounding his body glistens in the soft light.

Nancy Kramer is standing behind a pale pink armchair, wearing a white turtleneck sweater and dark trousers. She's holding on to the left arm of Tedesco and her face is very white. Malzone stands behind them. On the seat of the armchair is a nickel-plated snubnosed revolver that looks like a .38 but isn't.

While everybody else is saying, "Oh, my God," and like that, chief's barking orders: "Rawlings, check 'em both out; Daniels, call Homicide and the ME office; everybody else, clear out of this area and don't touch a thing." Then, walking to Nancy Kramer: "Are you all right?"

She tries to speak, can't, nods her head.

It may seem dumb to check vital signs under such obvious circumstances, but sometimes a guy's appearance can be deceptive. I go over to McCabe, step through the frame of the coffee table, get down and feel the carotid artery, then look at the pupils of his eyes: fixed and dilated. Same with Ferragamo.

While we're waiting for the teams from Homicide and the ME, chief takes Mrs. Kramer into the bar area off the dining room, pours her a brandy, tries to be helpful. Crenshaw, Big John, and I join them in there. Tell you what, this broad has to be seen to be believed. Sits on a stool, lights a cigarette, sips the brandy, dials her attorney. She's real pale, but no tears, no hysteria. Tells the attorney it's an emergency and she needs him immediately, period. Chief's sitting there, taking it all in, he looks like he needs a brandy more than she does.

Without going into the whole nine yards, here's the story we get from her attorney, William D. Bradley, later that evening: Mrs. Kramer left her apartment at approximately 3:45 that afternoon. When she returned about an hour later, Ferragamo was illegally in her apartment for the stated purpose of robbing her wall safe. Despite threats of torture and disfigurement, she refused to give him the combination. Ferragamo then telephoned his partner, McCabe, who arrived at the apartment about 5:30. An argument between the two men ensued almost immediately. While the argument was in progress, Mrs. Kramer took a revolver from her desk drawer and shot them both dead. The weapon was legally owned by her, to wit: Smith & Wesson .357 Combat Magnum, Model 19, serial number 76K6715, City of New York Police Pistol License number C-24524 (78).

As legal justification for the homicide, Mr. Bradley then quotes excerpts from the Penal Code, City of New York, Principles of Criminal Liability, dealing specifically with the use of deadly physical force in defense of person, premises, and property. Bottom line, Mrs. Kramer was legally justified in using deadly physical force under the given circumstances and, pending an investigation, could not be prosecuted for doing so.

How in hell did she get a pistol permit in the city with the toughest handgun laws in the entire country? Simple—if you know what you're doing. For the past four years, Nancy Kramer has been a dues-paying member in good standing of the West Side Rifle & Pistol Range, 20 West Twentieth Street. Under the law, any adult male or female permanent resident of the city who's a bona fide member of that club is entitled to (and, in the case of pistols, required to) apply for a New York City permit. After submitting the necessary documents and photographs, and being fingerprinted by NYPD, a lengthy investigation is conducted (three-to-four months minimum) by local, state, and federal enforcement agencies. If you come up clean, and if you have a letter from a NRA certified pistol instructor attesting to your competence with a handgun, you're issued a permit that entitles you to: (a) purchase a handgun from a licensed dealer; (b) purchase ammunition from a licensed dealer; (c) carry the weapon to and from the registered gun club; (d) fire the weapon at the club under supervision; (e) keep the weapon in your place of residence.

That's what Nancy Kramer did. I checked it out personally. Her license application had been submitted to and processed by the Nineteenth Precinct, which has jurisdiction over her area of residence; the permit was issued February 16, 1978. She purchased the .357 magnum February 20, 1978, from Continental Arms Corporation, 697 Fifth Avenue; price, $302.50, not particularly exorbitant for a nickel-plated handgun of such superb quality. In fact, the .357 Combat Magnum, Model 19, is considered by many handgun authorities to be possibly the finest type revolver made by Smith & Wesson.

Thanks in no small measure to the chief's astute insight into the philosophy of effective press relations, the double homicide becomes an immediate cause célèbre for the media gang. A carefully planned, coordinated, time-synchronized press briefing is held in one of the hotel's large conference rooms at 7:30 that evening, systematically orchestrated by the chief for maximum effect, with attorney William D. Bradley serving as eloquent spokesman for his client. No questions for Mrs. Kramer, but he allows her to be photographed in a dark, quietly elegant, high-necked Albert Nipon and—I love this touch—dark glasses, which render precisely the right dramatic aura. Here's the role model incarnate for all average, honest, hard-working women caught in the jaws of you-know-what, the personification of lib versus lob, the Liz Taylor face in the Brooke Shields body with the Gloria Steinem brain and the Bella Abzug heart. Late editions of the *Post* that night carry her picture on the front page, of course, chin up, under the headline:

HOTEL ROBBERS
SHOT DEAD BY
FEMALE VICTIM

Pistol-Packin' Momma Blows 2 Away!

Next afternoon, while Big John's coordinating with Homicide and waiting for the autopsy results, I drive down to the West Side Rifle & Pistol Range. Basement of an old office building on West Twentieth between Fifth and Sixth. Impressive place, large, clean, modern, probably as good as, if not better than, the range at the Police Academy. Electronically operated targets, built-in intercom between rangemaster and each individual station; air-conditioned, smoke-free, lobby separated from the range by bulletproof glass. I identify myself to rangemaster Bob Cavallo, clean-cut heavyset guy with gold aviator's glasses, about my age. Turns out to be a retired NYPD detective, spent most of his career in the Sex Crimes Analysis Unit at headquarters. Range isn't crowded that afternoon, so he has time to rap. Knows what I'm after before I ask, he's read the front-page story in the *News* that morning. Fact is, he's debating whether or not to stick it up on the bulletin board.

"One of my protégés," he says smiling.

"Know her well?"

"Not really. Comes in here maybe an average of once every two weeks. Turns heads all over the joint, y'know?"

"Good shot?"

"Excellent shot, considering that cannon she's got. Still, she's been at it about four years now. Likes rapid-fire combat these days, pulls 'em off as fast as any lady in here."

For some reason, that intrigues me. I hang around a while longer, keep talking with the guy, then he invites me to shoot fifty rounds as his guest. I sure need the practice. Proud to say I still use the same service revolver I bought new when I became a detective in 1958 (you buy them, they're not issued), an S&W .38 Chief's Special, Model 36. Blue finish, two-inch barrel, five-round cylinder, serrated-ramp front sight, checkered walnut Magna-type rounded grips. Model 36 was introduced in 1950, the first of the snubnosed lightweight belly guns of postwar design. Extremely popular model in our department, and with reason. Chief Vadney has the stainless-steel Model 60, which came out in 1966, a flashier version of the original, what can I tell you?

So Cavallo offers me fifty rounds on the house, I select .38 Special wadcutters, designed to cut a clean hole, profile-type targets, and I concentrate on rapid-fire combat shooting at a distance of twenty-five yards. During that session, I think a lot about Nancy Kramer. And I come up with an idea I'm very anxious to check out.

Police Academy's directly crosstown at 235 East Twentieth between Third and Second, so I decide to drive over there and see my buddy Stu Kahan in the Ballistics Unit. You'd absolutely love the Academy, it's a world in itself, they've even got an NYPD museum in here, open to the public. I went to the old Academy, this one's relatively modern, built in 1964 when Abe Beame was mayor, eight stories of light tan brick, and

Ballistics is on the top floor. Even though you have to show your shield and sign in to get in the building, now you get off at eight and you're in a big steel cage, security is extremely tight up here. You show your shield, you're buzzed in, you sign in, you turn left, walk down a short hall. Outside the door to the Ballistics Unit, on the wall to the right, there's this enormous glass display case holding just about every type of handgun you can imagine. It's not strictly for display purposes, they use it for training new officers in the unit, teach them how to strip down unusual pieces and put them back together, and sometimes they borrow parts from the display weapons in order to test fire guns that come in damaged and inoperable.

To give you a quick rundown on what goes on in NYPD Ballistics, approximately 15,000 weapons per year are tested and catalogued in here. The unit has a staff of twenty-two, including two civilians; most are firearms examiner-investigators and seven are assigned to microscopics. Basically, you test fire a gun for two reasons, to determine the operability of the weapon and any unfired cartridges found in it, and to establish a permanent file for the information. Today, virtually all handguns are test fired into a special ballistics water tank, nine feet long, five feet wide, four feet high; holds 500 gallons of water. Not too long ago, handguns used to be test fired into a cotton-filled ballistics box, but cotton tends to "polish" the high-speed stuff, which results in microscopically altered rifling readings. Water is far superior. Two test firings are made on each weapon. One slug and its spent shell are placed in a plastic evidence envelope with the gun, sent to the property clerk to await disposition of the case. The other slug and shell are placed in a small brown paper envelope marked with the appropriate information and kept on permanent file. When the case is finally adjudicated and the D.A.'s office releases the weapon, it's sent to a smelting plant in Jersey and melted down. Years ago, tons of weapons were loaded on a barge and, once a year, dumped far out in the Atlantic, but that practice stopped when ecologists started to squawk about upsetting the balance of marine life.

Now I go in and ask for Lieutenant Stu Kahan, who happens to be commanding officer of the Ballistics Unit now. Known him for years. Stu comes over, hasn't changed much, weighs all of 150 pounds soaking wet, dark hair's receding quite a bit now, oval face dominated by big glasses, looks more like a college professor than a cop. We shake hands, kid around, he knows what I want before I ask, he reads the papers too. This morning Homicide sent Nancy Kramer's .357 in for the standard tests, along with the six slugs they dug out of her apartment walls. Reason those slugs hadn't stopped inside the bodies of Ferragamo and McCabe, as most .38-caliber slugs would have, is due to the tremendous difference in velocity and energy of the .357 magnum. Kramer's apartment walls are constructed of the old-fashioned, eighteen-inch-thick plaster you don't see in modern buildings. Although the rifling on four of the slugs was too damaged for positive identification, the copper jackets on the other two slugs had retained relatively good rifling; I'd seen them myself. Therefore, to obtain a positive rifling match on the .357, Stu's squad will have to test fire it into the water tank, retrieve the slug, and examine its rifling under a ballistics comparison microscope together with one of the two good slugs from the apartment.

Okay, they haven't gotten around to it yet, which is what I expected. Stu says he'll do it himself, finds the sealed evidence envelope with the weapon and slugs in a pile of identical envelopes that arrived the same morning; not necessarily homicide cases, just your run-of-the-mill Wednesday night shootings from all five boroughs, ho-hum, the natives are restless. Now he takes me into the test-firing room, a long rectangular area to the left of the squadroom. It's bright with florescent lights, has soundproofed walls, a bulletproof observation window the size of a door that faces the squadroom, and the nine-foot-long steel water tank is against the right wall, with a two-foot-high catwalk around two sides. Half of the tank's top is open to allow viewing of the slug as it's stopped by the water. Stu closes the heavy door, tosses me a pair of ear protectors, puts on his own pair. He stands at the firing end of the tank, loads the weapon with two cartridges of the identical ammunition Kramer used, .357 magnum, high-velocity, 158-grain, copper-jacketed soft-point.

Now he sticks the weapon in the funnel-like opening and fires two quick shots. I'm watching the water. Both slugs stop at about the middle of the viewing area, drop to the bottom. Stu removes his earmuffs, flicks open the cylinder, ejects the two shells, places the gun on the ledge. He walks toward me, scholarly as you please, grabs the long clay-tipped pole, sticks it in the water, individually retrieves the slugs, hands them to me. Both are perfect, of course.

Next, I follow him through the busy squadroom all the way to the microscopics room in back. It's a compact area with desks holding a total of seven ballistics comparison microscopes, five of which are Leitz and two American Optical. They cost about $21,000 each and they look the money. Four men are working in here at the time, typewriters click, telephones ring and—if only the chief could be here—there's a transistor radio playing. Softly, but guess what that little mother's playing? Right the first time. Rock. Yeah! Swear to God, I can't help smiling at this, it's the Beatles, no less, belting out "Hard Day's Night" on WYNY, ninety-seven on your FM dial. Ballistics people are human too.

Stu sits down at one of the Leitz microscopes. Now, as we all know, the rifling inside the barrel of any given weapon is always microscopically different from that of any other given weapon and, for purposes of positive identification, the rifling marks on a spent slug are considered comparable to a fingerprint under the law and accepted by all courts. Ballistic identifications start with the establishment of what are called class characteristics, the width and direction of the rifling. For example, all Smith & Wesson barrels are classified as "Right-

Five," that is, five grooves, five lands (surface between grooves) and a twist to the right. All Colt barrels are classified as "Left-Six," and so on. Now, a ballistics comparison microscope is actually two microscopes combined optically. Take a silver dollar, split it in half, place the left side under the left lens, right side under the right lens, focus both, then turn the knobs to bring the two images together optically. That's essentially what we're doing here.

Okay, Stu takes one of the relatively "good" .357 slugs from the evidence envelope, places it on a piece of synthetic wax under the left lens; now he takes one of the "perfect" .357 slugs he just test fired, places it on the wax under the right lens. He gets the evidence slug in clear focus and tries to find the best rifling marks on the copper jacket. The soft-point lead tip is flattened, of course, and much of the jacket is badly damaged by impact with the wall, but one side is better than the other, so he turns the slug with his fingers until he has the clearest grooves in focus. Many grooves can be seen with the naked eye, but the microscope lets you see the fine details of the lands, the tiny scratches on the surface between the grooves. All right, now he can establish the class characteristics. The evidence slug is definitely a "Right-Five," Smith & Wesson. Next, he brings the test-fired slug into focus, turns it until he finds the side with grooves and lands similar to those on the evidence slug. Now he turns the knobs, brings the two images together optically so that only their sides appear to touch. From this point on, it's a matter of making very fine adjustments, tapping both slugs gently again and again until the lands and grooves of each side are in relatively perfect alignment.

All this takes time, of course. Typewriters click, telephones ring, the Beatles are replaced by The Who, who are replaced by the Slime, whatever. I'm standing there with my teeth in my face, listening to Stu mutter to himself, he's carrying on a scholarly conversation, happy as a pig in shit.

Finally he sits back. "Positive match."

"Ever have any doubt?"

"Always have doubts, John."

"Now what, the shells?"

"Not necessary in this case, but I'll run 'em under if you want."

"No, no. So now what, that a wrap?"

"Soon as I do the paperwork, right."

"Paperwork? You?"

"We're all equal in God's eyes, John."

"Lieutenant Stuart *Kahan?*"

"Especially when we're two-three weeks behind."

"Commanding officer of the whole—"

"All equal. Jews, Micks, Dagos—hell, even Protestants."

"In that case, I'd like to ask a little favor."

He rolls his eyes, pushes on the nosepiece of his big glasses. "Funny, had a feeling you might."

"Won't take a minute, Stu."

"They never do."

"Remember the slug they pulled out of Jimmy Ferragamo's belly up at Lenox Hill?"

"You mean *the* Jimmy Ferragamo?"

"The late-great, God rest his soul. Got it in the files?"

"That slug? No. No, you're too late on that one, John."

"Yeah, huh?"

"Just this morning we donated it to the Guinea Hall of Fame."

"Thoughtful gesture. Like to see it."

He gives me this look, picks up the telephone, punches a couple of buttons. "Tony, pull an envelope for me, huh? Ferragamo, James. Uh-huh, same guy. No, no, this one came in from Lenox Hill about two weeks ago, remember? Right. Scope room. Thanks." He hangs up, turns to me. "So what you got in mind?"

"Just fishing, Stu."

"Uh-huh. Care to enlighten me?"

"Not really. Hate to be laughed at in public."

"I'm a compassionate man, John."

"Yeah, I know. Transistor radios right in the scope room. Hard rock, yet."

"Helps ease the constant pressure. Tremendous pressure in this squad, John. Incredible responsibility. Life and death in the balance."

"I hear you. Just."

"Besides, the clowns in here like rock."

Tony comes in, good-looking Italian kid with a dark mustache. Hands Stu a small brown envelope. Stu thanks him, hands it to me. I read the information on the front:

BULLET GROOVE TO LAND IS: N (E) W

B.S.#: 7648 DATE OF OCC.: 6/12/81

DECEASED:

INJURED: Ferragamo, James, W/M/C

NO ONE INJURED ☐ PROP. DAMAGE ☐ VOUCHER #533

TO B.S. ON: 6/14/81 BY: Lenox Hill Security

SOURCE: Abdominal surgery, 6/13/81, Dr. A. Vivera

EVIDENCE: .38-cal., Right-5

PCT.: 19 61#: OFF/#/CMD:

B.S. DET.: Anthony S. Tota BK#/PG:

I open the string clasp, pour the slug into my palm. It's almost perfectly intact except for a slight flattening of the lead point. Copper jacket has easily visible rifling marks. Smells of disinfectant.

"Need me for anything?" Stu asks.

"Promise you won't laugh?"

"Word of honor."

"Take this slug, place it under the left lens."

He gives me that look again, takes the slug. "This is a thirty-eight, you know that, right?"

"Right. Humor me."

"Ho-kay." He shrugs, swivels around in the chair, removes the damaged .357 evidence slug from the wax under the left lens, replaces it with the .38, adjusts the focus, turns the slug around, looks for the best grooves on the copper jacket. Next, he turns the knobs to bring the two sides together optically. Now he starts tapping both slugs very gently, tries to bring the lands and grooves into alignment. Finally, he pauses, frowns, adjusts his glasses, continues to frown as he looks up at me. Never forget the expression on his face. He pushes at the nosepiece of his glasses, hunches over, takes another long hard look.

"I'll be a son of a bitch," he mumbles.

"Mind if I take a look?"

He stands up slowly, steps back. "I'll be a son of a *bitch!*"

I sit down fast, hunch over, adjust the focus. Well, okay, to be honest, I'm so elated I feel like laughing out loud. So I do, only softly. I mean, it'd been strictly a hunch, a very long shot at best, but it's the kind of intuition you tend to develop in this business after twenty-six years. The lands and grooves on the copper jackets of the .38 and .357 are absolutely identical.

Question: How is this mechanically possible?

Answer: It's not only mechanically possible, it's relatively simple, although only serious handgun nuts would know about it: All .38 Special cartridges can be chambered and fired in .357 magnum revolvers, but not conversely. As a practical safety measure, the .357 magnum cartridge is 1.290 inches long, as opposed to the .775-inch length of the .38 cartridge. Therefore, it's impossible to chamber a .357 cartridge in a .38-caliber revolver.

Remember what I said about women being so much harder to figure than men? Full count, money pitch coming, she's got you guessing up there, total suicide? Now what's she do? *Ziiiiing!* The high-hard fastball she wasn't supposed to have, straight down the pipe, Sandy Koufax/Nolan Ryan, 98 mph., the aspirin tablet, forget it, go sit down. Am I right or am I right?

Perfectionist that he is, Stu's already at work. He goes through his cartridge boxes, selects a .38 Special, copper-jacketed soft-point identical to the one used on Ferragamo June 12, marches into the test-firing room, me on his tail, chambers it in Kramer's .357 magnum, fires it into the water tank, retrieves the slug, marches back to the scope room, places it under the right lens, focuses, finds the best grooves, the whole nine yards, then brings the sides of the two .38 slugs together optically. Now he's into the delicate tapping routine, patience personified, looking every bit the scholar, determined to bring the lands and grooves into absolutely perfect alignment. Finally, he sits back, looks up and me and nods.

"John," he says quietly, "you got yourself a case."

15

WHEN THE CHIEF FINDS OUT, he goes totally nuts, he's so excited he actually offers to let me be the arresting officer, but I defer—magnanimously—to his obviously superior diplomatic expertise. "Chief, we've already collared Kojak," I tell him. "Elizabeth Taylor I just can't handle." He understands perfectly. Agrees to do it himself. *Some*body has to. First order of business, attention to details, this collar has to be clean-cut all the way, so we get a warrant for Nancy Kramer's arrest on the single charge of attempted murder, which will hold up in any court. It's now 4:10 in the afternoon, Thursday, June 25, chief's got plenty of time for effective media staging, maximum utilization of time and space within given parameters of minimum lead-times necessary, da-da. Jerry Grady in Press Relations gets on the horn fast, alerts the TV networks, newspapers, newsmagazines, wire services; can't tell them exactly what's up, but he stakes his professional reputation on the fact it's lead-story stuff, sets it up for six o'clock sharp, Nineteenth Precinct.

Wait a minute, hold everything. At 4:26, Grady gets a call on his private line from Mike Wallace of CBS. Yeah, *the* Mike

Wallace, personable, lovable, hatchetman Mike "Are-You-Saying" Wallace of "60 Minutes." Wants to know if this thing's connected in any way to yesterday's double homicide. Grady hesitates: "Yesterday's—uh—?" Wallace gets tough: "Are you saying you don't *know,* or are you saying you're not *saying?*" Grady says he's saying the chief says not to say. All right, no more nice guy, Wallace demands to speak to the chief. Hold on.

I'm in the chief's office with Mat Murphy and Big John, who's just arrived, we're having a last-minute briefing on strategic deployment of personnel at the hotel, ring-around-the-collar, chief calls it. Phone rings. Chief picks up. "Yeah, Jerry. *Who?* You puttin' me on? What's he want? Yeah? Okay, wait a minute." Punches the hold button. Left eyebrow's into a nervous spasm, never saw this before. Fumbles for his Sony TCM-600 under his console, presses the red record button, discovers he doesn't have the telephone pick-up suction cup attached to the receiver, grabs it, licks the cup, sticks it on, plugs in the other end. Takes a deep breath. Glances at us. Glances at the telephone squawk box on his almost-empty desk. Punches the button, now we can all vicariously share in the excitement of celebrity. We lean forward. Chief leans forward. Yanks his tie down. Takes three deep breaths, basketball freethrow style. Clears his throat. Punches the flashing button. Click. "Hello, Mike, what can I do for ya?"

"It's Grady, chief. You set?"

"Grady, get the fuck off the *line,* will ya! Put him *on!*"

Click. Pause. "Hello?"

"Hello, Mike, what can I do for ya?"

"Hold on for Mr. Wallace, please." Click.

"One-upmanship," chief mumbles. "God damn bureaucrats."

Click. "Chief Vadney?" No mistaking that voice. It's him!

"Hello, Mike, what can I—"

"Grady tells me you got a major story about to break, true?"

"Sure do, Mike. Unbelievable."

"Connected with yesterday's homicides, right?"

Chief grins a twitch, sits back. "Grady tell you that?"

"Are you saying it's *not* true?"

"I'm not confirming or denying, Mike. What you got in mind?"

Wallace yells to somebody in his office: "Who? *Rather?* Tell him to hold, I'm on another line!" Back to the chief: "Listen, Vadney, I don't have time to play *games!* Is this connected with the homicides or *not?*"

Chief's grin vanishes. "Absolutely, yeah."

"Worth our time?"

"Absolutely, Mike, no question."

"What's it all about?"

"Uh, strictly off-the-record?"

"Yeah, right, sure."

"I got your word on that, Mike?"

"Vadney, are you for *real?!*"

"Okay, okay. I'm gonna make an arrest today that'll knock your socks off, Mike."

Wallace yells off the phone again: "Tell Redford no, positively no, we're not doing his Utah story." Now to the chief: "Go ahead."

"Mike, I'm gonna make an arrest today that'll knock—"

"Yeah, I *heard* all that! Bottom line, Vadney, come *on!*"

"Nancy Kramer, I'm gonna arrest her."

"Uh-huh. Charge?"

"Ready for this? Attempted murder!"

"Uh-huh. Go ahead."

"Attempted *murder,* buddy, that's what we're—"

"Attempted murder of *who?!*"

"Jimmy Ferragamo, June twelve."

Pause. "All right, I'm interested."

"All kinds of complications involved, Mike, tip a the iceberg, goes without sayin'. Now, we're talkin' a 'Sixty Minutes' segment here, right, buddy?"

"Chief Vadney, let's get a few things straight. In the first place, I'm not your *buddy,* I've never met you in my life, to the best of my knowledge. Secondly, we'll send a crew to cover this, but there's no guarantee we'll use the footage. You understand that?"

"Oh, yeah, sure."

"All right, now what's your timetable on the collar?"

"Hotel Champs-Elysées, ETA five o'clock sharp."

"*Ridiculous!* It's now—four thirty-one!"

"Well, we're just about to leave."

"Are you saying you don't *want* the story?"

"No, no. No. No, I'm sure as hell not saying *that.*"

"Well, what *are* you saying?"

"I'm saying—how's five-fifteen?"

"Five-thirty, earliest."

"That'll screw up the rest of the media boys, Mike. I've called a press conference for the book—"

"I *know* all that! Call 'em *back!* Better yet, let 'em *wait!*"

"Jesus, you drive a hard bargain, buddy."

"Take it or leave it! And quit calling me *buddy!*" Off the phone: "*Who?* Brando *again?* Tell him to take a walk, we're not doing his Indian story, *period!*" Into the phone: "Five-thirty, Vadney, that's my final offer!"

"Okay, okay. You got it, Michael. Now, listen up, we gotta orchestrate this thing a little here. Your crew goin' in with a coupla mini-cam remotes, right?"

"Mini—? Vadney, leave the technical stuff to us, huh?"

"I read ya, Mike. Now, we arrive at five-thirty, coupla unmarked cars, we'll be movin' pretty fast, buddy, bing-bing, y'read me?"

Off the phone: "I can't *believe* this!"

"That's the way we operate, Mike, no advance warnin' to anybody. Way I figure it, we pull up in front, you guys hustle over and join us, we go inside in tandem, right? Remote crew right on our heels, shootin' away, *cinéma-vérité.* You with me?"

"*Cinéma-vérité?*"

"No problem."

"Amazing. Haven't heard that in years."

"No problem, partner. Through the lobby, touch base with the security boys, show 'em the arrest warrant. Commandeer an elevator to floor thirty-eight. Knock on 'er door, identify ourselves, state our purpose. She opens, you follow us right in, *cinéma-vérité,* I'll do all the talkin' needs to be done. Shoot reverse angles if you want. After she's cuffed, tossed, read 'er rights, pan around the apartment, pick up lots of color. Tilt down, zoom in on the bloodstained white carpet and furniture, I'm sure it's still there."

"Chief Vadney, may I ask a question?"

"Absolutely, Mike."

"Naturally, you want appropriate screen credit for directing this particular scene, is that correct?"

"Well, I hadn't really given—"

"All I'm saying, you'll have to join AFTRA, it's mandatory, you understand that, right?"

"No problem."

"Initiation fee is a little steep."

"Uh-huh. How much we talkin' here, buddy?"

Pause. Then, softly: "Forget it."

"No problem, I'm sure we can iron out the details, Mike. Now, long as we're on the subject, listen up, this is important. There's at least some degree of danger involved in a collar like this, naturally. You and your crew, you'll have to sign a general release. Standard operating procedure in these situations, Legal insists on it."

"Chief, as a matter of fact—"

"No problem, I'll bring the forms with me, you can sign 'em like in the elevator."

"Well, as a matter of fact, I hadn't—"

"But now, hold on a minute, listen up. Now we knock on her door, right? Most dangerous time of all, Mike. Single most dangerous time of all on any collar. Want you and your crew positioned flat-out against the wall. Flat-out. Read me?"

"Flat-out."

"Why? I'll tell you why. Truth is, you just never know what's goin' on in the sick brains of these slimebags, if you'll forgive the expression. Goes double for these high-strung, trigger-happy broads. You just never know. *Never* know! Particularly if they're on the rag and like that. Liable to go hysterical on us, shoot through the door, shit like that. Happens. Me, no problem. You kiddin'? Bulletproof vest, shotgun, all standard. Tell you what, if the network's antsy, be glad to bring along vests for you and your boys. Be my pleasure."

"That's very kind of—"

"Be my pleasure, Mike."

"—you, Vadney, but I think not."

"Suit yourself, Michael, it's your neck. This weird broad shot two men dead just yesterday, y'know. Shot 'em *dead.* Cold *blood.* Blew their fuckin' *brains* out, literally, if you'll excuse the expression."

There's a slight pause, then Wallace's voice turns suddenly warm and, yes, even friendly, he's into the actor-journalist role known and loved by millions, the change of pace polished to perfection: "Matter of fact, chief, I hadn't planned to be there with the crew. But now, frankly, after listening to you describe this thing, I gotta admit I've changed my mind. Actually, I think this whole story might have definite possibilities. Might go all the way."

"Now you're talkin', Michael."

"Call me Mike, please."

"Like your style, Mike. Call me Walt."

"All right, look, let's get down to cases. Tell you what I'd like to do, Walt. If you have no objections, I'd like to hop down to headquarters with the crew and ride right along with you to the hotel."

"Be my pleasure!"

"*Cinéma-vérité* style, Walt, y'read me?"

"All the way, partner."

"Here's how I see it: You drive, I sit next to you, cameraman and sound technician in back. Tape a little candid rap session on the way to the collar. No big deal, we'll have the lights on, but that—hell, that shouldn't bother you."

Chief flashes a grin that gives me goosebumps. "Hell, cameras and lights come with the territory, Mike, don't even know they're around. Where you at now, West Fifty-second, right?"

"Right."

"What time can I expect ya?"

"Let's say—five-fifteen?"

"Five-fifteen, lobby, security desk."

"See you then."

Chief snaps off the squawk box, he's positively beaming, can't hold it in, slams his fist on the desk. "Hot-fuckin'-diddly-*damn!* Hit the *jack*pot, men, 'Sixty Minutes'! Top a the Nielsen ratings, most popular show on TV, thirty million viewers! Wait'll I tell *Grady!*" Grabs the receiver, suddenly freezes, stares fixedly at the Sony suction cup still attached to it, still recording hot air, then glances at the squawk box. Now his eyes close tightly in pain. "Oh, my God," he says hoarsely. "I can't believe this. Just lost a whole conversation with—! Can't believe I'd be that fuckin' *dumb!*"

Believe it. Five-fifteen we're in the lobby by the security desk, intrepid three-man team, chief wearing his spotless-white BPV and holding a gleaming twenty-gauge Ithaca pump, Big John and me wearing our gleaming shields and holding our spotless-tan Dutch Masters panetellas. Five-twenty, Mike Wallace shows with his bearded young camera-man and bearded young sound technician, both wearing denim. Wallace looks much better live than on TV, younger, slimmer, wears a battle-scarred safari jacket and tan cords. Takes one look at the chief, purses his lips, realizes his instincts were right on the money. We take the elevator down to the garage.

"We're goin' full sirens and lights," chief announces proudly.

"No *way!*" the young sound guy tells Mike. "No fuckin' *way!*"

"No, huh?" chief asks Mike.

"Screws up the sound track, Walt."

"Yeah, huh?"

"Vest has to go," the young cameraman tells Mike.

"Vest?" chief asks Mike.

"Too much glare in the lights, Walt."

"Yeah? Huh."

Elevator reaches garage level, we step out, chief struggles to unbuckle the heavy vest. Cameraman puts down his shoulder-mounted videotape camera, takes a small jar from his pocket, opens it, whips out a brush, starts applying makeup to the chief's face without a word.

Chief slaps his hand away. *"Hey!* Get *outa* here!"

"Wanna look like a *ghost?*" the guy asks indignantly.

"Pancake makeup," Mike explains. "I'm wearing it myself, Walt, it's necessary, believe me."

"Yeah, huh?" Chief shrugs, lets the guy brush it on, glances at us nervously.

Couple of detectives walk in from the garage, press the elevator button. I happen to know them, John Gaulrapp and Dan Forget (pronounced Forj-ay), from the old Fourth District Robbery Squad; they shared responsibility for solving the famed Hotel Pierre robbery back in 1972. Chief knows them too, of course, now he starts to look very uncomfortable.

"John, Dan," I say. "Like you to meet Mike Wallace."

They step over, shake hands, say hello.

"What's going on?" Gaulrapp asks.

"Chief's going on 'Sixty Minutes,' " Big John says.

"Yeah?" Forget says. "What're you playing, chief, a black guy?"

"Not funny, Dan," chief says.

"No, it's not," Gaulrapp agrees. "*Any*body can see he's playing an Indian."

"An Indian *chief,*" Forget adds. "*Got* to be."

Chief's not amused. "Get the hell outa here, will ya!"

Few laughs later, elevator doors open, Gaulrapp and Forget step in, exchange a whisper, turn around. Real pissers, these guys. As the doors start to close, they pat their mouths rapidly in the old Indian war cry: "*Wo-wo-wo-wo-wo-wo-wo!*"

Breaks everybody up, even gets a grin out of the chief. Makeup's finally finished, we go into the garage. Chief's dark late-model four-door Chevy's parked right at the gas pumps, freshly serviced, recently washed, sparkles right down to the hubcaps, rank has its perks. Chief and Mike jump in front, crew in back, slam-slam-slam-slam. Big John and I go to our dirty old beat-up piece of shit, climb in humbly, the real stars of this whole drama, the unsung heroes, but who knows, who cares?

We're lead car, Big John's driving, off we go, straight to FDR Drive, it's packed, of course, height of the rush hour, but fast and smooth, no lights, who needs a siren? I look back, chief's staying right on our tail, I've got a front-row seat at a silent film. Lights on the videotape camera flood the front seat, chief seems relaxed, in his element, answering questions, talking easily, an occasional turn of the head, a hand gesture now and then. Speeding along in soft June twilight, on his way to collar a beautiful young murderous *femme fatale* at Park Avenue's ultra-chic Champs-Elysées, "All in a day's work, Mike, comes with the badge," *cinéma-vérité* with every pimple exposed in choke-shot focus, "Hill Street Blues" with Manhattan class.

Streak off FDR at Seventy-ninth, shoot west to Park, hang a squealing right, now north to Eighty-fourth in a swiftly flowing river of yellow steel. Pull up at the canopied entrance behind a couple of elegant gray limos, jump out fast. Supersonic set out front stands suddenly aghast at the fast-breaking spectacle here: Bronze-faced man runs for the door, shotgun in hand, badge on blue suitcoat, bathed in the bouncing lights of a shoulder-mounted videotape camera in hot pursuit, flanked by a bearded kid with a microphone and big black box, followed by—Christ, isn't that Mike *Wallace* in the safari jacket?—followed by—Harry, look, it's Senator *Moynihan!*—followed by a little man who's—Dahling, why is that man *laughing?*

We're in the lobby now, everybody scatters, women scream, men yell, we follow the leader straight toward the bank of elevators. Our lobby team is there, Nuzhat Idrissi, Roger Stephenson, and lovely Carol Tedesco, attaching badges to their jackets as we approach. Two figures sprint across the lobby, catch up to the chief at the elevators: Harold Crenshaw and one of his security guards. Chief whips out the arrest warrant when he spots them.

Crenshaw takes a quick swipe at his hair before stepping into the bright lights, Dick Cavett in a rare snit: "Chief Vadney, this is out*rageous!* What's the *meaning* of this, who *are* these people?!"

Chief hands him the warrant. "Mr. Crenshaw, I have a court order for the arrest of Mrs. Nancy Kramer, a resident of this hotel."

Crenshaw looks at it incredulously, he's dumping bricks now. "You can't be *serious!* You're going to arrest Mrs. *Kramer?* After all she's been *through?* Good God, man, haven't you done enough damage to her *already?*" Believe it. Bricks.

Idrissi and Stephenson have an elevator now, they hold the doors as we march in, all of us, close quarters. Up we go, nonstop to thirty-eight. Camera's turned off, sound's off, bearded boys are busy changing their respective cassettes.

"What's the *charge* against her?" Crenshaw demands.

"Attempted murder," chief says softly.

"Attempted *murder?*"

"Attempted murder."

"Excuse me, sir," Mike Wallace says. "Are you the manager of this hotel?"

In the absence of the bright lights, Crenshaw looks directly at Wallace for the first time. "Oh, my God, is this—? Oh, Jesus, are we on 'Sixty Minutes'?"

"Yes, sir," Mike says. "Are you the—"

"Oh, my *God!*"

"—manager of this hotel, sir?"

"This is positively out*rageous!*" Crenshaw yells. "I want you and your film crew out of this hotel *immediately!*"

"Mr. Crenshaw," chief says quietly, "they have official permission to film this arrest. They've signed a legal release entitling them to accompany us at their own risk. I warn you not to interfere in any way. When the elevator reaches thirty-eight, I want you and your security man to stay in the elevator for your own protection. Is that understood?"

"I'm the *manager* of this hotel!"

"Don't care if you're the *bellhop!*" chief snaps. "Stay in the elevator for your own protection, both of ya! That's an order! Idrissi, Stephenson, stay with 'em, hear?"

"Yes, sir."

"Yes, sir."

Elevator stops at thirty-eight, doors open, hallway is empty. Chief checks his watch, I do too: 5:56. Lights, camera, sound, action. Chief leads the way down the long hall, his back brightly lighted, shotgun gleaming at his side. As we near Suite 3827, Big John and I draw our service revolvers, hold them at our sides. Chief reaches the door, stands to the left. I position myself against the wall to his left, Tedesco behind me, gun drawn, Lee J. Cobb in color-blind drag; Big John's flat against the wall to the right, Wallace behind him, crew last.

Chief uses the butt of his shotgun: *Wham—wham!—wham!* "Police officers! Open the door!"

Silence except for the soft whir of the camera. Ten seconds.

Wham!—wham!—wham! "Police! Open up!"

Whir of the camera. Five seconds. Ten.

Pffft. Peephole slides open. Muffled voice sounds like Nancy Kramer: "What the hell's going on?!"

Chief holds the warrant up to the peephole. "Have a warrant here for the arrest of Mrs. Nancy Kramer. Open the door, please."

Click! Clack! Door opens a crack to reveal a heavy chain lock; interior is dimly lighted. Chief pivots back automatically, shotgun across his chest. Nothing happens. Camera whirs.

"Chief Vadney?" It's definitely Kramer's voice.

"That's correct."

Her figure appears in the crack. "What's this all about?"

"Open the door, lady."

"What's that bright *light* out there?"

"Mrs. Kramer, I have a warrant here for your arrest. Now, I'll ask you once more to open this door. If you refuse, I'll have no recourse but to break it down."

"Break it *down?* Are you *crazy?*"

"Open the door, lady!"

"What's—what's that, a *shot*gun?"

"Open the door, make it easy on yourself!"

"All *right!* For God's *sake,* put that *gun* down!" Door closes a fraction, chain lock is removed, door opens wide enough to reveal Nancy Kramer standing there in a light blue shorty bathrobe. Looks like that's all she's got on. She's holding it tight at the neck now.

Chief looks her up and down. "Step back, please."

She complies, he shoves the door back all the way, glances left and right, shotgun at the ready. Finally, he lowers the weapon, walks inside. Big John and I follow, revolvers at our sides, camera and sound boys right behind us, Wallace behind them; Tedesco is last, closes the door. We're in a mirrored, white-carpeted entry hall. Soft piano music comes from the living room, Chopin's familiar Nocturne *No. 2 in E-Flat.* Kramer's dark hair is nicely disheveled and in the bright camera lights it's obvious she's not wearing makeup; doesn't need it either.

"Who the hell are *these* people?" she demands. "Get that camera *out* of here! How *dare* you!"

Chief hands her the warrant. "Mrs. Kramer, it's my duty to—"

"Turn those *lights* off!"

"—place you under arrest."

"Who the *hell* do you think you *are,* marching in here—"

"Place your hands against the wall," chief says calmly. "Elbows straight, legs spread. Tedesco, search her, Rawlings, check—"

"*Search* me?! I'm *nude* under this robe!"

"Up against the wall, lady," Tedesco says happily.

"I can't *see!* Turn those lights off *immediately!*"

"Tedesco, search the lady; Rawlings, check the other rooms."

Tedesco's face starts to color as she escorts Kramer to the wall; fascinating contrast in figures—fireplug versus hourglass. As I walk away from the bright lights, the chief begins reading her rights in a flat monotone that provides a nice counterpoint to the nocturne. I snap on the lights in the living room. Nobody's sitting at the blond mahogany piano; stereo must be on, excellent sound reproduction. Large square chrome coffee table is still there, minus the glass top, white carpet underneath is covered with a big, spotless-white sheepskin rug. Another sheepskin covers the carpet in front of the long white couch, which isn't white anymore; slipcovers have been removed, exposing the original upholstery, once probably white, now shades of dirty yellow. I continue through, snap on the lights in the kitchen, take a quick look in the dining room, then walk down the hall to the first bedroom. It's obviously a guest room, relatively small but tastefully decorated, even has its own Zenith color TV. I check the bathroom and closet; both empty, spick-and-span.

Go down the hall to the next door, accompanied by Chopin, soft chords played andante with a delicate, sure touch. Turns out to be the master bedroom. No lights, but the wide windows face west over Park, investing the room with a red-orange sunset glow. Chopin would approve. I snap on one of the jade-and-brass floor lamps. Handsomely framed Oriental watercolors against pale-green Japanese "grass" wallpaper. Graceful Ming-design rosewood furniture, Persian carpets with floral and avian designs woven in rich, harmonious colors, laid over the fitted white carpet. Bed looks like a double queen, positively gigantic, you could roll over a dozen times in this thing. It's unmade, flowered-silk top sheet pulled all the way down and off, on the floor with the spread. Bed unmade? Six o'clock? I go in the large bathroom. Double commodes are real marble, fitted with elaborate gold-plated fixtures. Sunken marble bathtub is surrounded by lush tropical plants, à la Harcourt and Tent. Two fluffy sheepskin rugs on the black-and-white marble-tiled floor.

Back to the bedroom, open the closet door, snap on the light. Walk-in closet? Try drive-in. Eighteen-wheeler. We're in a *haute couture* boutique here, where's the saleslady? Stroll down the carpeted aisle, both sides are padded-hanger perfect with m'lady's spring and summer wardrobes, literally hundreds of selections, must be traumatic to decide. Above, wraparound two-tier shelves hold our elegant spring and summer handbags with a decided preference for Courrèges, Gucci, Harrods, Crouch & Fitzgerald, a few from Bloomies, here's one from Lord & Taylor, must've been a rainy day. Floor has our expandable double-decked shoe racks, *chaussures pour printemps et été seulement.* we lean here toward Givenchy, Bernardo, Pappagallo, Capezio, and Gamba, although you're apt to find a few A'mano, Bandolino, even Pandiani. All neatly arranged with one exception: Pair of Bernardo sandals have fallen off the lower rack to the right. Destroys the symmetry. I glance up. Directly above the sandals, the hangers of two long evening gowns are slightly askew. Careless chambermaid, no doubt, but try and find decent help nowadays. Artur Rubinstein, or whoever, is into the coda of the nocturne, and the final notes are played solemnly. Last chord is very low and seems to linger on in the silent fragrance of expensive new leather.

Well, what the hell, life is full of little mysteries just crying for investigative expertise. I glance around, pick up a dainty hand-painted silk parasol, examine the pointed wooden tip. Now, carefully, I walk toward those two out-of-line evening gowns, aim the parasol at the approximate thigh of one, and jab quickly.

Somebody jumps back fast.

I draw my revolver. "Step out with your hands in sight."

Out hops a tiny fawn-colored Pekinese puppy, no more than six inches long, maybe four inches tall. Huge lustrous brown eyes gaze up at me, pink tongue showing, fluffy tail wagging. I'm standing there in a combat crouch, both hands on my gun. "*Wo-wo-wo-wo!*" Peke's up on its hind legs now, paws waving, obviously warning me to back off. This is no shit, these little Pekes make excellent watchdogs, unlikely as it seems. Known for their courage, wouldn't run from the devil himself. This one's a bitch, she bounces out of the closet now, tail held high, off to report an intruder. "*Wo-wo-wo-wo!*" I straighten up, holster the gun, adjust my tie, follow her inside. It's been a long day.

I'm met in the hall by the whole "60 Minutes" cast and crew, on the way to the bedroom; seems Nancy K's been allowed to change into a more appropriate outfit. Nice gesture, chief, although I suspect viewers might prefer her as is. Lights flood the bedroom now, follow her into the closet, puppy on her heels, gives the cameraman a valid excuse to include her legs, which are eminently worth closer inspection. Nancy's obviously elected to ramain silent until represented by counsel, so we can assume Wallace's voice-over narration during this scene, if they use it, which I expect they will, since it includes the totally unexpected element of—there's no other term for it—Nancy's Tongue.

Nancy's Tongue. Maybe destined to become a "60 Minutes" classic. Here's how it happens, folks, eyewitness report: Nancy prances into the closet in her tease-robe, pauses, finger to chin, looks over the racks of glad rags, crosses her ankles, at ease with the camera. I'm suddenly aware the stereo's playing "Don't Cry for Me Argentina," vocal in the damn-near heroic style of Patti LuPone:

It won't be easy, you'll think it's strange
When I try to explain how I feel,
That I still need your love after all that I've done.

Whirrr, cameraman pans around the dazzling drive-in boutique, slowly, comes full circle, tilts down, zooms in on the puppy who's happily licking mommie's Estée Lauder-ed toes.

You won't believe me, all you'll see is a girl you once knew,
Although she's dressed up to the nines, at sixes and sevens with you.

Camera stays in tight as we ascend the Bain de Soleil-ed legs, oh-so-gradually, lovingly.

I had to let it happen, I had to change,
Couldn't stay all my life down at heel,
Looking out of the window, staying out of the sun.

Slowly ascending camera picks up every subtle nuance in the light blue shorty robe, casually open at the neck now—to put it delicately—apex of the V having plunged to perhaps indelicate depths for family viewing. Gol-*lee,* Dad, lookit them *bazooms* on 'er!

So I chose freedom, running around trying everything new,
But nothing impressed me at all, I never expected it to.

Up, up, climb every mountain, cross every stream, finally stops on her screen-filling face, dark smoldering eyes riveted on the camera, flawless complexion beaded with sweat, glossless lips pursed, changing to an almost-sullen pout, and then, suddenly, boldly, defiantly, the kid sticks her luscious pink tongue out at thirty million delighted viewers as the music swells to crescendo:

Don't cry for me Argentina!

Now that's a freeze-frame. Got to be. Commercial-break man's dream. " 'Sixty Minutes' will continue after these messages." Super the big stopwatch, second hand sweeping: *Click-click-click-click-click.*

That night at Hal Kendig's Speak Easy Saloon, Big John and me are sitting at the bar, smoking our cigars, sipping our martinis, and I just can't seem to shake that image of Nancy Kramer sticking her tongue out at the camera. A bunch of detectives from the precinct are there, Idrissi, Stephenson, Brendan Thomas and them, they're having a ball, all laughing and talking about the booking, what a media circus it turned out to be, which it did in spades. But me, I keep seeing Nancy Kramer's smoldering eyes, her face beaded with sweat, her tongue sticking out at the camera. Image just won't quit. In a sense, that tongue says it all. Swear to God, it gives me a spooky feeling. Maybe it's different in other cities, maybe I'm magnifying it out of proportion, but these days, in this city at least, that's what an awful lot of people seem to be doing. Sticking their tongues out like kids. Looking society straight in the eye and saying, Fuck you! Ripping off as much as they can carry, legally, illegally, doesn't seem to make much difference. Know what I mean? That's all I'm saying, nothing profound. They just don't seem to give a damn. Me, I do.

I'm sitting there, I look through the smoke and see my face in the mirror behind the bar, cigar stuck in the side of my mouth, I can't help smiling. Face of a forty-seven-year-old detective who still gives a damn. Big John does, too, only I suspect he has more fun. In fact, I know he does. Trick with him, he doesn't kill himself with abstractions. Plays it as it lays. Takes two and hits to right. He's looking at me in the mirror now, elfin eyes sparkling with mischief.

"So what brings that smile to your poor sad puss?" he asks.

"Nancy Kramer's tongue."

"It's a sin to think impure thoughts, lad."

"Can you keep a secret?"

"Can I keep—? Did Jesus love the lepers?"

"I think I'm going nuts."

"So are we all, lad. Be specific."

"Hallucinations."

"Hallucinations?"

"Last a couple of seconds, maximum."

"How long's this been going on?"

"Off and on since last summer. Average maybe two a month. Had two in one week during this case."

"When they happen, what do you see?"

"Quick cuts, like in a film."

"Quick cuts of what?"

"Variety of things. Memories from childhood mostly."

"Real memories or—?"

"I think so, yeah."

Big John smiles, shakes his head. "Great minds think alike."

"No. *You?*"

He looks me up and down. "Behave yourself, lad. Big, healthy chap like me? It's only the little scrawny fellows have problems with their poor undernourished brains. I happen to know one who had a similar problem to yours. Maybe he still does."

"Who?"

"Idrissi."

"Yeah?"

"Idrissi. Told me himself. Sounds like the same thing, had him worried for a while there. Didn't tell anybody, didn't even tell his wife. Thought he had a tumor on the brain or something. Went to a GP, of all people, who promptly sent him to a neurologist."

"What'd he find out?"

"*I* don't know. What'm I, a fuckin' neurologist?" He sticks his cigar in his mouth, turns, looks down the bar. "Hey, Nuzhat!"

Idrissi's rapping with Stephenson and Thomas at the far

end. Looks at us through the hanging smoke, adjusts his gold-framed glasses. Big John waves him over. He makes his apologies, weaves his way through the crowd, holding his usual glass of vodka on-the-rocks with an olive. Rarely eats the olive; only reason he orders it, Kendig has this stubborn habit of giving him a lemon twist, unasked for, and he hates lemon twists. Classy little detective, Idrissi, about my age, heavyset, dark complexion, neatly trimmed mustache. Dark gray suit, white shirt collar, pale gray shirt, tie with thin gold stripes against a dark blue background. Born in Nazareth, grew up in Jerusalem where his father was chief of police. Still has traces of an Arabic accent.

"What can I do for you?" he asks.

Big John jerks a thumb at me. "Blue eyes here has some medical questions for you."

"Medical questions?" Nuzhat's eyes dart around to the people near us.

"Hallucinations," I tell him quietly. "If that's what they're called. I don't know the medical terminology."

He nods, clears his throat. "You have them, John?"

I nod, clear my throat. "Afraid so."

He frowns, leans closer. "Can you describe them?"

"Just quick flashes at odd times, maybe twice a month. Very fast. Over in seconds."

"Yes. And afterward?"

"Sick feeling. Slightly dizzy."

"Yes. And that's over quickly, too?"

"Right. Understand you had something similar?"

He glances at Big John.

"Didn't tell him anything," Big John assures. "Sounded like the same thing, so I thought you might be able to help."

"Sounds very similar," Nuzhat says. "Let me ask you a question, John. Have you been to see a doctor?"

"Not yet, no."

"And how long have you had these?"

"I'd say close to a year."

"I'd suggest you see a doctor. If it's the same sort of thing I had, it's no big deal, apparently. Not all that unusual."

"Mind telling me what the doctor said?"

He sips his vodka, reaches his left hand in his trouser pocket, pulls out the familiar string of white worry-beads, holds them at his side, starts massaging. "Well, I went to a neurologist. Excellent neurologist, I'll be glad to give you his name and address if you want. He gave me the full treatment, neurological consultation, examination, impression, recommendations. Sent a copy to the doctor who referred me. The fact of the matter, apparently people like us, late forties and older, in our type of occupation, it's not unusual to have these problems. The way he explained it to me, he said the body's a marvelous machine, knows how to tell you when something's wrong. Same with the mind. In this city, in this day and age, adjusting to the—what'd he call it?—adjusting to the 'rapidly accelerating rate of change,' that was it. Making that adjustment on a daily basis causes problems for some people. Particularly if you happen to be under a certain amount of constant stress. The mind will accept and try to absorb maybe ninety-nine percent of all significant change on a daily basis, then, when you're in danger of an overload, it gives you a warning. It tells you in a split-second or, in my case, in a matter of several seconds. He said you don't actually hallucinate, that's not technically accurate. Your mind simply flashes back to real memories, usually from more stable times. Memories you don't even know you've retained."

"Memories from like childhood?" I ask.

"Precisely. Happens to be the case with me."

"Ah, great minds think alike," Big John says.

Nuzhat gives him an indignant look, then turns back to me. "Of course, the mind is constantly flashing back, it happens to all of us many thousands of times a day, that's what memory is all about. Happens so often we're oblivious to it most of the time. Now, what happens in an abnormal flashback—that's what he called it—what happens, the mind is giving you a signal, a distress signal. He gave me an example, headaches. Not serious, chronic headaches like migraine, just common—he called them 'vascular-flow' headaches. Although no one knows what actually causes common headaches, the physical effect is of course well known. Pain-sensitive nerve endings in the head are affected when the blood vessels dilate; distress signals are being sent to the brain that more oxygen is needed. In the case of abnormal flashbacks, the brain itself is warning you that it's receiving too much disturbing information simultaneously. In effect, telling you to back off for a while."

I wait, then: "And that's it?"

"Essentially, John. That's the bottom line, as I understand it. He didn't prescribe any medication, said I didn't need any. Said I should seriously consider biofeedback therapy so I could learn to recognize the trigger mechanisms and avoid them. Man was quite right."

"So you did that?"

"Oh, yes. Biofeedback was extremely helpful."

"What the hell's biofeedback?" Big John asks.

Nuzhat thinks about it, sips his vodka. "Basically, it's relaxation training. Developing voluntary control over responses once thought to be involuntary. This neurologist has a biofeedback office and a professional therapist. You go in, you sit down, he hooks you up to the equipment. What it is, it's a differential amplifier combined with a small computer. Three rectangular boxes on top of each other, looks something like stereo equipment: EMG amplifier, digital computer, temperature amplifier."

"What's EMG?" I ask.

"Electromyogram. Therapist then tapes three wires, called transducers, to your forehead and one to an index finger."

"Wires?"

"Transducers, yes. Sounds complicated, but the only function of the equipment is to monitor. For example, the EMG amplifier monitors electric currents associated with muscular action in your forehead and feeds back that information to you by a needle on a display meter. You clench your teeth, the needle swings to the right of the numbered scale, indicating muscle contraction in your jaw and face. Same basic principle for the temperature amplifier. What I learned to do, for the first time, is increase my sensitivity to exactly what mental and physical processes are necessary to make me relax. Results are fed back instantly. Later on, you take a series of progressive relaxation exercises."

"What kind of time we talking about?"

"Forty-five minutes, twice a week to start. Then it depends on individual progress. I stayed on that schedule for six weeks, reduced it to once a week for the next four weeks, then once every other week, finally once every month. The idea is to wean you off the instrumentation."

"You off now?"

"Oh, yes."

"No more flashbacks?"

He sips his vodka, massages the worry-beads. "Still have them once in a while. Very infrequently, John. I've simply developed voluntary control over responses that most people think are involuntary."

We talk a little longer, he gives me the neurologist's card, the therapist's card, suggests I give it a shot. When he's gone, Big John and I exchange glances. I know why he's grinning like Pat M. He sees me sitting there in the biofeedback seat with three wires taped to my forehead and one to an index finger, studying the dials, trying to get in touch with my brain. Frankenstein's midget.

Now I squint at myself in the mirror, I have to smile too, I can visualize the whole routine. And I'm thinking: Is that what it's all come down to? After twenty-six years in the department, you end up with your head wired to a biofeedback machine? Me? No way. Tell you the truth, I'd rather have the little flashbacks once in a while. Fact is, they're not half bad. Besides, I already know how to relax, it's never been a real problem.

Big John looks at me in the mirror. "So what brings that smile to your poor sad puss?"

"Nancy Kramer's tongue."

"We're back to that, are we?"

"How much time you think she'll pull?"

"Nancy K?" He puffs on his cigar, thinks about it. "Should be a devil of an indictment, lad, all counts considered. Complicated case. But I figure—now this is conservative, mind you, plea bargaining to the contrary notwithstanding. But I figure, by the time that lovely young lass gets out, she'll look like Elizabeth Taylor looks today."

I nod. "Some people have all the luck."

About the Author

John Minahan is the author of ten previous books, including the Doubleday Award novel *A Sudden Silence* and the million-copy best seller *Jeremy.* An alumnus of Cornell, Harvard, and Columbia, he is a former staff writer for *Time* magazine and was editor and publisher of *American Way* magazine. Mr. Minahan and his wife, Verity currently live in Miami, where he is writing the second novel in this series, *The Great Daimond Robbery.*